𝒜

"Twenty years from now you will be more disappointed by the things you didn't do than by the ones you did do. So throw off the bowlines. Sail away from the safe harbor. Catch the trade winds in your sails. Explore. Dream. Discover!"
~ Mark Twain

It is incredible how time flies. It was twenty-five years ago, to this very day, when Luke Davis left everything behind, moved to Hawaii, bought a cruising yacht and sailed into the adventure of a lifetime. He never could have imagined the unbelievable direction his life took at that very moment. All he had hoped for was to escape the rat race and live a simple life. What he found was nothing close to simple, but he wouldn't be where he was today if he had taken a different path or made different choices. He drank a toast to fate and allowed his memories to take him back.

Chapter 1

Cracking open a cold beer in the cockpit of his Gulfstar 50 ketch, *Tranquilo*, Luke Davis settled back to watch the sun set over the horizon west of Waikiki Beach. He was hoping to finally see the ever-elusive "green flash" which had been described to him by many cruisers and fellow sailors since he arrived in Hawaii and purchased this, his first sailboat. Supposedly, due to the curvature of the earth's surface, the last bit of reflected light from the setting sun passes through the top of the ocean, casting a green flash of light. Well, Luke had yet to see this phenomenon, and having been raised in Missouri, the "Show Me State," he was beginning to believe some folks out there were pulling his leg. But he kept hearing about it from many unrelated sources so every chance he got, he would set himself up to have a clear unobstructed view of the horizon at sunset.

Oh, how he wished right now that he were anchored in a calm bay watching this particular sunset, rather than twelve-feet off the ground where *Tranquilo* was mounted on jack stands in dry dock. After spending the last nine hours sanding the boat's bottom in preparation for the four coats of bottom paint he would apply in the next few days, his muscles ached and he was covered with dirt and grime. He yearned for a swim in the clear blue, seventy-eight degree waters off the islands of Maui or Lanai. It was mid-November, and he had just heard over the radio that an early winter storm had just dusted Buffalo, New York with two-inches of snow. Well, at least this was a great climate in which to work.

When he first came to Honolulu for a stockbroker's convention six months earlier, he was drawn to the marina next to the hotel. Rather than sitting in a convention hall listening to award presentations and new corporate promotions all day, then being herded like cattle to take a *Mai Tai* sunset cruise on a tourist party boat, he'd sneak out and walk the docks, admiring the sailboats and cruising yachts. On one such afternoon of playing hooky, Luke struck up a conversation with a fellow working on his 35-foot Columbia sloop and eventually got himself invited for a sail to Maui. That did it: Luke was hooked on cruising. He returned to Chicago, quit his job, sold everything, and returned to Honolulu to "buy him a boat."

When Luke arrived in Honolulu, he arranged for a hotel room that honored his frequent flyer miles, overlooking the Ali Wai Yacht Harbor right at the edge of Waikiki Beach. Right away he hooked up with his friend, Gus Lassen, who had taken him sailing to Maui. Gus, a high school teacher in Honolulu, had lived aboard his sailboat in the Ala Wai Harbor for a few years and had a good feel for what was going on there. He gave Luke some advice on the variety of yachts that were built well enough to withstand the demanding sailing conditions of Hawaii. However, there were so many different types of sailing craft that it would ultimately boil down to whatever appealed to Luke and what he wanted in a boat.

Every day Luke would walk the harbor, looking at the boats, striking up conversations with sailors of all types and from countries all around the globe. Each one was so proud of their vessel and talked on and on about why theirs was the best type of yacht. It seemed that he never ran into an owner who regretted the type of yacht he had. Maybe there was a little ego involved, or maybe they each had given a great deal of thought and research into the yacht to which they would entrust their investment and their lives.

Luke quickly learned this was not going to be an easy process like buying a new car or a new home. Not that those purchases in his life had been simple, but it was very clear that there were so many different designs of sailboats and if he saw one or another that interested him, it was never for sale. Money was not really the issue, although he wasn't going to blow all of his cash on the nicest yacht in Hawaii, because he intended to cruise, and that would require a sizeable reserve of funds. Yes, this was settling in to be a long and somewhat arduous process.

Some of his inquiries required him to contact yacht brokers who held the listings of some of the boats he was interested in. The brokers were mostly *live-aboards* in the harbor who were trying to make some money while living a life in paradise. Many of their respective "representations" of the yachts were bordering on the professional approach of a used car salesman, *"Since this is your first yacht, let me highly recommend to you this exquisite steel ketch that will take you around the world and never sink." "This here glorious sloop was only sailed on Sundays by a little old lady who never took her past Diamond Head."* Luke became discouraged as the weeks wore on without even coming close to the possibility of starting his cruising adventure.

Friday nights became Luke's most anticipated part of each week because the Hawaii Yacht Club always held the "Friday Night Beer Can Races" and they knew how to host a good time. At precisely 5:00, the Rear Commodore would ring a ship's bell in front of the Hawaii Yacht Club, signaling the start of the race out of the Ala Wai Harbor, a sharp turn to starboard (right) and on to the Honolulu Harbor entrance buoy, and back to the starting line in front of the yacht club. The cruiser fleet started first, and then every five minutes another fleet of sailboats, based upon their size and racing ratings, would start. The more "racy" the boat, the longer they had to wait to get started. The winning sailboat was rewarded with a case of beer. After all of the sails were stowed away, the party began.

One thing racing boats always need to be competitive is crew. In the beginning, because Luke hadn't a clue as to what to do or what was going on, he was asked to just sit on the rail as "ballast" for the boat. Even being "rail meat" as they referred to him, was an important function, especially if you brought a cold 12-pack of beer to add to the boat's cooler, and you picked a light displacement racing boat that seemed short on crew.

After a few weeks and a little experience, Luke was asked to come back and race on one of the competitive racing boats for their Saturday series races. He was meeting a new group of sailors, a different breed from the cruisers he had been so early focused on, and gaining more experience trimming sails and working as part of a racing team. More and more he was gathering information and storing it in the back of his mind, which kept giving him a clearer picture of the kind of boat he wanted.

He was always sure he wanted a boat that he could handle alone, and now he was learning just how the winches and different types of sails were used to make the most efficient use of the wind and sea conditions of the day. Sailing downwind in very light air takes a whole different physical and mental process than trying to sail against the wind on a stormy *heavy air* day. Getting this racing experience was proving very helpful.

Luke was also meeting some wonderful people at the Hawaii Yacht Club, which was formed at the turn of the century and founded in a true spirit of *aloha*. They built a beautiful club in the Ala Wai Yacht Harbor, complete with a clubhouse, racing dinghy storage for their members' small boats, slips for members' yachts, and slips for sailors who visited from an outer island or from other countries. Atop the clubhouse was a great bar and restaurant with views overlooking the harbor and out to the Pacific. Many a night while sitting at the bar or around the huge barbecue grill, Luke would listen to stories of passages, beautiful anchorages, and tropical adventures from visiting sailors and local members. Luke was like a sponge, absorbing every line, just like the days of his childhood when his dad spoke of the South Pacific. All he needed was his boat.

After six weeks, his frequent flyer miles certificates were about used up, and he had to make a decision whether to lease an apartment or possibly fly to California and investigate the sailboat market there. He'd hoped to begin his cruising adventures in Hawaii because of the wonderful first cruise Gus and he had shared going to Maui, Lanai, and Molokai. Each island was unique and the people were so wonderful and very friendly. Luke had spent enough time in California every year on business to develop a genuine dislike for the place. Too much traffic, smog, and crazy people, *"the real land of fruits & nuts,"* he used to say. However, it was starting to look like that would offer the best selection of boats. Surely, somewhere on the West Coast he would find his dream yacht.

After a Friday night beer can race, in which the boat he had crewed won, Luke and his mates were sitting around the barbecue at the yacht club savoring the taste of their 24 aluminum "trophies," when he first saw her. She was being towed into the courtesy dock by a sport fishing boat, and as heads turned in her direction, anyone with time at sea could tell she had just been through a rough passage. Being towed rather than coming in under her own power was the first sign that something was seriously wrong. Even with Luke's lack of experience compared to those around him, he could tell there were some really "unhappy campers" ready to find a warm shower.

As soon as the disabled yacht was brought along dockside, what must have at one time been a very lovely young lady jumped on the courtesy dock and quickly headed for the clubhouse, not bothering to assist with securing the boat to the dock. Her male companion, who Luke supposed was the Captain, tended to securing his vessel, but in a manner even Luke knew was not the most appropriate way of securing the lines. Luke and a couple of his buddies walked down and offered a hand, but the "Captain" said he had everything under control and appeared in no mood for any help. So the three crewmates headed back to their lawn chairs by the smoldering coals and opened another round of "trophies."

Even with all of the disarray onboard this new "lady" in front of the club, Luke felt a feeling of excitement just looking at her that he had never felt when checking out other sailboats in the past six weeks. She was somewhere between forty-five to fifty-five feet long, ketch-rigged, with a center cockpit, with plenty of big and new self-tailing winches for handling the lines that controlled the sails, which was about as close to what Luke was looking for in the design that most excited him. Maybe a bit bigger than he had considered, but the way she was rigged with a self-furling headsail and those winches, certainly a boat which could be sailed single-handed. But most of all, she was beautiful. Luke hardly noticed the torn headsail, and passed off the shredded mainsail as to a poor job of stowing it in the rush to tie up to the dock. This feeling of awe was just like the memory of seeing that new girl who transferred to his high school back in his sophomore year, who just happened to also be the most beautiful girl ever to appear in the whole state of Missouri. He was blinded by her curves and beautiful face, and she left the entire male portion of the student body hearing nary a word that was said the rest of the day. This night, this new "lady" also overwhelmed him.

Luke's mates were commenting on all of the broken equipment, the filthy stains, the lack of following proper docking and security procedures, and most of all, not following the proper notification protocols of a foreign vessel entering Hawaiian waters. Although she was documented and registered in the USA, she was still required to notify the U.S. Coast Guard and display a yellow quarantine flag serving notice that she had yet to clear a customs' inspection. Something was clearly wrong, and as the weary sailor headed up to the bar, Luke nonchalantly followed, interested to see what his story was.

The young lady companion had headed

into the lower level of the clubhouse, and began sobbing uncontrollably, talking a mile-a-minute to the first group of people she came to. One of the female club members, obviously a lady of great sailing experiences, empathized and immediately helped her to the lady's room and out of the embarrassing situation in which she had placed herself. A couple of other ladies followed so it appeared the mate was in good hands.

Luke headed on upstairs to the bar where the Captain had just finished his second shot of whiskey and was calling for more. He appeared to be in his mid 50's, a bit overweight, had the appearance having a lot of money, with his *Henry Lloyd* jacket and *Rolex* watch, but also appeared on the verge of a breakdown. The Dock Master of the Hawaii Yacht Club, Vern, was in the restaurant having dinner with his wife and left his meal to come over, introduce himself, and inquire of the new customer's credentials. With most yacht clubs, as private organizations, they have the right to require, and it is proper form to present a yacht club card from your homeport in order to receive reciprocal guest privileges. After downing his third shot of whiskey, the newcomer stated with arrogance that his name was Ron and said, "I am a member of the Los Angeles Yacht Club. If it's quite all right I would like to be left alone and not bother with any administrative requirements until morning."

Vern was about as easy-going a fellow you could find, and being retired from the Navy after a 30-year career he didn't need a "job" that entailed a whole lot of stress. In fact, Vern could be seen daily inspecting the yacht club and overseeing the maintenance and upkeep on the grounds as well as handling the few administrative procedures for the visitors to the club. However, *Rolex* watch and a *Henry Lloyd* jacket or not, one did not speak to the former Chief Petty Officer 1st Class like that. "Cut 'em off!" Vern exclaimed to the bartender. "And fellow, you are no longer welcome here. Back to your vessel and be prepared to cast off in the morning!"

"But our engine seized up about three weeks ago, and we have been fifty-four days at sea from Los Angeles! Please, I'm terribly sorry. We are exhausted. I really am sorry. What can I do? I...I..." Then the second emotional breakdown of the evening began.

Vern and Luke sat down for the next hour with the distraught man and tried to help him through his traumatic and weeping version of his first voyage with his new wife. Los Angeles to Honolulu should have taken around eighteen to twenty-two days in a yacht like his. But on their ninth day out, not having reefed the mainsail or the headsail, which most prudent seaman will do prior to darkness setting in for the night, they encountered a storm in the middle of the night and both sails were torn beyond use. Also during the storm, because their batteries were not properly secured in place, a battery came lose and started an electrical fire, which shorted their entire electrical system, and they lost all electrical power. They tried in vain to change sails a couple of days later after the seas calmed down and the normal trade winds returned, but they hadn't even the basic skills to master the changes. They motored on towards Hawaii, but evidently the cooling system intake became obstructed and the diesel engine overheated and seized.

Having had enough of her husband's inability to take charge, his young wife eventually was able to discard the shredded mainsail and hoist a smaller back up sail. Without a headsail, they could only make 50 to 100 nautical miles a day. Ron had intended to navigate to Hawaii with his new Satellite Navigation Technology, Sat Nav, however, without battery power they became lost. They had no idea where they were, how to read the sun and the stars, nor could they broadcast for help on their single side band radio.

This morning, they were spotted by the sport fishing boat that towed them in, having no idea they were anywhere near Hawaii. Their second mainsail had also blown apart in an accidental jibe, and when the fishermen spotted them flogging about, they knew there was a problem. The couple woke up to the sound of, "Aloha, is anybody aboard?" They promptly came topside and couldn't believe they were actually going to be rescued. Ron offered to pay the fishermen handsomely to tow them in, but even without the monetary offer, they would have been assisted. It was just the way of the sea. Even as he was securing his boat to the courtesy dock, the fishermen eased on out of the harbor, not expecting any reward.

The ladies downstairs had calmed the young wife down and gotten her into a hot shower, and she stayed in the lady's room for the better part of the hour that her husband was reliving their ordeal up in the bar. With a borrowed hairbrush, some deodorant, and new Hawaii Yacht Club t-shirt & shorts, she was feeling better and willing to come upstairs for a meal. Vern arranged for the cook in the restaurant to stay on as it was getting late, and they were able to get the couple to sit together and eat a hot meal. The tension between the two was very apparent during the meal.

Even though Ron was humbled and emotionally distraught from the telling of their crossing from the mainland, he still carried an air of arrogance that caused the locals to lack sympathy for him. It was agreed that they would deal with the administrative check-in procedure in the morning, but Vern advised them not to leave their vessel until the Coast Guard came aboard and they cleared the customs inspection. Ron's wife emphatically stated she would not spend one more minute on that boat and insisted that her husband set her up in a hotel for the night and arrange for her to fly home the next day.

Vern knew this would cause a problem with the Coast Guard, so he slipped to the back office and gave them a call to explain, if possible, why they should try to come over to the yacht club right away. Vern was well known at Coast Guard Headquarters for his hospitality and assistance whenever they needed to do their inspections, so they sent a team out within the hour. Of course this infuriated Ron, but he had no choice. This didn't sit well with his wife, both because it was delaying her ability to get to a hotel and it caused her to spend more time on the boat.

A little after midnight they were cleared, and with some cash and credit cards in hand, off the young bride left alone in a taxi, "to the nearest Hyatt." Embarrassed, dejected, and frustrated, Ron asked Luke if he knew of a local yacht broker in Honolulu so he could sell his boat a soon as possible. He echoed what his wife had earlier stated to the Coast Guard, "I'm through with sailing and want to be on the first plane out of here." He assumed Luke was a local yacht club member because he had been there to assist him with getting squared away for the night. Although it was now in the early morning hours, all he could think about was going back to his home in the hills of Malibu. Luke stated he knew every broker on Oahu, but tonight wasn't the time to be making this kind of decision. He offered to help Ron early the next morning set up a temporary slip with Vern and to take a look at getting his boat inspected by a mechanic. Ron refused Luke's attempt at reason, and had he not acted like such a snob, Luke would have offered Ron help with finding a hotel room.

"I'll be by in the morning with a fresh pot of coffee, and we can get started then if you wish," said Luke before heading back to his hotel. Ron was left without a chance to take a shower, since the club was closing, and he returned to his boat alone.

Chapter 2

The events of the night and the thought of this boat possibly becoming available kept Luke up most of the night. After waking up at sunrise, he headed for the club and, sure enough, some of the older retired gentlemen had their coffee on and newspapers all strewn about, trying to get the low-down on the new boat at the courtesy dock. All the commotion of the previous night had happened way past their bedtime.

Ben, a retired sugar cane plantation manager, had befriended Luke a few weeks earlier and was teaching him about fishing and rigging fishing lines and lures. He was usually the first person at the club every morning and had a pot of *Kona* coffee ready before most of the other early risers drifted in. Ben was the first to ask Luke about the new boat, assuming Luke had been at the club the night before with the racing crowd. Over the course of a couple cups of coffee, Luke filled them in, except the part about Ron wanting to quickly unload his boat. If that story got out before Ron was certain that it was what he really wanted, every broker in Oahu would overcome him before lunch. Understanding the condition Ron was in when he retired last night, arrogance notwithstanding, Luke wanted the opportunity to at least give the guy a chance to be more objective.

On his third cup of coffee and having satisfied the curiosity of the guys in the clubhouse, Luke took a chair next to the barbecue grill and evaluated this very pretty lady tied up out front, although she appeared much more disorganized in the daylight. He was still excited with her lines and the overall setup, and not knowing for sure all that needed to be done, he visualized the possibilities of her becoming his new home. Yes, she was bigger than he initially imagined he could manage single-handed, but she looked so right. A couple of new sails, a rebuilt engine, maybe some new paint if the stains and grime of fifty-four days at sea didn't come off; yeah, she warranted some real consideration. Luke contemplated waking Ron up and seeing if he had had a change of heart, but he decided to be patient so as not to appear too anxious. One of the keys to being a successful stockbroker was knowing how to be patient and make your move at just the right moment. *Let Ron come to me*, he thought. *It's got to be his idea.*

The Saturday morning activities at the club began early with dinghy races for the children starting at 10:00 in front of the courtesy dock. At about 9:00, the youngsters and the sailing coaches began bringing the sails and boats down to be rigged, and the noise from all the activity wasn't conducive to sleeping in late. Ron appeared from his cabin, cussing the children and getting a return scolding from the two coaches for his foul language. As Luke observed this from his chair just up from the dock, he laughed at the despicable character and could see this guy was way out of his element. Luke was certainly not going to try to get Ron to take a look at his experience and learn from it. This guy's romantic notions of sailing the South Pacific should not be encouraged lest the image of the United States be further damaged. About the only suggestion Luke would like to give him would be to get back to Malibu as soon as possible and build on to that big home, maybe add another three-car garage or a second pool.

Luke's heart rate was elevated in anticipation of a chance to get a closer look at the boat, but he tried to stay composed as he offered a cordial greeting, "Aloha, want some coffee?"

"Cut that aloha crap! Let's just get down to business," barked Ron, reaching for the cup with the desperation of a junkie buying his morning fix. After a sip, he realized he hadn't invited Luke aboard. "You can come aboard if you can stand the mess. Did you bring the list of brokers?"

"So, you're sure you want to sell her?"

"That's what I said, isn't it? If you'd had all the trouble with this lame excuse for a yacht as I have, you would too. I'm only interested in getting out from under it and trying to salvage my marriage and what little sanity I have left. How I ever listened to that vacuous wife of mine and let her convince me to buy this piece of crap, I'll never know. Boy, was I ever taken for a sucker. When I get back to LA I'm going to sue the shirt off the back of that yacht brokerage for misrepresentation, faulty equipment, and anything else my lawyers can think of!"

Luke saw his chance to pounce. "Ron, if what you say is true, with the engine seized, the sails shredded, and I imagine major permanent structural damage from flogging about for days on end, you're going to have a real headache unloading this boat. I suspect before anyone would even consider representing it in their brokerage, they are going to want a surveyor appointed by the boatyard to oversee her refurbishing. Surveyors in Honolulu run about $50 per hour and the yard fees for a project like this will run into the tens of thousands. Then after you get her ready to sell, the way I see it, there is no way in the current market that you'll even recoup your costs after broker's fees, slip fees, etc. I've come to know how laid-back and slow the pace is here in Hawaii, and unless you are here to personally supervise the work, it could be many months before she is even close to being marketable. Also, you have to consider the availability of a slip here in the harbor. A boat this size has a three to four year waiting list just to get a slip!"

Rubbing his tired and blood-shot eyes, Ron replied, "Look Luke, I appreciate you helping me last night and being candid with me, but I don't give a damn about surveyors, slip fees, boatyards or whatever else is involved in getting rid of this piece of crap. I just want out from the liability and the possibility of ever seeing it again. I intend to head home and as soon as I can get out from under it, the sooner I can try to salvage my dignity. Find me a buyer, and I'll make it worth your while."

"Well I've been looking for a project to keep me busy, but I've only got $25,000 in my savings account, if you'd consider selling her for that." Luke would never have insulted any other yacht owner with that kind of offer, but "Captain Ron" was the most arrogant, self-centered, obnoxious, dislikable character he'd met since leaving Chicago. In the wee hours of the morning, Luke had considered asking Ron what it would take to buy the boat and he figured if the diesel engine was a total loss, maybe he could steal her for $100,000-150,000. But the more time he spent with this

22

whining, overgrown baby, $25,000 just popped into his head. Luke was not sure of the replacement cost of a yacht like this, but she must have cost a quarter of a million new, and she couldn't be older than a year or two.

Ron paused, looked Luke in the eye, and said, "Have a cashier's check ready for me first thing Monday morning and I'll sign over to you the Certificate of Documentation. I will be flying out on the first flight I can get to LA and to hell with this piece of shit!"

Luke had worked some big deals in his former profession, but none carried the thrill of closing this sale. He wished the banks were open—wait, they were still open until noon! It was a quarter till ten; he could get the check and possibly have this scumbag on his way before he had a chance to change his mind.

"Tell you what, Ron: I don't mean to rush you, but if you want to try to join your little lady on that flight back to LA, I'll do my best to get back here in an hour with the check. I'd hate to see you lose her, and maybe you two can start to mend your relationship. Besides, if we act now you will be able to avoid having to deal with Vern and paying your fees with the Hawaii Yacht Club."

"I'll start packing our things. Do you know where she went last night?"

"She said something about the nearest Hyatt. There's a phone next to the coffee pot in the clubhouse you could use to try to find her. I'll introduce you to Ben and you can ask him if the club secretary will be in this morning or if he knows of a notary we can call to document the transaction."

The entire transaction ended up taking less than an hour, and during the time they were waiting, Ron had found that his wife was registered at a Hyatt at the other end of Waikiki Beach, although she didn't answer when the operator called up to the room.

Luke agreed to help Ron move their personal belongings off the boat while Ron kept trying to reach his wife to arrange their trip back home. He wasn't sure she would be open to speaking to him again, but his vanity wouldn't allow him to give up on her, especially with Luke showing concern for Ron's well being. Luke was all for anything that would speed up the process of getting this asshole off *his* boat and out of this state. By 3:00, Ron was loading his belongings into a taxi headed for the Hyatt. He still hadn't spoken to his wife but with some semblance of pride and a cashier's check in hand, he was happy to be rid of this part of the nightmare at least.

Luke informed Vern of the situation, excluding the purchase price, and Vern was more than happy to accommodate him with a temporary slip rather than having to put up with anymore of "Captain Ron's" obnoxious attitude. Ben brought his fishing boat around next to the crippled Gulfstar and they worked together to guide her into the new slip. Luke was as excited as a little boy on Christmas morning. He couldn't wait to start cleaning up and taking inventory of his boat. They say the best day in a sailor's life is the day he buys his boat and the second best is the day he sells it. Well, today was the most excited Luke could recall ever having been, even more than the day he got married.

"Tranquilo" was an expression Luke had learned when on a business trip to Mexico City the year before. He had gone there to check on a start-up company making dashboards for General Motors, which were to be shipped to Michigan and added to the assembly of their midsize line of cars. Luke met and began a romantic encounter with the secretary of the owner of the Mexican company and he extended his business trip an extra week to be sure he captured all of the data needed for the upcoming stock offering. Coming from Chicago and the fast-lane lifestyle in which Luke was ensnared, he became very relaxed in the lovely senorita's presence. Because Luke was so intense and his shoulder muscles were always tight, she kept saying, "tranquilo," meaning "take it easy." The expression, "tranquilo" and her unique ability to help Luke unwind were such pleasant reminders of relaxation, that Luke had always envisioned naming his boat *Tranquilo*.

Even though it was said to be bad luck to rename a vessel, with all of the bad vibes coming from this boat's previous owners, Luke wanted to "ward off" any of their bad karma and begin anew. He even had the hull from the waterline up to the decks painted dark blue with a new epoxy "bullet-proof" paint, which required about six-days of fine sanding and preparation before painting. He hired a professional painter to spray on three coats over the course of three days, and *Tranquilo* was beginning look like a brand new and different boat. The painter had a cousin who was an artist, and he was hired to paint *Tranquilo* in script lettering on each of the side aft quarters of the hull. It was amazing to watch him scroll the name on the newly painted dark blue hull. He used white, with shades of gray to give it a shadow effect. Each day, more and more, she was becoming Luke's boat. After the four coats of bottom paint were applied, they launched her back into the water and tied her up along side the yard's work dock to evaluate the engine.

The boatyard at the Ala Wai harbor was

an interesting place full of characters who told many fascinating stories. The owner was a Russian immigrant whose nickname was "Pirate Pete." He wasn't called that because he had a patch over one eye and a peg leg, however; it was that he was accused by more than a few patrons of "pirating on land." Most of those who complained were used to paying for equipment and supplies at mainland USA prices and didn't take into account that everything except pineapple and sugar cane had to be shipped to Hawaii. And if you wanted something immediately, which most yachtsmen did, you would have to pay extra for airfreight or having it made special. Pete was a hard-working, hands-on type of manager, always moving around to ensure things were running his way. Luke actually found Pete very helpful and not really overpriced compared to the other boatyards. Pete wouldn't allow any whining or arguing and his deep, booming voice could be heard all over the harbor if a disagreement ensued.

Pete's yard foreman, Steve, was a shipwright who seemed to know everything about boats. When Luke met with Steve and Pete the Monday after buying the Gulfstar, he was upfront with them about this being his first boat and needing a lot of advice. Luke also explained he wanted to do as much of the work on his boat as he could, which was allowed in the yard, but he would leave the major engine and structural repair to them. Pete and Steve seemed to appreciate Luke's sincerity for not coming off as a "know-it-all," and their respect for him grew the more they saw Luke toiling in the hot sun everyday.

Sure enough, the diesel engine was ruined, seized to the point of a total loss, and another like it would be six to eight weeks coming from the mainland. Gus and Luke went shopping at all of the junkyards, auto dealerships, and parts stores trying to find a replacement to no avail. Ben from the yacht club came by to check on the progress one morning, and Luke filled him in on his engine dilemma.

Ben had an idea to help Luke out. He had a friend whose teenage son had recently wrecked their brand new Mercedes 300 SD. It had a six cylinder turbo-charged diesel engine, which was about the only thing in the car that had not been damaged. It was a very dependable engine and a lot more powerful than the engine that Luke had just had removed from his boat. With a few adjustments to the motor and transmission mounts, Luke soon had one of the most powerful engines in a sailboat in the entire Pacific region.

"Aloha *Tranquilo,* anyone aboard?" called Gus, distracting Luke from the setting sun and from yet another chance to witness a "green flash."

Being brought back to the moment, Luke replied, "Yeah, come on up. Just opened up a cold one."

Chapter 3

Luke's 90-day transient permit for a slip in the Ala Wai Harbor passed quickly. He was anxiously making plans to begin cruising the islands, had completed all of the systems' checks, and felt he had adequate spare parts and all of the necessary equipment he could foresee needing. He purchased and reviewed detailed charts and cruising guides, and a route to Molokai, Maui, and Lanai, then on to the island of Hawaii was to occupy his first several months of cruising.

It was now early spring and the normal flow of the Pacific high-pressure system was returning the normal trade wind pattern of *"10–15 knots out of the Northeast"* as the daily weather report would state. Based on some cruising tales of outstanding anchorages he'd heard from experienced sailors at the Hawaii Yacht Club and the great trip he and Gus shared almost a year before, he was setting his sights for familiar anchorages first, before exploring new destinations.

Luke wanted Gus to come along, however, school was still in session, and Gus just couldn't get away at this time. One huge advantage the Gulfstar had over Gus's boat was the autopilot. The Columbia had to be steered all the time, whereas Luke had the advantage of being able to move about the Gulfstar to make sail adjustments, fix a meal, or lie in the cockpit, while just keeping a visual watch to ensure the boat held her course. Because of a lot of inner island barge and shipping traffic, taking a nap was out of the question for fear of a collision, however, the distances between the islands are short enough that a person can remain alert and awake for each crossing.

Gus advised Luke to keep an eye out for compatible crew to join him who might be able to add to the experience as well as be of help since this was his first crossing. With five days to go until his planned departure, Luke taped a sign on the gate to the temporary slip where he had resided for the past three months. It read:

"Going to Maui this weekend,
May need some crew,
Hail 'Tranquilo'...
To see if you'll do."

Two days later, on a sunny day perfect for varnishing, Luke had just finished applying another coat of varnish on the toe rails and was completing a coat on the bow pulpit, when he heard a woman's voice with what he thought was slight New England accent, "I hope you are a better Captain than a poet."

Luke had become as tanned as a local boy from working in the sun every day and though he kept his newly grown beard trimmed, his hair was now approaching shoulder length. The morning routines of exercise, running, and swimming had Luke in the best shape of his life. He was six feet tall, a very firm 180 pounds and usually worked without a shirt, wearing only a pair of shorts and flip-flops. Never having the discipline or desire to become a muscular guy, he stayed away from working out with weights. Now he had developed a leaner, more agile body, much improved from the stressed-out, improperly nurtured one of his most recent past.

He looked up and was astonished to see that a white limousine had pulled up in front of *Tranquilo*, and the chauffeur, who looked exactly like the Asian bodyguard "Oddjob" from the *007* movie *Goldfinger*, was holding open the rear door for one of the most exquisite and beautiful women Luke had ever seen. She was tall and slender with long shiny black hair and a slight trace of an Asian look. Luke tore his eyes briefly away from the woman to check out the chauffeur to be sure he didn't have one of those metal derby hats which could be flicked at an adversary's throat to sever his head.

Luke's attention quickly returned to the young woman. She was impeccably dressed with dark blue pleated pants and a white silk blouse. She probably had a suit jacket to match but because of the late morning sun, opted to leave it in the limo. As she walked toward Luke, she removed her *Wayfarer* sunglasses and he could see amusement in her almond shaped eyes and a smile forming on her beautiful lips.

Straightening up from his work, he replied, "Well, fortunately I spend more time studying nautical charts than I do poetry. However, if my limerick was able to get your attention, then possibly it should be worthy of a Pulitzer Prize!" They both chuckled. "If you don't mind me asking, you seem a bit lost. Can I help you with something?"

"Oh, quite the contrary, Mr. Davis, I am exactly where I want to be and, if I may, I would like to have a moment of your time." She opened the gate with self-assurance and walked onto the dock next to Luke's boat as if she'd been invited.

Luke eased back to meet her halfway, wondering how she knew his name. "Well, come on aboard and have a seat in the shade while I put this brush up to soak." He extended his hand, "Here, let me help you up."

She promptly removed her high-heel shoes and ignored his offer to assist her onto the deck, grabbing the starboard upper shroud and pulling herself up like a pro. As she took a seat in the cockpit, her driver, leaving the car running in front of the row of boat slips, tried to follow, but he was so stout and short legged, Luke knew he would have needed a set of stairs to make it up to the deck of *Tranquilo*. In the end, the driver didn't even try pulling himself up, instead taking a casual stance on the dock while watching Luke's every move.

As Luke went aft where he had a bucket with paint thinner for soaking his varnish brush, *Oddjob* followed, walking on down the side of the dock along the starboard side of *Tranquilo*. He kept an eye on Luke as well as scanning the harbor and sending an unspoken message that he was very close should he be needed. Luke noticed an earpiece with a wire discreetly running down the back of his shirt. *What in the hell is all this about?* Luke wondered.

As he returned to the cockpit, the woman stood, extended her delicate hand, and introduced herself with a firm handshake. "Hello, my name is Teruyo Boudreaux and, yes, I was quite taken with your poem. I'm here to introduce myself and inquire as to the possibility of hiring your services and your boat to take me sailing to some of the other islands. I saw your poem two days ago, and because of the necessity to be extremely cautious, I have had to wait until now to approach you with my request."

"Cautious? I realize I haven't shaved or cut my hair in the last five months, but didn't believe I was that scary looking," he replied with a slight grin.

"No, not at all, and please don't take this the wrong way, but in order for me to proceed with this charter, I first must assure my security team," she said giving a slight tilt of her head in *Oddjob's* direction, "that my safety is not compromised. Again, please don't be offended, but we have been doing a thorough background check on you as well as maintaining constant surveillance to ensure you are a man of worthy character, as well as being capable of returning me safely.

"Mr. Davis, I am the granddaughter of Masashi Tanaka, founder and Chairman of Tanaka Industries, one of Asia's largest industrial conglomerates. Because one of my cousins was kidnapped and murdered four months ago, elite security professionals now constantly escort members of my family. Before it is possible for any of us to ever venture out alone for personal reasons, we first must have the approval of the security team. At times I feel I'm a prisoner in my grandfather's domain, but he loves us very much and it is his way. He certainly has the power to ensure his family is protected from the greed of those trying to get to him."

"Whoa, whoa, whoa! Hold on there,

little lady." Luke held his hands up to stop her. He didn't mean to sound like John Wayne in a western movie, but this was not at all resembling any conceivable scenario he'd imagined coming with ownership of a sailboat. "If you did in fact do a background check on me and keep me under surveillance, which I don't appreciate one bit, you will have found first of all, I'm not in the charter business and secondly, have never even sailed alone or been in charge of a boat other than on day trips out of this harbor. And finally, I don't even have a Captain's License or any credentials other than my boat registration, insurance, and driver's license! Do you really expect me to believe you want to, how'd you say it, hire my services and my boat to take you sailing to some of the other islands?" Luke's voice elevated with confusion and irritation.

"Yes, Mr. Davis. I do expect you to believe my story," she firmly replied. Softening her voice, she continued, "However, I understand why you are overwhelmed with this sudden intrusion into your privacy, especially at the beginning of your new adventure. You see, when I was going to school in Rhode Island, I became infatuated with sailing and I truly love every aspect of it from racing to cruising. I worked hard to earn a place on the Brown University sailing team, competing and becoming a medalist my last year there. And this past year, I was fortunate enough to crew on a forty-two-meter mega-yacht returning from southern France to England. I have been to Hawaii many times and have longed to sail here and sincerely, Mr. Davis, I am really interested in chartering your boat.

"When I was walking along the harbor two days ago admiring the boats, I was truly taken with your poem and the Bristol condition of your yacht. I watched you work from a distance when you were stowing your inflatable dinghy. You seemed so focused and at the risk of sounding like a giddy schoolgirl, I felt excited to ask to come with you. Yes, I've found out you don't have your Captain's License, and you are not looking for financial gain in finding a crew. I have all the confidence that if you do choose to sail on alone, you will be fine, and the cruising experience will be all you have worked so diligently towards.

"I have pursued this proposition to you only for my own personal desire to sail and explore the islands in the few short weeks before I must return to Japan. I offer to hire you so no misunderstandings can come of us sailing off together as well as to further prove to you my sincerity that I just wish to spend my remaining few weeks here sailing to a few of the Hawaiian Islands. I will continue to look for a boat and Captain should we not agree, but may I stress, from what we do know of you at this point, the security team and I are confident in your boat and your abilities to return me safely."

"And how many in your security team will be going along should we agree on this?" Luke asked, his tension easing due to her composure.

"I would be in daily contact with them, and they will be near but they will not intervene unless called for or feel my security is in jeopardy. I really am quite good at taking care of myself, and perhaps you will find my sailing skills and knowledge of certain aspects of cruising to your benefit." She smiled confidently.

"Ms. Boudreaux, this has caught me quite off guard. I mean, I was only looking for someone to help crew. I have no reservations of going it alone." Luke paused for a moment, then continued, "This is more complicated than I had considered before I placed my sign and I'm sorry, but this is all a bit hard to believe."

"Please, call me Teruyo. May I call you Luke?" she asked softly.

"Sure, that's fine," he replied cautiously, wondering at the turn of events.

Teruyo continued softly, leaning towards Luke with her hands on her knees, "First of all, Luke, this doesn't have to be complicated, and yes, as I said in the beginning, I am very sorry to have had to look into your background. I sincerely am, but it is the only way they will allow me to go along with this idea. They have a tough job to do, and in the past I've even tried to avoid them to pursue my own freedom, but I have found it is better to work with them, rather than against them. As long as we have no trouble and I keep in contact, they will keep their distance, and we feel confident in your character that you will do me no harm."

In almost a whisper, Luke leaned toward Teruyo and asked, "Okay, Teruyo, let's say we do this. How am I supposed to believe I don't end up deserted on Molokini Crater with my throat cut, and you guys leaving with my boat?"

With a slight giggle, she tilted her head back and rolled her eyes. "I have proper identification, passport, and credit cards and I will answer any questions you have to assure you of my real intentions. And if you like, feel free to verify my identity by any means you desire." Leaning forward again, she softly added, "Besides, Luke, if I wanted, I could buy a much larger boat. But as I said, you are about ready to go and I have only a very limited time, so this feels like it could be opportune timing for both of us."

"Alright, tell me this. Why is such a

beautiful and apparently well-off young lady not here with a boyfriend or newlywed husband like ninety-nine percent of the other Japanese ladies your age visiting the islands?"

After a moment's hesitation, Teruyo leaned back and straightened up, replying firmly, "As you wish, I did state you could ask any questions. Actually, I was in a relationship until a few months ago. It came to a very messy end, and I have been traveling since, trying to get my life back in order."

Luke pondered that for a moment then asked, "You like something to drink?"

"Some water or juice would be nice."

"How about your driver; would he like something?"

"You could ask, but he will probably decline."

Luke went below and retrieved a couple of glasses of ice water and a beer. He returned, handing a glass to Teruyo, and then took one to *Oddjob*. Surprisingly, he accepted it and acknowledged Luke with a slight bow of his head but no smile. Teruyo came out of the cockpit and leaned over the lifeline, saying something in Japanese to him. He handed her the empty glass and left the dock. Luke didn't see where the driver went; he just drove away.

Luke went below to fix a snack tray of cheese, crackers, and pineapple. As he was almost finished preparing the snack, he noticed over his shoulder that Teruyo was looking down into the cabin. "Come on down and look around. You'd just as well get a good look at her for yourself."

With the invitation to enter his cabin, her mood immediately changed from melancholy thoughts of her breakup back to the proposal at hand and she bounded down the companionway stairs. She complimented Luke on the finish of the teak woodwork. Except for some scratches resulting from unsecured items having been flung about during the previous owners' crossing, the interior teakwood was beautiful, however, Luke wanted more of a glossy finish on it. He was so impressed with the interior of Pirate Pete's 1960's schooner, that Luke wanted that kind of finish as well. Little did he know what he was getting into on that project, but three weeks later, he had mastered the art of varnishing and was very proud of his efforts.

Fortunately everything in the cabin this day was pretty tidy, and because Teruyo's appearance was totally unexpected, Luke was grateful he wasn't deep into a major project, which usually had the cabin in disarray. He showed her both the fore and aft cabins, each with its own head (toilet) and shower. He told her the aft cabin was his, but if this trip together was going to happen, as the "paying" customer, she could chose which cabin she preferred.

Luke could tell Teruyo was familiar with the cabin of a sailing yacht, especially the way she appreciated his chart table and navigation station. She recognized he'd recently installed a ham radio next to the single side band and VHF radios that came with the boat. Without asking permission, she opened the lid on the chart table and looked through the charts laid out flat with his plotting instruments on top. He didn't mind; he'd have done exactly the same thing if the roles were reversed. He could see she knew what to look for.

They returned to the cockpit with snacks and fresh drinks and spent the rest of the afternoon talking about sailing, a little about their pasts, and why Luke was heading towards Maui first. Luke asked her for identification and she produced her passport, Rhode Island Drivers License, credit cards, and even a photo of her with the Brown University sailing team after they'd won a trophy at a regatta. Luke had traveled out of the United States in the past and was familiar with not only the necessity for having the proper identification, but the proper types of credit cards as well. She appeared to be legitimate.

"So, how much are you willing to pay me to take you around the islands?"

"How much do you want?"

He snickered and with his slow Missouri

drawl said, "Well let's see... How about five dollars a day plus expenses? But it has to be cash under-the-table, the *gov'ment* can't find out about it or it could put me in a higher tax bracket."

She giggled. "Oh, you don't come cheap, do you?"

"I'm not cheap and I'm not easy," he replied with a grin.

Teruyo was becoming easier to talk with but was still more composed and relaxed than Luke. Being confident around women was not usually a problem for Luke, but this lady was different. Add to the mix that they were most assuredly being watched, and it all was a bit overwhelming for a small town boy from Missouri.

Gaining confidence, he said, "You may not fully understand this, but the crossings between the islands are usually pretty rough. The way the wind funnels between the tall islands' mountains increases the size of the waves and causes some pretty rough sailing. Have you ever been seasick?"

She replied matter-of-factly, "We had some heavy-weather sailing along the Bay of Bisque off the west coast of France and we were all affected to some degree, however, after a couple of days, I had stabilized and the motion become second nature."

"Obviously you've logged more miles in

a sailboat than I have, but I do remember my trip to Maui with my friend Gus. He was pretty sick the first few hours after getting into the channel. For some reason it hasn't bothered me, but a few of the crews I've raced with turn a bit green as soon as we round Diamond Head. I thought you needed to know; it can get real steep and deep right away out there."

Teruyo leaned slightly forward and spoke with a calm assurance that was very sensual, "Rest assured, Luke. I'm not as fragile as I may appear."

Luke related the story of his sail to Maui with Gus and emphasized how they chose to depart the harbor in the evening, which made for slightly lighter winds and smaller waves. Gus had also warned Luke that it would be rough and how it usually takes most of the crossing to Molokai to get his stomach under control after leaving the stillness of the Ala Wai Harbor. Luke assured Teruyo that his boat was worthy of any passage, but there were risks and it could be very uncomfortable. She wasn't put off by the warnings at all, so they proceeded to discuss the possibilities that lie ahead. The longer they talked, the more their excitement grew.

Luke showed Teruyo around the deck of *Tranquilo*; the masts and rigging were solid with stainless steel rod rigging of the highest quality to hold the masts true. The oversized self-tailing winches, which had caught Luke's eye that first evening, were the best money could buy, and he had completed a thorough inspection, cleaning, and greasing of each of them. That had been another three-day project in and of itself. It seemed every boat project took twice as long as expected.

As evening approached and they were becoming more relaxed with each other, they decided to meet back at *Tranquilo* for dinner around seven o'clock. Earlier that morning, Ben had brought by some fresh Mahi-Mahi fillets from his catch the day before, and since Luke was planning on cooking them tonight anyway, he invited Teruyo to join him. Ben had taught Luke some incredible, yet simple recipes for cooking fish on a boat. Over the barbecue grill was best, so a grill had been another purchase for *Tranquilo* that was deemed a necessity.

Luke told Teruyo, "As long as you are not allergic to ginger, this could be the best dinner you've had in the islands yet."

She got up to leave and again offered her hand with a firm shake. "Thank you, Luke, for trusting me so far. I know this is all unexpected and I hope we can continue to explore the possibilities."

She jumped down onto the dock and, without putting on her shoes, walked to the end of the dock and closed the gate. Immediately, the white limo appeared from nowhere. She let herself in the rear door and they slowly drove away.

Luke just sat in the cockpit for a few minutes, amazed at what had happened. They were becoming a little more comfortable with each other, but it was still hard to believe this was actually happening to him. Although her story seemed reasonable, the whole security team was unlike anything Luke had ever encountered. It was kind of like she was some sort of celebrity. She sure was beautiful, though, and the granddaughter of Masashi Tanaka: all the more reason to be suspicious.

It wasn't extraordinary for Luke to have relationships or business encounters with beautiful women. It's just that Teruyo was so well educated and very self-assured. Plus she knew how to sail. *Now that is an interesting combination in a woman! Better do some serious inquiries into this one.*

After a hot shower at the yacht club and a quick trip to the grocery store for some fresh fruit and vegetables, Luke returned and lit the charcoal grill on the stern pulpit of *Tranquilo*. As he turned around to make his way down to the galley to start the rice cooker and prepare the fish, he saw Teruyo getting out of the limo, this time without the driver opening the door. As she stepped away from the vehicle, it slowly drove away. She had changed from the more business-like pants and blouse she wore for their earlier meeting to a light-colored casual summer dress with a matching jacket over one arm and a shopping bag in the other. She looked even lovelier than she had earlier.

She entered through the gate, wearing a big smile, and quickly slipped out of her shoes and climbed aboard. Lifting her sunglasses to rest on the top of her head, she pulled a bottle of chilled wine out of the bag and sensually asked, "Would a Chenin Blanc be appropriate with the Mahi-Mahi?"

"Yeah, that'll be great. I'm afraid I'm a real sucker for a nice wine with a good dinner."

She could have confirmed that from the surveillance over the past two nights, but didn't want to spoil the moment. She understood how her security team could make anyone nervous; they had done it enough over the past few months. Luke and Teruyo went below to the galley where he placed the wine in the freezer to keep chilled.

"Can I help with dinner?" she asked earnestly.

"How about making a salad while I see if I can duplicate a Samoan recipe I learned for cooking fish? I met this fascinating young

Samoan fellow when I was rafted up to the dock at the boatyard. They were working on a fishing boat tied up next to me when I was in the process of replacing the diesel engine. He'd prepared some of their fresh catch with ginger, butter, and lime juice, and it was absolutely the best fish I have ever eaten."

They ate under lantern light in the cockpit on the expanding teakwood table that folded out from the binnacle. "Luke, you're right. This is wonderful, the best fish I've ever eaten! The way this Mahi-Mahi melts in my mouth with the aroma of the fresh ginger is fabulous."

They continued talking right where they had left off in the afternoon, just talking and listening to each other.

"How is it that a Japanese lady has a New England accent?"

"Actually, I'm only half Japanese. My mother is Japanese and my father grew up in Louisiana, hence my French last name. They met and married in college. I was actually born and raised in Connecticut and I wanted to study at an Ivy League school. I graduated from Brown two years ago with a biology degree. The past two years, I've been doing research and working on my graduate degree in Environmental Science, studying the effects of pollution on marine environments."

She added that the study of martial arts

was her other passion next to sailing and biology, and mentioned having a fifth-degree black belt, but didn't elaborate. Luke could see that much of her poise came with the fact she could probably easily take care of herself in almost any physical encounter. Her dream was to make some contribution towards furthering awareness of marine ecology and the environment through continued research or teaching. Her father was an archaeologist before he was stricken and passed away from cancer at the age of thirty-five, and he'd had a large impact on her desire to become involved in ecology. She, her mother, and her younger sister were very close, and now were kept very well guarded under the protection of her grandfather.

"Everything came to a stop for me when I fell in love with the captain of the Brown Sailing team. I was attending a social event, held in his honor to recognize his long string of victories, when we met. It was love at first sight that turned into a two-year romance. We'd even been living together for the past year and had begun seriously discussing marriage. Fortunately, one plus of having a security team is they discovered he was not faithful to me, and this news was totally devastating. It appeared he was more interested in marrying into my family's money and had no real concept of true love or fidelity.

Although I've been badly hurt, I'm glad I found out before we continued any longer. I've taken some time off from graduate studies and traveled a little in Europe and now I'm on my way to our home in Japan."

"I know a little about infidelity," Luke replied with disgust. "When I was in 'Nam, I received a *Dear John* letter from my wife. The Army doesn't let a soldier leave a war zone to take care of personal problems, so I took care of the paperwork through the Army and before I knew it, I was divorced and have never seen or heard from her again. Don't have any regrets either. If they can't be true, they ain't worth wastin' time on."

As the last of the wine was evenly divided up between their glasses and the alcohol and meal were taking effect, Luke was having a difficult time remembering to be cautious. This was becoming just like a date, and she could see he was not as guarded and more of his real personality was coming out. Luke started showing Teruyo his humorous side. As the evening progressed, he would respond with little amusing quips. It was good for her to be able to laugh, and the more he could see her eyes and extraordinary smile light up her face, the more Luke continued to joke around. In their own ways, they were both learning about each other and even easing into a romantic mode.

She asked to be excused to use the head, so Luke gathered the dishes from the cockpit and took them to the sinks below. When she returned, she assisted with the cleanup, and for the first time other than their handshake, they were touching. Passing the clean dishes lent a couple of opportunities to touch her hand, sexual energy vibrating through him with every brush. Logic and reasoning were being taken over by an attraction that he had not felt in many months. This was not the time to ruin a very pleasant evening, but Luke was feeling a most anxious desire to embrace and kiss Teruyo right at this instant. He'd had just enough wine that he was losing his inhibitions.

She was also feeling his touches, but with more control to maintain a proper appearance, and careful not to give the wrong impression, Teruyo was doing her best to dry the dishes. She was also feeling aroused, and when they were finished, they just stood facing each other in the galley. Looking into her eyes, the feelings overcame him and he reached to embrace her. Teruyo melted into his arms. Their lips locked in a kiss of passion and exhilaration that was breathtaking.

The extent of the passion caught them off guard; it was not planned, nor was it remotely expected. They had realized they were attracted to each other, but not to this degree. The embrace was totally unlike any either had experienced with anyone, ever. They stopped, both shocked at this completely spontaneous, intoxicating kiss. They looked deeply into each other's eyes, at a loss for words for several seconds.

All Luke could say was, "*Wow!*"

As intense as the moment was, and as electrifying as their first kiss felt, his exclamation brought a giggle from Teruyo, then uncontrollable laughter from them both. They fell into the soft cushions of the salon, laughing and holding each other.

"Hey, if you won't tell anyone, I won't either," stated Luke, which drew another laugh.

"Oh please, no one can find out we're acting like this. My reputation at Brown would be ruined," Teruyo giggled.

"Let me guess: you're the serious one, right?"

"Yes, yes. Oh, this is so funny. Luke please, that was precious... I mean that kiss was so intense, then... 'Wow!'" She started laughing again.

They continued to hold onto each other as the laughter subsided into the still of the evening. The wake of a passing dinghy caused a slight motion on *Tranquilo.* The lapping of the waves against her hull returned their thoughts to their embrace. Silently for each, it began to sink in: that kiss, that embrace was incredible.

"You're not wearing a bug are you?" Luke softly asked.

"A what?"

"You know, a bug... a remote microphone that is making your security team wonder what I put in your Mahi-Mahi to cause this crazy outburst. Maybe they're calling in a S.W.A.T. team to take me out."

"Do you watch a lot of James Bond movies?"

"Haven't missed a one."

"No. No bugs, Mr. Davis."

"Are we being watched?"

"I must confess, I'd totally forgotten about them. Yes, we are being watched. Whether or not they can see or hear us now, down here in the cabin, I have no clue. For now, until we gain their complete trust, we are being watched."

"Hey, let's cast off the dock lines and cruise the harbor. That should shake them up. Besides, it's such a beautiful night, and you can show me how good you are at driving a boat in close quarters."

"Oh, I'd love to!"

Luke started the engine and let it slowly warm up as they worked together to take down the awning and stow it below in the forward cabin. He unhooked the electrical shore power connection and turned on the navigation lights, leaving only two of the dock lines attached. He then slid in right behind Teruyo as she had taken the position at the wheel and explained to her how to operate the throttle and forward-neutral-reverse lever. She allowed him to explain and welcomed his touch, although she had already figured out the controls.

"Now, the stern torques to port when in reverse, so you'll need to slightly steer her to starboard as we back out."

She assumed this as well, but his suggestion was appropriate since there were concrete pilings on either side of the stern that could put marks on the beautiful new dark blue paint. When everything looked ready, Luke cast off the remaining two dock lines, and Teruyo carefully and expertly backed *Tranquilo* out of the slip, turned the stern to port, then forward into the channel. She slowly drove past the many rows of slips, looking at all of the boats, and occasionally waved at other sailors lounging in their cockpits.

They sailed in front of the Hawaii Yacht Club. As it was a Tuesday evening, only a few people were lounging by the barbecue, but they knew Luke's boat and waved. When it dawned on them Luke wasn't driving, that made for some speculative conversation.

"This ought to start some gossip in the morning for Ben and his crew." Luke beamed.

All the while, Luke was admiring Teruyo's skills at handling *Tranquilo* in the tight confines of the harbor. The key to handling a fifty-footer in a harbor this crowded was to anticipate what was coming next, as well as handling the boat. She was taking things slowly, not only for the enjoyment of the moment, but keeping out of trouble in the event another boat came out of a slip or the wind picked up and necessitated an adjustment. Gus had spent hours coaching Luke in and out of the harbor in windy and rainy as well as calm conditions. Luke could tell Teruyo knew how to drive a boat.

Though Luke was standing above and behind her by the main sheet, Teruyo was amazed he trusted her already with his boat. She was having such a great time, but for him to allow her the chance to prove her story on their first evening together showed that he was willing to believe in her. That was a great feeling. Maybe she could finally be more trusting with a man again, too.

Chapter 4

Luke didn't awaken the next morning until well after 7:00. He'd usually have been at the yacht club for coffee and a shower and headed to his favorite breakfast hangout by then. After returning from their evening harbor cruise the night before, they had decided to call it an evening in order to appear to the security team that everything was still proper. They made plans to meet for breakfast at 9:00 at *Eggs & Things,* Luke's favorite place for breakfast with which Teruyo was familiar. He had walked her to the drive in front of his slip. In just a few seconds, the limo appeared and Luke held open the door. Just as Teruyo was sliding into the seat, their eyes met once again, and for an instant, they both felt the intensity of their earlier embrace in the galley.

Of course, sleep was difficult for both of them. In fact, Luke had as tough a time falling asleep as the first night he had seen the Gulfstar arrive at the yacht club. It was equally difficult for Teruyo. Their embrace lingered as though it had never been broken. It had been electrifying, and she couldn't wait for the next day to arrive. She had never felt this excited around any man before. *What did he put in that Mahi-Mahi?*

Eggs & Things was a little hole-in-the-wall place that served the best breakfasts in the entire free world, according to Luke. Their pancakes were light and fluffy and hot, with *real* melted butter. Luke preferred dousing his in their rich, delicious coconut syrup. Luke wondered how he could have lived 34 years without coconut syrup. It was the most amazing stuff, and Luke couldn't think of a better meal to start off the morning. He had been living in Honolulu now for almost six months and could probably count on one hand the number of days he hadn't had pancakes with coconut syrup at *Eggs & Things*. The owner was an avid fisherman, frequently bringing in his catch for breakfast the next day. Fresh Ono, Ahi, Mahi-Mahi, Swordfish, and Uku were some of the many fresh fish choices. Their eggs were farm fresh too, always fixed just right, and the waitresses were friendly and efficient. This was a very busy place; it was no wonder why. Most mornings, there was a line outside to wait in until a seat was available.

By 9:00 on a weekday though, it wasn't too busy that a table couldn't be found, and as Luke came through the door, he saw that Teruyo was already seated at a table for two and waved him over. She was just as excited to see him, as he was to see her.

"Mind if I sit down and join ya, Lady?" Luke asked with his relaxed Missouri drawl.

"Well, okay, but count yourself fortunate. I've already refused two fishermen, three surfer dudes, and something out of a *Star Wars* movie."

"Yeah, this place attracts Honolulu's finest," he laughed. "How are you this morning?"

"Tired, really tired."

"Me too, didn't sleep well… must have been all the traffic in the harbor last night."

The waitress, knowing that Luke always wanted coffee and ice water, arrived with a cup of *Kona* coffee and cheerfully greeted him, "Good morning, Luke. We have fresh Ono this morning."

"Oh, you sure know how to take advantage of a boy early in the morning."

"Early! You call *this* early? We were about to call the Harbor Patrol to go looking for you!" She winked mischievously at Teruyo and asked, "How about you, Miss?"

"Tea please, and I'll have the fresh Ono as well."

After the waitress hurried back to the kitchen, Teruyo asked, "Traffic? It seemed really quiet when I left."

"Traffic and every other sound from the harbor… fish jumping, bilge pumps pumping, cars honking... you name it, I heard it."

"I also lost a lot of sleep thinking about last night," she replied. "I was a little afraid that once you had a chance to think, you might be uncomfortable with my situation. I thought you might not show for breakfast this morning and sail on away without me."

"You know, I even thought about that, but as crazy as this seems, I was anxious to see if you'd show up here as well. Listen, I've spent the entire night thinking about last night. I don't know why I grabbed you like that. I'm sorry, but yet I'm really not."

"No, don't be. Last night was wonderful. I'm actually grateful you're willing to even talk about it. I can tell you are just as nervous and unsure as I am. Should we just flow with it and see where this leads?"

"Well, I was kind of hoping you were still counting on coming with me tomorrow."

"Oh yes, now more than ever! I'll have to finalize a few details with the security team, with your permission of course, and we should be all set."

"You mean they have already cleared me?"

"Yeah, they'd pretty much done that before I approached you. It's just been a matter of my input and some final observations."

"Did they see me kiss you?"

"I don't know. They didn't mention it or

seem anxious when we discussed this morning the further possibilities of this trip, though they did get a little nervous when they saw us taking down the awning and leaving the slip last night." She grinned.

"Well, I'm not at all thrilled to know someone is possibly watching my every move. I really don't want to put you in a compromising situation, but I'm more of a free spirit than they may approve of."

"Well, let's just see how it goes."

Their breakfast came, taking up every millimeter of space on the tiny table. Luke devoured every bite. Teruyo was very pleased with the flavors and with watching him eat. They agreed to meet back at *Tranquilo* in two hours. Luke got on his bicycle and headed back to the harbor.

Before Luke had gone to *Eggs & Things* that morning, he'd first gone to the yacht club and showered. He was glad Ben had not been out fishing because he needed someone he could talk with about this remarkable story. Ben could see Luke was troubled with something so they went outside and sat next to the barbecue grill where they could talk in private. Luke told him the whole story of meeting Teruyo and asked Ben if he could do some checking around to see if anyone in Honolulu could verify this Tanaka Industry and the "security team" story. Ben said he'd get right on it, and for Luke to check back with him after their breakfast rendezvous.

True to his word, Ben had done some checking on Teruyo Boudreaux. She was indeed the granddaughter of one of the richest men in the world. Tanaka Industries was one of Japan's largest conglomerates and held a tremendous amount of real estate holdings in Hawaii as well as in the mainland states. Ben's contacts assured him that a security team was not only very probable, but also most likely had even checked him out. They were the type of organization that wanted to know everything about anyone they dealt with, not leaving anything up to chance. Yes, this bordered on privacy issues, but they had the means to do it, were discrete, and had connections in the right places so as not to be discovered breaking any laws.

Ben gave Luke all that he had found out so far and advised him to be very careful with this lady. He assured him that his "friends downtown" described this organization as a very tight-knit family. "Not the Yakuza, the Japanese mafia, but very protective and with the resources and the desire to keep their family closed to the outside. Luke, this is not just a pretty girl you're dealing with," Ben cautioned.

On the one hand, Luke was glad to hear Teruyo was truthful about her situation, but the burden of being attracted to or even just having her and all of her family "baggage" with him for a few weeks was unsettling, especially now that he was set to head out on his much anticipated cruise to Maui. Sure, he knew of Tanaka Industries—anyone who read the Wall Street Journal did—but to suddenly find himself involved with the granddaughter of the head of one of the world's largest corporations made him nervous. But what was the worst that could happen? As long as he didn't try to hold her for ransom, why should he worry about harm coming to him? Well, he'd see how things went today with Teruyo, and find out just how she was going to setup communications with her security team.

Teruyo anxiously arrived at noon, about a half-hour before they had planned to meet, but that was just fine with Luke. She had really dressed down from their previous encounters, wearing shorts, a t-shirt, and sandals.

"Hey, looks like you came to work."

"Well, *Sir*, if we are leaving tomorrow, we probably have lots to do."

"Hmm, I like the sound of that, but from

now on, you will address me as 'Sir, Captain Sir,' and no snickering allowed on this ship!" Luke had to work hard to keep from laughing.

"Very well, *Sir, Captain, Sir*! May I please scrub the bilges, change your engine oil, and fix you lunch?"

This was getting a bit silly, as they were both hamming it up, but it was fun. Teruyo pulled herself onto the deck and sat on the cabin top, anxious for her first orders of the day.

"Well, we could belay the bilge cleaning and the oil is still fresh, but we do need to get a list of food and necessities that you'd prefer. Also, I was wondering about how you are planning on keeping in touch with your team, and what's my role in all this?"

With a seductive smile that accelerated Luke's heart rate three-fold, Teruyo leaned towards him and purred, "First of all, I want you to be sure to provision us with lots of ginger."

Straightening back up, she continued, "Actually, I found in the trip I took last summer from the Riviera to England, it was very helpful having plenty of freeze-dried meals and instant soups such as Saimin, like we can find at the Japanese market *Shirokiya* in the shopping center."

"I love *Shirokiya!* We could load up on all kinds of treats that last a long time. Have you ever eaten there for lunch?"

"Oh yes, they have great sushi and bento."

"What about your 'big brothers'?" Luke tilted his head towards the parking lot, from where he was sure someone was watching them.

"I know how that must be bothering you. I would like to suggest a meeting today with Shindo, my driver from yesterday. He is in charge of my security, and you should hear from him what he expects of you. I have found these people are very dedicated to my grandfather, and it is best to work with them."

"Ok, set it up."

"Yes Sir, Captain Sir!" At that, she jumped off onto the dock, ran to the gate, and waved. A moment later, Shindo appeared and she brought him over to the starboard side of *Tranquilo*. Teruyo was actually excited to be introducing Shindo to Luke. This seemed a bit odd, but maybe it was because she was looking forward to taking the next step in getting on with this adventure.

"Luke, may I introduce you to Shindo. He is in charge of my security."

Luke jumped down onto the dock and offered his hand. "Pleased to finally be introduced, Mr. Shindo."

Accepting Luke's handshake and with a slight bow, Shindo replied, "I am also pleased to make your acquaintance, and thank you for the glass of water yesterday. Shindo is my first name, thank you."

"You're welcome. Would you like to come aboard and look my vessel over? Wait a second, I have something to help you step up to the deck." Luke went up to get an old plastic milk crate to assist Shindo with stepping up to the deck. However, before Luke was even in the cockpit, he felt his boat list to starboard and when he turned around, Shindo was up on the deck right behind him. How that happened Luke would never know, as Shindo was so stout and short-legged, Luke couldn't imagine he could have made it up on his own.

"Sorry, I didn't mean to imply… I just thought…"

"That is understandable, Mr. Davis. Thank you for the courtesy."

"Well, if you would like to look around, you'll see I have no guns or weapons. I do have a spear gun for diving, and a flare gun, which holds 12-gauge flare shells. Other than that, I don't believe in carrying weapons."

Taking a seat in the cockpit, Shindo replied, "Yes, Mr. Davis, we know. I am confident that Teruyo is satisfied your vessel is seaworthy; she is more experienced with that aspect of our concerns. What I need from you is your assurance that if you feel at any time you may be in danger or you suspect anything even remotely suspicious or not right, you will make every effort to contact me. I know you have good radio capabilities, and here are two frequencies where our team can be reached immediately." He handed Luke a card with a radio frequency on the UHF range that Luke could use with his SSB radio and another frequency to use with his ham radio. "When you are away from your boat, you can contact us using the toll-free phone number on the front, which is also manned twenty-four hours a day. We must know when you plan on sailing to an island where you may be staying for a day or more so I can fly there or have one of our other team members there before you arrive. Teruyo will call or radio us your estimated departure and arrival times and we have coded all of the harbors and most of the anchorages in Hawaii so she can refer to them when she calls. In the event you need our help, we will have a better chance of promptly responding.

"We will not be intrusive and only respond if you call. However, understand very clearly, we have been entrusted with the safety of Teruyo and we will not hesitate to ensure that if we cannot work together with you on this, we will no longer allow her to continue."

Luke answered, "I understand and appreciate the tough job you have. Do you want me to communicate in plain language over the radio or in a code?"

"Teruyo will make the radio calls in a code she is experienced with when you are not close to a telephone. In the event you need to call, do so with the most clarity to avoid misunderstanding."

Luke felt this was all pretty straight-forward; obviously they were prepared to keep in contact with his radio capabilities. Very professional, simple, and... *how'd they know I didn't have any guns?* "You have my assurance, Shindo, that I'll do everything to keep you informed. Would you care for anything to drink?"

"Please. Some water would be nice."

Chapter 5

They spent the rest of the afternoon shopping at the Ala Moana Shopping Center, just a few blocks from the harbor. First, they looked for clothes for her that would be more practical and comfortable for life aboard the boat, but when she started looking at swimwear, she suggested Luke should look in another department for foul-weather gear. Ron's wife had left her foul-weather clothing on the Gulfstar in her haste to get to a hotel, as did Ron, however Teruyo was a bit taller than the last lady of the Gulfstar, and a proper fit was very important for keeping dry and warm. Luke had found what he felt she needed, but not the right quality he was looking for, so he didn't buy any.

They loaded up on many flavors of Ramen, which made for a fast, hot meal. She bought some practical but beautiful Oriental bowls and plates, which had a non-skid type of bottom to prevent them from sliding off the table. There were several other treats that Teruyo purchased, which were foreign to Luke, but, as they say, *When in Rome—or when in a Japanese department store with a lady who is Japanese...*

When they were all shopped out, Shindo appeared at the entrance and assisted with loading their purchases into the limo. This was a real luxury for Luke, as his usual trips to the store were on his bicycle, meaning that everything had to be carried home in his backpack. Next stop was the market, where they shopped for fresh fruits, vegetables, and some canned foods that were not in Luke's current stock, but Teruyo assured him would be most welcomed for preparing meals if they were away from markets for a long time. And of course ginger, plenty of fresh ginger. In case they didn't catch any fresh fish, the market had a nice selection of Ahi, Mahi-Mahi, Ono, and Papio. He would freeze those so they would have plenty in case the fishing lures he and Ben had made didn't live up to their reputations.

When they returned to *Tranquilo*, Shindo helped them unload the trunk of the limo and left them to stow away their supplies. This "charter" was beginning to come together, and they were both very excited as they worked together stowing everything in its place. After everything was stowed away, and there was nothing left to do, they sat in the cockpit and mellowed out for a while as the sun started to set over the break wall at the harbor entrance. Luke grabbed a beer and Teruyo was happy with a glass of water, each lost in their own thoughts, but both wanting the journey to begin immediately.

"Since this is our last night in the harbor, would you like to have dinner at the yacht club?" Luke asked.

"That sounds great, and I'd like to grab a shower and change into one of my new outfits."

"We can do that there if you want."

"OK, I'll send Shindo on and tell him I'll call him in the morning. If it's alright with you, we can say my charter starts tonight?"

"It'll cost you an extra five bucks," Luke teased.

Teruyo grabbed a new pair of shorts and a long-sleeve top she had just bought, and they headed towards the club. On the way, she informed Shindo of their plans, and he gave a slight bow of his head before driving away. At the club, they went to the respective showers and afterward, met upstairs in the bar where Luke had arrived first, visiting with his friends Ben and Vern. He introduced Teruyo, and in the true aloha spirit, they welcomed her to the club. Teruyo thanked Ben for the Mahi-Mahi from the previous night. They were very impressed with her sincerity, as well as her beauty.

Luke felt they couldn't find a nicer place to have their last dinner before leaving the Ala Wai Yacht Harbor. The food wasn't the best in town, though very good. It was just the whole feeling of this place that Luke loved so much. The view at sunset was incredible, and surrounded by all of the beautiful yachts and watching the boat traffic entering and exiting the harbor added a unique quality to the atmosphere. When Luke joined the club as an associate member right after purchasing the Gulfstar, he became part of a family as well as a member of a club. He could have invited Teruyo to a fancier restaurant, but to Luke this was like a home away from home.

Teruyo was also happy to be here. Meeting Ben and Vern was a great chance to validate her choice of signing on with Luke for this sail. She could see the mutual regard Ben and Vern had for Luke, and that Luke appreciated the advice and encouragement they shared with him. She recognized the significance of a man beginning his first voyage on his own. There is a tremendous responsibility with heading out to sea; the safety of you and your crew is always on the line, the investment of all the hours of labor as well as the money into your boat, and even one's reputation and character as a man. This takes a large amount of courage, especially for one's first crossing in the extreme conditions between the islands of Hawaii.

As the restaurant was closing down, and the club getting quieter, they knew it was time

to be heading back. When Teruyo notified
Shindo that she would call him in the morning,
she didn't make a big deal about it. They
looked at each other about halfway back, and it
dawned on him that this was going to be their
first night together alone. Without saying a
word, Luke took Teruyo's hand, and they
resumed walking. She couldn't have asked for
a better sign of assurance.

They walked without talking back to
Tranquilo, now with the nervousness and
anticipation of what lie ahead. Luke was
considering putting on some soft music and
low lantern light, but he didn't want to frighten
Teruyo off by coming on too strong. However,
she *was* still holding his hand. Teruyo,
although ten years younger than Luke, was
actually feeling more relaxed with what she
hoped was happening.

He gave her a hand stepping up on deck
and then went about checking and double-
checking all the dock lines as if a big storm
were brewing. She noticed he was a bit
preoccupied with checking everything on deck
and seemed to be delaying coming down into
the cabin, so she went on below. When all was
determined to be secure and there was nothing
left to do, Luke nervously took a deep breath,
like he was about to free-dive to check on his
anchor, and he started below, closing the
companionway hatch as he descended the

steps.

Teruyo had put on a tape of soft jazz and was just finishing lighting the two kerosene lanterns as Luke turned around from closing the hatch. Her eyes were seductive and when she blew out the match, she did so without taking her eyes off of Luke. The question of whether to follow his desires or not was answered. They joined in an embrace and kissed with all of the passion and heat two new lovers could generate, and he led her gently to the aft cabin.

Chapter 6

"Good morning."

"Hmm, good morning, Captain. So much for an early start."

"Well, it is *your* charter."

"Ah, then let's stay in bed and leave tonight."

"Aye, except the Harbor Master said check-out time is noon."

After a few kisses and more snuggling, it became apparent there were still more important things to be attended to than hopping up and checking out with the Harbor Master. They were going to take this at their own pace.

By 9:30, they had managed to make coffee and get dressed, but were still moving with the urgency of starry-eyed lovers on a rainy Sunday morning. Teruyo brought Luke a cup of coffee to the cockpit as he was just finishing a thank you letter to the Harbor Master and his staff for their courtesy. She wasn't a morning coffee person, but enjoyed serving him his coffee and watching him clear the cobwebs. They talked about the last minute things they had to do: buy her a set of foul-weather gear, break down his bicycle and stow it in the forward berth, get out the charts, remove all of the dock lines he had rigged for that slip, top off the water and fuel tanks, pump out the holding tank, and cast off. Teruyo also needed to notify Shindo when they were departing and give him an ETA for Maui. They dropped the letter off at the Harbor Master's office on their walk over to *Eggs & Things* and were back by noon with her new set of "slickers," ready to cast off for the fuel dock.

Tranquilo held 100 gallons of diesel fuel in two stainless steel tanks and 210 gallons of fresh water in four stainless steel tanks distributed throughout the voids under the cabin sole. The holding tank for sewage for the two heads held 35 gallons, and it had to be pumped out to a sewage-holding tank at the fuel dock. When at sea, a valve can be reversed and the sewage and *grey* water emptied into the ocean, but that was only legal and proper if you were three nautical miles offshore. Luke wasn't sure what the fuel consumption rate for the newly installed Mercedes diesel would be, so he started a log to determine an estimate of fuel-per-hour usage. Teruyo called Shindo, everything was topped off and secured, and by 1:35 they cast off from the fuel dock for Maui.

The marine weather forecast was calling for 15 to18 knots of wind out of the NNE, but that meant it could easily be 20, gusting to 25 knots in the Kaiwi Channel between Oahu and Molokai. Luke asked Teruyo to hold *Tranquilo* into the wind in front of the yacht club while he set a double reef in the mainsail. It was great to have a crew who knew how to hold a boat steady while tending to the sails, especially under the watchful eyes of the sailors at the club. When Luke was satisfied with the mainsail's trim, he set the mizzen, unfurled the genoa then gave a sign for Teruyo to bear off (turn down wind). He returned to the cockpit to adjust the set of the sails to the wind coming now off the port quarter. Ben and Vern waved from the balcony of the yacht club, and Luke yelled, "Aloha!" The couple's excitement was really building now as they sailed out the harbor channel. The shiny blue hull of the Gulfstar with her three new white Dacron sails made for a postcard picture that Ben and Vern would relay to the other yacht club members each time anyone would ask about Luke.

After they rounded the channel buoy to port and headed east toward Diamond Head, the wind was now coming off the port beam and Luke trimmed the sails to adjust for the new direction they were going in relation to the wind. He knew he would need to reef the genoa (roll it in some) when they left the lee of Diamond Head, but for now, they were sailing well. He asked Teruyo to idle down the engine for a few minutes so it could cool before shutting it off, and they gave each other a big hug—they were finally on their way.

Teruyo was as excited to be sailing as Luke, and he was letting her steer even though he was dying inside to take the helm. But he kept himself busy down below double-checking the hatches to be sure there were no leaks in the engine room. He also checked for anything that may have fallen out of any unsecured cabinets. Back on deck, he asked, "How do the sails look? Watch the heading. What's our depth?"

"Hey Captain, tranquilo, tranquilo...take it easy."

At 1447 (2:47 p.m.), they passed the Diamond Head lighthouse and entered the Kaiwi Channel. The wind freshened, and Luke reefed the genoa to about a 100% jib shape. *Tranquilo* dug into the waves close reaching at six and a half knots. Right away, the spray from the six to eight-foot waves bounced off the dodger, and they lurched up and down over each wave with the thrill of children on a roller coaster. Teruyo had a grin the size of Texas, and Luke was on a huge natural high. He was finally cruising on his own boat.

Luke got right down to setting his fishing lures. Ben had helped Luke with the purchase of a couple of good-quality fishing poles with the right type of line, and they had attached pole mounts on the stern rail. They had spent some mornings at the yacht club making lures and talking about the types that worked best for different conditions. A hand-held line was secured to each port and starboard stern cleat, which held smaller lightweight lures. Luke had already mounted the fishing poles in the holders prior to leaving the fuel dock so all he had to do was read the clouds and clip on the appropriate color of lure. Since it was a typically partly cloudy day, he selected "The General" for one side, which was a squid-type pink, blue, and white lure. For the other side, Luke chose "The Teacher," a green and white-skirted lure. Ben had a story for each lure, and Luke felt it could be good luck to carry on with their names. He staggered them behind *Tranquilo* so they wouldn't get tangled, but not so far that they stopped popping out of the water. Ben said the more surface action you can get from them, the more it would resemble a wounded or frightened baitfish. If the winds were to back off and their boat speed decreased significantly, then Luke would need to reel them closer to the boat so the lures would still be close to the surface.

With everything set, Teruyo offered get a couple of beers if Luke would take the helm. "Bummer...oh well, let me have it," Luke teased, grinning, and settled in behind the wheel. Everything was perfect: *Tranquilo* was sailing really well, it was a beautiful day, and Teruyo had just returned wearing a skimpy bikini and handing Luke a cold beer. She was gorgeous! It was the first beer he had seen her drink, and maybe it was just a show of camaraderie, because she only attempted a few sips. He could tell she didn't like it.

He set the autopilot to be sure it was working properly, however, he shut it off shortly afterwards because it felt great to be driving. The autopilot would get plenty of work later on. He advised Teruyo to apply plenty of sunscreen. She had prior to leaving the fuel dock, but now she had much more area exposed. It wouldn't do getting sunburned on their first day out. They didn't bother with setting the bimini top to protect them from the sun; they were enjoying soaking in all of the elements too much. With the wind, saltwater spray, the sun, and Jimmy Buffet belting out *"Cheeseburger in Paradise"* over the speakers, they were off to a great beginning.

From the Diamond Head lighthouse to Haloe Lono harbor on the southwest tip of Molokai was about 35 nautical miles. Gus and Luke stayed there on their first crossing together the year before, and making for this harbor was a possibility for Luke and Teruyo. The plan had been to sail directly to Maui, however because of their late start, which neither regretted, they would be arriving there sometime late at night. Luke was not all that comfortable anchoring off Maui in the middle of the night. The first area they were going to on Maui, Ka'anapali Beach, was not the calmest anchorage as the wind and the waves frequently came in from different directions, making for an uncomfortable rolling motion when at anchor. There were some good spots to pick, but one needed daylight or more local experience to set the hook and be safe as well as comfortable.

After maintaining a speed of about six and a half knots for the first two hours, they decided to make for Haloe Lono harbor to spend the night. Haloe Lono was a private, manmade harbor with no channel entrance lights, and if you didn't know exactly where it was, you would not know what to look for. Keeping a close eye on the depth sounder and nervously watching the heading, they made it past the small surf break and around the breakwater.

The harbor used to be a facility at which they loaded barges with sand to spread over Waikiki Beach. Teruyo slowly drove up to a point where it was very calm and with plenty of room to swing about the anchor if the wind changed. Luke dropped the anchor in twenty-two feet of water. It was 1905 (7:05 pm) and they had successfully made their first crossing together.

There were no other boats in the harbor that evening. They had forty-five minutes before sunset, plenty of time for a shower and a few appetizers. Luke hoped this would be his chance to see a green flash.

Showers on a sailboat must be short and sweet. Freshwater is a precious commodity, and hot water is a luxury. Fortunately, when they were running the engine on their approach to the harbor and while setting the anchor, they were also heating hot water. Teruyo knew of this luxury from her crewing on the large yacht from France the previous year, but Luke, who remembered staying pretty salty while sailing with Gus, especially appreciated it. The proper way to shower on a sailboat is to get wet, shut the water off, lather up, then turn the water back on and rinse off. Teruyo showered first, as Luke went through the boat, checking on everything to ensure there were no leaks or surprises. When it was Luke's turn to shower, Teruyo started making pupus (appetizers), and in short order, they were snuggled up in the cockpit sipping frozen margaritas and watching the sunset.

"I wonder if we will see a green flash," Teruyo said.

"Have you seen one?"

"Oh yes, they're so beautiful. Haven't you?"

"I must admit they've plum evaded me."

Giggling, Teruyo asked, "What does 'plum evaded me' mean? Is that a southernism or what?"

"I'm not sure, but it comes from a Jimmy Buffet song and I think it means 'one without the capacity to see.'"

That brought a laugh, and at that moment they both saw the sun dip over the clear horizon without the slightest puff of green.

Their second full night together was better than their first. Their lovemaking was passionate, and being together alone on *Tranquilo* coupled with the emotion of the successful crossing and exhilarating sail was amazing.

Luke was awoken by an unfamiliar noise a little after midnight. He bounded out to the cockpit and was relieved to see that the wind had only changed direction and the anchor chain was making a slight rumble on the bow roller. Everything was secure. The ground tackle (anchor and chain) was very undersized originally, especially for Hawaiian waters. Gus took it as his personal mission to insure this new beauty of Luke's would stay put when setting the hook. Since she had a good electric windless on the bow to assist with retrieving the anchor and chain, he procured a 66 lb. *Bruce* anchor, which more than did the job.

While he was out, Luke sat on the foredeck and admired the stars; he had never seen so many stars. It was totally dark around them; there were no city lights of Honolulu to keep the eyes from seeing the more remote stars. Teruyo came on deck, and they held each other, soaking in the beautiful night.

"See that?" Luke asked as a falling star zipped overhead.

"Yes, and I made a wish."

"Going to tell me what it is?"

"No, I can't or it might not come true."

Teruyo gently eased Luke to his back, and they made love on the foredeck.

Chapter 7

"Sleeping late is getting to be a habit," Teruyo teased.

"You sure are a stickler about keeping on schedule."

"Sorry, Sir, Captain Sir. More discipline Captain, please. More discipline!" Teruyo laughed.

After breakfast and a long relaxing spell just holding each other in the cockpit, they decided to move on towards Maui. Teruyo called on the single side band radio to announce their coded position on Molokai and their expected arrival at their next coded position on Maui by early evening. The message was acknowledged, and her responsibilities to the security team were complete for the day. Luke gave *Tranquilo* another thorough inspection and was pleased to see everything below was dry and in working order. They started the engine early, while still doing dishes and tidying up, to give the refrigeration systems a chance to keep up the charge for the freezer and reefer. It was a very sunny day, so they rigged the bimini top to protect them from the sun and applied lots of sunscreen. Then Luke hauled the anchor.

Ka'anapali Beach was another forty-five

miles, but sailing along the lee of the island of Molokai would not give them the strong trade winds they had yesterday until they got closer to Maui. For the first few hours, as long as they stayed fairly close to shore, the wind was blowing onshore from the south. It was very smooth and calm, compared to the previous day.

A pod of dolphins appeared, playing and crossing right in front of *Tranquilo's* bow, and Teruyo was quick to go to the bow pulpit to watch them. Luke set the autopilot and joined her until the dolphins concluded their friendly visit and moved on. Luke grinned as he held Teruyo while sailing in flat water, the boat in perfect trim, driving herself.

They debated pulling into the harbor town of Kaunakakai on Molokai, because the cruising guide indicated it was a well-protected harbor with really nice people. However, they were making such a good course to Maui that they decided to save that stop for another day. Not long after passing the entrance to the Kaunakakai harbor, the sea breeze gave way to the trade winds, so it was time to reduce sail area. Teruyo feathered *Tranquilo* slightly into the wind so Luke could reef the headsail and the mainsail. He also lowered the mizzen and stowed it securely on its boom. After all was trimmed, they were back to six-plus knots and "steep & deep" in the channel again.

The farther into the channel they traveled, the more the wind was setting them away from Maui towards the island of Lanai. Luke's cruising guide as well as the charts warned of a reef extending out from the northeast point of Lanai that was nicknamed "Shipwreck Beach." The guide mentioned a World War II Liberty Ship that had run aground and is a landmark reminding sailors of the danger of this reef. Sure enough, even from a few of miles away, they could see it lying off shore, still being pounded by the surf. The West Maui Mountains were now visible in the distance as well. Three more tacks and they should be able to fetch to Ka'anapali Beach.

All of a sudden without any warning, the fishing reel on the portside started screaming. Luke had let out more line after their speed had picked up, and as they were preoccupied checking out the wrecked freighter, they were caught off-guard by the alarm of the fishing reel. The heavy-duty pole was bending like it was light fishing tackle as the reel unwound. Luke scampered back to the rod and reel and slowly tightened the drag setting a quarter of a turn like Ben had advised him. This slowed the reel, but line was still playing out rapidly.

"It must be a big one!" cried Luke as he was trying to balance himself to reel the fish in on the stern pulpit and at the same time, keep from falling off into the eight-foot waves.

Teruyo took the helm and shut off the autopilot. Luke asked her to try to slow *Tranquilo* down. She was able to head the bow up into the wind about fifteen degrees and then furled in the rest of the genoa. This slowed the boat speed to just over four knots and also helped reduce their listing to starboard. Luke was amazed how quickly and efficiently she handled the lines and the helm.

Luke's next concern was the reef ahead; although they were a ways off, he didn't want to get too close. He was able to slowly reel in a few turns on the reel, but then the fish would pull more back out. Ben had said, "If you get a big one on, you must be patient. The more line the fish has, eventually, the more tired it will become." Luke kept trying to bring it in, and Teruyo kept heading more into the wind then falling off a bit to maintain steerage. Luke called for her to set the autopilot and to come back to help with bringing in the other three fishing lines so they wouldn't get tangled. This was getting intense: big fish on the line, dangerous reef ahead, eight-foot seas, and the wind blowing twenty to twenty-five knots.

After Teruyo stowed the two hand lines and secured the lure on the other pole, she went back to the helm. Luke called for her to tack over to starboard so they could keep away from Shipwreck Beach. When she did, Luke was able to reel in a lot on the fish, as that brought the stern of *Tranquilo* closer to the fish. Teruyo was being cool under pressure, and Luke was stoked. This was one big fight. The fish flew out of the water about two hundred feet aft of the stern. Luke wasn't sure if it was a marlin or some other big fish, but it seemed to him just like watching those fishing shows on TV, except he was hanging on for dear life with one hand and trying to bring the fish in inch by inch with the other.

"There he is again! Teruyo, did you see him?!" Luke yelled at the top of his lungs.

"Yes! Be careful back there!" she shouted back.

"In the port side cockpit lazarete just aft of the propane gas bottles is a gaff and a small baseball bat clipped to the bulkhead. See if you can get 'em ready for me."

Teruyo found them right away. The gaff had a rubber tip to help prevent injury, and the half-size baseball bat had a strap to go around one's wrist so it wouldn't fall overboard. Ben had made the half-size bat for Luke from a discarded broken softball bat. Teruyo laid them on the floor of the cockpit for now and continued keeping *Tranquilo* going as slowly as possible without turning downwind and running over the line in the water. Now that they were on a starboard tack, they were listing to port, so this would be easier for Luke to gaff the fish, if he could just guide it to the port quarter.

Luke's arms were giving out. Never in his thirty-four years had he battled anything like this. The largest fish he'd ever caught was a Walleye, maybe four pounds, at a lake in Kansas. He wouldn't give up though; he kept reeling whenever the fish slowed. What seemed like forever but probably was twenty to twenty-five minutes, Luke could see the fish about ten feet away.

"Can you hand me the gaff, then stand in front of the helm? I'm going to try and lift it into the cockpit."

She handed him the gaff and went back to the helm. *Tranquilo* was still lurching up and down in the waves, and when the fish came up on the low side, Luke was able to hook the gaff under the gills and through the throat. With one big heave, he lifted it out of the water and in one motion flung it into the cockpit. It was huge and not in a good mood.

"Hand me the 'Persuader'!" Luke yelled.

"The what?"

"The baseball bat...the bat!"

The fish was flopping wildly, and Ben told Luke if he ever got a good size fish in the boat, to kill it with a blow to the head or it could do some serious damage. Luke gave it a couple of strong hits. It was a Mahi-Mahi and as it was dying, it went through the most amazing color transformation right in front of their eyes. When he first brought it onboard, it was an iridescent, beautiful blue, but as it died, it slowly turned to a lighter shade of green.

"*Wow.*"

Luke and Teruyo fell silent. They didn't feel the motion of the boat in the rough seas, and the wind was still screaming through the rigging, but they didn't hear it. This was unlike anything they were prepared for. Luke's arms and whole body were aching, and he was exhausted. There was blood all over from the dead fish. Teruyo was still driving from in front of the helm, but only by instinct, still amazed by the whole experience. Luke pulled the gaff out and she handed him the rubber tip she was still clutching in her hand. They didn't celebrate; they just slowly went about putting the gaff and the "Persuader" away. He got a bucket out and started filling it up with seawater to rinse the blood off the decks and the cockpit.

Next, Luke fed a small piece of line through the Mahi's gills and secured it so he could carry it up to the cabin top, forward of the dodger. There he lashed the fish to the handrail on the deck and then placed a wet towel over it and tied it with more line. The fish was slippery, and Luke wasn't about to lose it over the side. After all of the blood was cleaned up, he dowsed the fish again with water so it wouldn't get too hot. He went back

90

to the cockpit where Teruyo handed him a cold beer.

Chapter 8

They eased into a small cove at Ka'anapali Beach next to Black Rock at 1830 that afternoon. As they arrived closer to the lee of the West Maui Mountains, the wind died so they motored on in to find a comfortable place to anchor before tending to the fish. Luke and Gus had anchored at this same spot the year before, and though it was a roller-coaster ride then, on this day, the cove seemed much calmer. After diving on the anchor to insure it was set in the white sand, Luke retrieved the dinghy and began inflating it.

A dinghy for getting to and from shore had been another important investment for the yacht. On the cruise to Maui with Gus, Luke had been dumped in the surf a couple of times in Gus's rigid dinghy. Gus was adamant that they were the only way to go, but other cruisers differed in their opinions when it came to stowage and getting through surf breaks. An inflatable dinghy with good oarlocks and a small outboard motor became Luke's choice because of the flexibility they have when trying to get through the surf. This makes them less prone to tip when getting in and out. They take more time to assemble and disassemble, but they can be stowed in a lazarete rather than on the deck like a rigid dinghy. So after a little research, an eight-foot Avon with a four-horse Johnson outboard motor became Luke's next boat.

Luke asked Teruyo to pack his backpack with a change of clean clothes for them both including flip-flops, and then she helped him lower the dinghy over the side. While Teruyo was below calling the security team to inform them that they'd arrived at Ka'anapali Beach, Luke put the fish in a large heavy-duty trash bag so it wouldn't make a mess in his new dinghy. When they were all set, Luke rowed them down the beach about one quarter of a mile and they came ashore in front of Whaler's Village, an outdoor mall with shops and a museum, and three beachfront restaurants where he and Gus had spent some time last year.

The fish felt like it weighed around thirty pounds and seemed twice that by the time they got it ashore. As he and Teruyo carried the Mahi-Mahi out of the dinghy to a grassy lawn in the middle of the entrance to the mall, a crowd of tourists gathered to see the fish. It was about eight-thirty in the evening, the height of the dinner rush, and they attracted some curious onlookers. Luke got the attention of one of the waiters from the Rusty Harpoon Restaurant and asked him if they bought fresh fish. About a half-second later, the kitchen manager came bounding out and held it up, proclaiming to all, "Tomorrow's fresh catch of dah day." The other restaurant managers were envious that all of the customers from the three restaurants with ocean view seating saw this fish being sold, knowing that the Rusty Harpoon would be busy the next day.

They took the fish into the back of the kitchen through the loading dock and weighed it. It was twenty-six pounds and the kitchen manager said he'd gladly pay $9.75 per pound, which was the current market rate.

Luke replied, "Sold, on one condition: I want two nice fillets for my lady and me and the opportunity to see you clean it."

"No problem, bruddah. I show you how to clean fish la dat." The kitchen manager, James, a native of the Philippines, beamed and said with his pigeon-English accent, "Be here tomorrow aftahnoon, I pay you den, too."

Luke explained that this was his first Mahi and they were trolling lures while sailing over from Honolulu. The restaurant's general manager, Willie, was also happy with the new catch-of-the-day and especially the show that James had put on out on the lawn. He said, "If you and your lady here need a place to clean up, we have a shower rigged out back for when our employees finish surfing and are in a hurry to get to work. You're more than welcome to use it, and we'll see you get a nice dinner."

Luke remembered there was a shower down by the beach for rinsing off sand and he had figured they could wash off the fish odor there, but this offer was much better, considering that it would provide more privacy for Teruyo.

They went to the back dock where a shower stall and a makeshift locker room allowed them some privacy and a hot shower. Luke thought of how adventurous and happy Teruyo was with this very casual atmosphere, especially compared to what he expected she would be used to coming from a wealthy and privileged life. She was having as much fun as he and was not at all fazed by the makeshift locker room.

After getting most of the fish scent rinsed away and changing into fresh shorts and t-shirts, they felt like millionaires. They were seated for dinner in a fine restaurant, with a bit of celebrity status in a very romantic setting. The waitress was personable and kept the food flowing, beginning with Maui Onion Soup and fresh salads. She recommended the prime rib as the best on the island and of course the fresh fish. They were both hungry, so Teruyo ordered one of her favorite dishes, the Alaskan king crab legs, and Luke asked for a large hunk of the prime rib. After desserts with coffee and reliving their fish story to the some of the servers who came by, they generously tipped their waitress and met with Willie. He had prepared their check for the fish, and "comped" their dinner as well. Luke and Teruyo expressed their sincere gratitude, as they felt he was way too generous.

After going down to the beach to check on his dinghy and ensure *Tranquilo* was riding well on her anchor, Luke and Teruyo strolled hand in hand through Whaler's Village. They were too tired to be interested in any shopping, but after a couple of days within the confines of the boat, it was nice to explore a new place with lots of activity around. Fortunately, the outdoor mall was not too big, and when they circled back to the dinghy, it was very easy to decide to head back to the boat. Luke rowed them back and though his muscles were sore and he was tired, he was very happy; it had been a day to remember. However, tomorrow, he decided, he'd mount the outboard motor on the dinghy.

Black Rock is just that, a big black flow of lava rock jutting out from the lush surroundings that encompassed the Sheraton Maui Hotel Resort. Luke remembered from his first time here, that each evening at sunset an employee of the hotel, dressed only in a Hawaiian tapa cloth, lit a series of tiki torches along the crest of Black Rock. When he reached the end, he held the torch high in the air as if to salute the gods then dove into the water fifteen feet below with a beautifully executed swan dive.

By the time they had reached *Tranquilo,* the diver had long since preformed his ceremony, but the drums from the luau were still beating from the lawn at the Sheraton. Although they were anchored in the midst of some of the most luxurious resorts and hotels in the world, being on *Tranquilo* next to the torch-lit Black Rock and hearing the drums in the distance made for a real "South Pacific" feeling. As tired as they were, they were still both anticipating making love as the icing on the cake to this extraordinary day.

Chapter 9

Early the next morning, the sounds of children and parents snorkeling by Black Rock awakened Luke and Teruyo. It was a novice divers' paradise with great varieties of fish and easily accessible to the many tourists staying in the area. Since most of the tourists came from mainland USA with a six to ten hour time difference, their internal clocks were still on mainland time for the first few days, so by sunrise, the kids were ready to start the day.

The anchorage was still calm, and after Luke and Teruyo were finally ready to greet the morning, they decided, "If you can't beat 'em, join 'em." So, they donned their snorkeling gear and explored along with the other tourists. The colors were magnificent, and the fish were plentiful. It appeared the concession stand was making a good profit selling fish food, and it was fun watching the kids react to having fish eating almost out of their hands.

Luke had fallen in love with the little town down from Ka'anapali Beach, Lahaina the year before. The former first territorial capitol of Hawaii, it was quickly evolving into a popular tourist destination, but still maintained the local flavor and ties to the whaling industry of its past. Luke mounted the outboard motor and fuel tank, and since the anchorage at Black Rock was still calm, they decided to leave *Tranquilo* there and follow the shoreline the two miles to Lahaina Town in the dinghy.

There were a couple of other anchorages they passed on the way, which they checked out in the event they would need to use them at a later time. Lahaina had a well-protected harbor right on the edge of town, but it was full of charter and private boats. It had a "dinghy dock" to accommodate the many sailors who are anchored or moored offshore for tying up their dinghies and tenders. The dinghy dock had a real personality of its own. There was every size, color, and shape of dinghy you could imagine tied up next to each other. When another one came in, it would just ease between the others, as Luke remarked, "Like piglets crowding in for supper." They secured their dinghy there and started their walk through town.

The first thing to greet them as they walked from the harbor was Hawaii's first territorial capitol building and in its courtyard, the largest banyan tree in the state of Hawaii. The tree covered almost the entire square block, providing shade and a gathering place for local residents hanging out "talking story" and amateur artists painting harbor scenes. Occupying the next block was the renovated

Pioneer Inn Hotel. Downstairs it held a bar that still gave sailors a place to have quite a time, and the rooms upstairs unquestionably held some interesting secrets dating back to the turn of the century.

Front Street, which was the main drag along the waterfront, held the charm of a town growing from the early plantation era that started with the arrival of immigrants over one hundred years ago. Sugar cane became a big business with a mill to process the cane built in 1885, and the town grew with workers from China and Japan, then shortly thereafter from the Philippines. Since the late seventies with the influx of the resort development, more of the local businesses were beginning to turn to tourist-type shops, but still maintained their local style facades. Hardware stores were replaced with art galleries and t-shirt shops, and every kind of souvenir with a Hawaiian theme could be purchased to remember your trip to Maui.

There were some outstanding restaurants along Front Street as well, and literally suspended over the water, was the Lahaina Yacht Club. This was more of a salty bar than a full-service yacht club like Luke belonged to back in Honolulu, but they welcomed the couple with "Aloha!" and it was a great place for lunch. The club was abuzz in anticipation of an upcoming Sauza Cup Regatta, and committees were busy decorating and getting the necessary entry forms ready for the weekend. Luke had heard some of his racing buddies talk of sailing over from Honolulu, but he was so wrapped up in his own adventure, he had completely forgotten about it.

Luke and Teruyo spent the rest of the day shopping and checking out the art galleries. Teruyo was also attracted to Lahaina, and the people were all so friendly.

When they returned to *Tranquilo,* they realized they had forgotten about watching James fillet the Mahi. They got back in the dinghy and motored up to the Whalers Village entrance, then went to the back loading dock of the Rusty Harpoon. James was in the kitchen but he had held off from cleaning the fish, hoping Luke and Teruyo would be coming before the evening dinner rush. They apologized for forgetting, but in typical local-style, he said, "No worries, I show you now."

James proceeded to explain what was going on at the same time getting every possible piece of eatable meat off the fish. It was not unlike filleting a bass in Northern Missouri, only much bigger. The key, James told them, is having a good knife and a flat working surface, not the rolling deck of a boat in six to eight-foot seas. Luke made a mental note of getting a good long cutting board for *Tranquilo,* something he could stow away and use in case he got in the habit of bringing in the big ones. James sold him a knife that was already "broken in." Luke asked him if he would like to go sailing, but James replied, laughing, "Tanks, but you no gettin' me on no boat!"

Luke and Teruyo took their fillets from the Mahi-Mahi and went back to *Tranquilo* for the rest of the evening. They were a little tired from the crossing the day before plus playing tourists that day. Teruyo wanted to cook dinner, and Luke couldn't argue with that, but he wanted to cut up enough ginger for the fish. They worked together in the galley, sipping on a fresh bottle of Chardonnay as they cooked. The water in the little bay was still calmer than when he'd anchored there the year before, but Luke knew with a small change in the wind direction or in the direction of the ocean swell, it could become uncomfortable. When dinner was ready, they savored every bite. Teruyo had sautéed the fish with lemon, butter, and the ginger. It was fabulous.

Just before sunset, they settled in the cockpit with the last of the wine, waiting for the diver to light the torches and perform his dive. They enjoyed their front-row seats, and after his beautiful swan dive, he surfaced only fifty-feet from *Tranquilo.* Many of the hotel guests came out to see the ceremony as well. The drums began to beat, signaling the beginning of the luau. It was another beautiful night in paradise.

Chapter 10

After another wonderful breakfast on shore and a nice sail with some new friends the next morning, Luke was getting the dinghy ready while Teruyo made a "rest stop."

A low voice beside him said, "Hello, Mr. Davis. How is everything?"

Luke looked up, startled. "Great, Shindo. Good to see you. Teruyo is having a wonderful time, and so am I. We just took some local people we met a couple of nights ago for a sail."

"Yes I know. I won't keep you, but wanted you to know I was here."

"I'm thinking we will cruise on down the coast a few miles and try to find calmer water. The waves are coming in a bit differently this afternoon, and it would be more comfortable if we could anchor off shore a little further."

"Thanks for letting me know." And with that, he turned and disappeared into the foliage. Strange, what kind of message was that? *Just letting you know we're watching everything you're doing.*

"Guess who met me on the beach when I was getting the dinghy ready?" Luke asked Teruyo after they were underway.

"Who?"

"Shindo. He told me he just wanted us to know he was around. I informed him we would be changing anchorages."

"Oh, I'm sorry Luke. I wonder what that was all about. I thought everything was going OK." She was having such a wonderful time that she had almost forgotten about the possibility of being watched. She was certainly used to it by now since a security team had followed her for the last few months. However, the intensity of getting to know Luke and the freedom of being alone as they went from island to island had made her nearly forget she was always under their watchful eyes.

They found the anchorage called "the Roadstead" just outside of the harbor entrance to Lahaina much calmer, so they chose this as their destination for the evening. Teruyo knew moving to a new anchorage wouldn't lose Shindo, but it did make for a more relaxing place, further from his eyes as well as more comfortable due to the calmer waters. She contacted the base in Honolulu over the radio to inform them of their new location.

They took the dinghy into the harbor and had dinner at a well-known restaurant noted for the chef's creative cooking. Teruyo was pleased with the way he had lightly seared the sashimi in spices, but for Luke, eating raw fish still took some getting used to. After dinner they strolled through the numerous art galleries. Because it was Friday evening, the galleries were featuring many local artists and it was a festive atmosphere. Luke purchased a wonderful small painting of two young island children titled "Jan Ken Po," which captured their smiling faces while playing the game of the title. It was nicely framed and would fit perfectly on the bulkhead of the salon in *Tranquilo.*

They spotted Shindo across the street, obviously keeping his distance while watching for any signs that the couple could be watched or followed. Teruyo knew him to be effective. They were not to make contact in public unless she felt danger. In Luke's presence and holding hands as they wandered in and out of the galleries and shops, she had no fears that anyone could do her any harm. Her feelings for Luke were getting stronger, and she could tell he was also feeling the magic.

When they returned to the dinghy dock, they struck up a conversation with a couple also returning to their boat. The two were very cordial and stated they had been living out in the Roadstead for about six months. She was a waitress in a restaurant, and he had just come in to pick her up from work. He worked for one of the charter boats that took tourists to the island of Lanai during the day and suggested Luke and Teruyo consider sailing to Manele

Bay at Lanai tomorrow, as the charter boats didn't use the slips in the harbor there on Saturdays and Sundays. He said it was a funky little harbor with close access to Hulopoe Bay, another prime place, which Luke had read about for its cleanliness and great snorkeling. He said the locals spend more time at the harbor on the weekends and were a lot of fun. Luke thought that would be a great place to fill the water tanks and give *Tranquilo* a good freshwater wash as well.

As they motored out of the harbor to *Tranquilo,* lying at anchor in the Roadstead, Luke glowed with the experience they were sharing, and as he spotted the shiny dark blue hull of his boat in the light reflecting from the town of Lahaina, he was indeed proud of the results of all his labors. He could never have imagined how special this was turning out. *Tranquilo* was a pretty lady in a beautiful setting, and riding with him was also a beautiful lady who, as a last-minute addition to this adventure, was making it even more wonderful.

After climbing aboard and securing the dinghy for the night, Luke did a thorough systems' check, including checking the bearings to shore he had established earlier to see if *Tranquilo* was still anchored exactly where they set the hook hours earlier. Right after they'd set the anchor that afternoon, Luke put on his mask, snorkel and fins and "dove the anchor" to check that it was digging in properly. The bottom here was a flat lava surface with little sand and nothing for the anchor to grab onto. He felt since it was still calm this evening with little wind to pull firmly on the anchor, they should be OK, but he wanted to check to be sure.

"Luke, is everything alright?"

"Yeah, so far. I'm a little nervous about the anchor holding properly here since it's so deep and not a good sand bottom for it to dig into. If the wind should pick up in the night, we could start dragging. When I dove on the anchor right after we set it here, I noticed some moorings just south of us that I wouldn't want to drag into."

"Why don't we sleep out in the cockpit tonight? It's so beautiful, and we would feel the wind come up sooner by being out here."

"Good idea. I've got a couple of sleeping bags and we can bring our pillows and blankets and build us a little nest here." Hugging Teruyo, he added, "Maybe even recreate a little of our foredeck adventures of Haloe Lono?"

With a sly grin, Teruyo asked, "Hmm, more discipline, Captain?"

Moving away from Black Rock was a good idea as there was less rocking motion here and the thought of sailing over to Lanai in the morning made for a great plan for their first weekend together. As if every day wasn't like a weekend!

Chapter 11

Black Manele Bay was a well-protected small boat harbor located on the southeast side of Lanai. There were only two slips not occupied which could accommodate *Tranquilo,* and they chose one that would allow them to stay longer than just the weekend if they desired. Teruyo had notified her Honolulu radio contact of their new destination just prior to them motoring over from Maui. There was no wind, so they used the forty-five minute run to charge the batteries and the refrigeration systems as they motored. Everything was still running well, however Luke was always inspecting the engine for the first opportunity to catch a nut or bolt working itself loose before any problems evolved.

It was nice to be secured to a slip again. There was no electricity at the harbor, but there was plenty of fresh water and restroom facilities. The fellow they'd met the night before who recommended them coming here for the weekend said if they would wait until the afternoon, when the sun had a chance to heat up the water in the pipes, they could have hot showers. Most sailors would plan their whole day around getting a hot shower, and Luke and Teruyo were no different, even though they did have the luxury of their own hot water system if they were willing to run either the generator or the main engine.

Teruyo called on the single side band radio to let the security team know they had arrived OK, but she was unable to make contact. The steep cliffs that surround Manele Bay could have affected the ability for the signal to be received, so they tried Luke's new ham radio. Again, no contact with anyone on the frequencies they were to call. They decided to try in the evening as Luke had learned from the ham Radio classes he had taken that there is much more radio interference in the daytime than at night. Combining the steep cliffs with that theory, they didn't give it too much thought and went right to work scrubbing decks and rinsing the saltwater from the sails and all of the rigging.

When *Tranquilo* was all clean and her water tanks filled, they headed for the beach at Hulopoe Bay to explore and relax. Just as Luke had read, this was a truly gorgeous bay with a white sand beach and turquoise blue water. They saw a pod of dolphins casually swimming in the middle of the bay and they had the whole bay entirely to themselves. The bay at one time was a very popular anchorage for cruisers, but Luke's cruising guide stated that anchoring there now was prohibited due to some problems between locals and some cruisers in the past. Too bad, as this would be a great spot to spend a few days and ride out a storm blowing from the North or West, but it was not worth causing any problems with the locals over.

They laid down their beach mats and headed to the water for some snorkeling. The bottom was sandy with very few coral heads but still many varieties of tropical fish. They were both pleased with how clean this beach and the water were. When they returned to their mats after their swim, they noticed the first of a few local families who brought their children to the beach. The adults opted for places in the shade, as their kids played and swam in the water.

As Teruyo lay in the sun drying off, Luke admired how beautiful she was and marveled at how quickly she was tanning. They were both careful to insure they were covered with sunscreen, as it didn't take much exposure in the tropical sun to burn and really damage your skin. It seemed kind of funny to be lounging on a grass mat in the sun because they were exposed so much of the time, but the whole experience of being at this beautiful bay was worth it.

As evening approached and they had enjoyed their "solar-powered" hot showers back at the restrooms, the harbor activity increased with the return of a few of the local fishing boats and their families waiting to greet them. Most of the locals worked for the pineapple plantation and on weekends, fishing from the jetty or in a boat attracted many to Manele Bay. There were well kept picnic areas with barbecue grills. The locals were filling up most of the tables in anticipation of fresh fish and plenty of dishes they had brought down from their homes. They were friendly and talkative, and some offered a ride to Lanai City if Luke and Teruyo needed anything. They said just stand by the road and someone would pick them up whenever they headed up the hill. For now, this was a very comfortable place to relax, and they thought that maybe tomorrow they would hitch a ride into town.

Some of the most memorable experiences that come with cruising are of the people you meet along the way. Luke and Teruyo were having a wonderful time throughout the afternoon visiting with the people of Lanai and during the day, three other sailboats came into the harbor to take advantage of the facilities. Cruisers love to checkout other cruisers' boats when all of their chores are done, and since Luke and Teruyo had put up the awning and had lots of shade, it made for a nice place to get acquainted. One couple that tied up to a slip next to *Tranquilo* was from Alaska and lived aboard their forty-five foot *Swan* during the winter months, sailing out of the harbor on Molokai. Another couple came in from Maui, and like the folks Luke and Teruyo met the night before, lived aboard in the Roadstead outside of Lahaina harbor. Another boat had just sailed from the island of Hawaii, crossing the Alenuihaha Channel, which is one of the roughest channels to cross in the world. They were wet, tired, and hungry, and really glad to have a place to rest and shower without having to anchor.

Luke had set some chicken out to thaw earlier in the morning, and he had some barbecue sauce his Mom had sent from Missouri to baste it with. With Teruyo preparing rice and a salad in the galley, and Luke frequently turning and basting the chicken, they had the makings for another great meal. It didn't take much coaxing for a potluck dinner to get formed with the other cruisers, and by sunset, a nice spread of food and drink was laid out on one of the large picnic tables. They all had a great deal in common, and though Luke didn't let on that he still had a lot to learn, he was like a sponge absorbing all he could. He and Teruyo were especially interested in the story of the sail from the big island of Hawaii and they picked up some valuable information to help them choose the best time to sail that channel.

They also learned a lot about what it was like living offshore of Lahaina, and some of the challenges that couple had dealt with. There were occasional Kona storms and with the difficulties anchoring and mooring, this caused many boats to be lost to the reefs and rocky shore, not to mention the ongoing "territorial battles" of who was where first, and who had rights to anchor or set a mooring.

Hawaii had more registered boats per capita than any of the fifty states but the fewest harbor facilities. One of the sailors who had just sailed in from the big island said, "There were more slips available for boats in North Dakota!" It wasn't that Hawaii didn't have good natural harbors for the development of marine facilities, but a large majority of the locals of each of the islands resisted the boating community. The 60's and 70's brought an influx of "hippie-types" and many of the people living on boats gave a bad impression for the yachting community as a whole. There were several young inexperienced sailors that, for whatever reason, made very poor decisions or were lacking in the seamanship skills with which to properly maintain their vessels, and some of the boats were abandoned or became wrecks on beaches and reefs. This made for problems with the locals, and the last thing they wanted was to build more facilities to attract more "yachties."

Another problem was many good "natural harbors" were also historically good surfing areas, and surfing has been a way of life for Hawaiians for generations. The Hawaiians have had their lands and their way of life taken away from them by the white missionaries of the past and current land developers building resorts and condominium projects by the score. The last thing they needed was to give up their surfing spots, and that carried a lot of local political clout. Before marina development could expand in Hawaii, the image of the yachtsman and the economic benefits would have to greatly improve.

All dispersed back to their own boats at a reasonable hour, and a few locals remained fishing on the jetty, but as the stars came out in their magnificent brilliance, Manele Bay transformed into a sleepy, quiet harbor. Luke and Teruyo decided that they would try to hitch a ride to go exploring the next day.

"Luke, we better try to check in with Honolulu before they send the Navy out after us."

"Yeah, that would be a mite em- barrassing to see a frigate trying to turn around in this little harbor basin," he joked.

They again had no success reaching their contact in Honolulu on either radio unit, so Luke tried to reach his friend Gus on his ham station's frequency. Luke had deemed it a priority to add the ability to communicate from anywhere in the world while at sea. A close family friend of his who owned a business back in Missouri was an avid ham operator and emphasized to Luke if he ever got a boat, to be sure to get his ham radio license and he would be able to keep in touch from all over the globe. This sounded like great advice to Luke, so right after buying the Gulfstar, he enrolled in an amateur radio class and over the next eight weeks learned the Morse code and necessary technical information to pass and receive his General Operator's License. This gave him the privilege of using the airwaves for voice as well as communication with Morse code, and in addition to Gus, he had several new "radio friends" with whom to stay in contact.

The main difference with communicating over a radio versus a telephone is both parties have to be on the same frequency at the same time to be able to make contact. Luke had a list of radio call signs and when they usually could be contacted. He was not able to reach Gus but had no problem reaching a frequent contact, Joe from Molokai. Luke and Joe had talked frequently when Luke was practicing his Morse code, and Joe was able to receive Luke strong and clear regardless of the cliffs surrounding the harbor. Joe suggested a couple of other operators in Honolulu and Luke was able to contact them with strong signals as well.

"Luke, something's not right. I've never had problems contacting the team."

"I doubt it, but when we go to town tomorrow, we'll try the phone lines and I'm sure we'll get through to them then."

To take Teruyo's mind off this unexpected situation, Luke brought out his guitar. He had purchased it at a pawnshop close to Pearl Harbor, and though he was by no means an accomplished musician, he did know the value of a Martin D45 acoustic guitar. He intended to practice daily after finishing the list of boat projects at the Ala Wai harbor and getting into cruising mode. The Martin produced as sweet a sound as there was from a guitar, and even with Luke's limited skills, he was able to ease Teruyo into a mellow mood.

He had first started playing guitar while in Vietnam, playing the folk ballads of James Taylor, John Denver, and Bob Dylan. Luke didn't have the vocal skills to project himself very loudly, in fact he kept the volume down so as not to scare away the locals. Teruyo enjoyed him playing for her, and though his style bordered much closer to Country Western, which of all musical styles she least preferred, she was still very complimentary and when he was finished, showed her appreciation in a most loving way.

Sunday morning was not the best day to go exploring on Lanai, as the locals were mostly involved in church services. The only store in Lanai City was closed, and though the Hotel Lanai was open, the lady who could rent them a jeep wouldn't be back from church until a little after noon. Luke and Teruyo had hitched a ride to the hotel with a fellow who had been out all night fishing, and though the little Toyota truck had seen better days, he was happy to give them a lift.

It was a whole new world in Lanai City, as there was a cool breeze flowing through the huge pine trees that make this setting idyllic for the small town. It was settled as a company town for the Dole Pineapple Plantation employees, with green lawns in front of well-kept homes and maintenance buildings. The hotel where Luke and Teruyo waited served a simple menu for breakfast, and although they had already eaten, the cook had made some fresh bread to go along with homemade jam and local coffee, so the wait was very relaxing. They had a pay phone, and Teruyo tried calling the number in Honolulu Shindo had left for them, to no avail.

It was a good thing they were able to rent a jeep, as some of the roads leading to many of Lanai's most beautiful lookouts were four-wheel accessible only. The possibility of getting stuck made for a more exciting adventure for the couple, and the views were magnificent. It was amazing to see forty-eight thousand acres of pineapple, but after all, the whole island had been purchased just for that. There was another harbor for special barges to be loaded with the pineapples, after which they were shipped to the canneries in Honolulu for processing.

There were rows of Norfolk pine, Ironwood, and Eucalyptus trees planted in the late 19th century with the intention of helping to trap the clouds and produce more rain. From Lanaihale, the highest spot on the island at 3,370 feet, they were able to view the islands of Maui, Molokai, Kaho'olawe, Hawaii and Oahu, the only place from which five Hawaiian Islands could be viewed. It was much cooler than in the harbor, and since Luke and Teruyo hadn't brought jackets, they didn't stay long. After buying two fresh pineapples and talking a handyman from the hotel to drive them back to Manele Bay, they descended the higher elevations of Lanai to the noticeable increase in temperature of the arid coastline.

Monday morning would bring the charter boats loaded with tourists, so Luke and Teruyo agreed to depart for La Perouse Bay on the eastern edge of Maui. This beautiful anchorage, they were told, was a great point off which to depart at night for the crossing of the Alenuihaha Channel on towards the big island of Hawaii. The other sailboats were still in the harbor as well, and all except the couple that just crossed from the big island were contemplating leaving. That couple wanted to stay and continue to relax before heading on to Oahu and the hustle-bustle of Honolulu.

Luke and Teruyo decided to prepare another dinner together in the cabin of *Tranquilo.* He had a very well equipped galley with a top-of-the-line propane stove and a large working area. With canned tomato paste, canned tomatoes, and some herbs she'd purchased on their last trip to the market, Teruyo happily created a wonderful homemade spaghetti sauce over pasta. This called for a bottle of Italian Chianti Luke had purchased to complement another of her creative salads and the aromas from the sauce floating in the cabin.

"Do you mind opening the wine a little early?" she asked. "The sauce needs to cook just a few minutes longer."

"Coming right up. I'm as hungry as a horse. You sure you have enough?"

"I hope so. I noticed they didn't have a pizza delivery service on Lanai. We should have packed a lunch today."

As Luke opened the bottle of Chianti and inhaled its aroma, he continued, "Yeah, quite a day. What a tremendous difference from the tourist-hustle of West Maui to the laid-back serenity and beauty of Lanai."

"The people are sweet and seem so happy. I don't know if I could live in such a remote location for very long, though. I think I'd get Rock fever. However, as happy and healthy as they all seem to be, it says something for their lifestyle here."

"Well, I can attest to the fast-lane living of Chicago and eating airport food every week, and I would take living here over there without a doubt."

"I think you are starting to finally relax and get into a 'tranquilo' state of mind. You're going to do just fine at this, Captain Davis."

The spaghetti was the very best Luke had ever eaten, better than any place in the many Italian neighborhoods in Chicago. He marveled that it was fixed by a half-Japanese lady 2,300 miles from the mainland.

"Wow."

Before going to bed, they tried contacting the team in Honolulu. Again, no answer.

Chapter 12

They were ready to back out of their slip just as the first boatload of tourists came into the harbor. The Alaskan couple had already departed to return to Molokai, and the couple from the Lahaina Roadstead was not quite ready to leave, although they were in one of the charter boat's slips, so they were informed they needed to be out in the next half-hour. As soon as the first charter boat was secure, Teruyo backed *Tranquilo* out while Luke handled the dock lines, and they waved goodbye to their new friends and set a course for north of the island of Kaho'olawe, the "Target Isle."

The Department of Defense leased the island of Kaho'olawe and the U.S. Navy used it for target practice. There were limits on how close you could sail, and no one was allowed to land on the island, but this particular week the restriction was one-mile off shore. Luke heard the fishing could be really good, and it was on the way to where they wanted to anchor for an afternoon nap prior to taking on the Alenuihaha Channel and their crossing to the big island of Hawaii.

The weather was calling for normal trade winds, blowing fifteen-knots out of the

Northeast, but they were still in the lee of the huge volcano on Maui, Haleakala, which towers to just over 10,000 feet above sea level. This made for a lack of wind in this area, so Luke used this as a good chance to recharge the batteries and the refrigeration systems by running under the full power of the Mercedes diesel.

The Gulfstar had a freezer and separate refrigerator boxes built into the countertop along the portside of the galley. They were top-of-the line systems, which operated on off shore power when the boat was at a slip in which electricity was available. When at sea under power of the Mercedes engine, they ran off a compressor like a car's air-conditioning unit. This was a big plus as most of the boats Luke considered only had an ice box which required hauling block ice every three or four days to keep food fresh. Ben had suggested for Luke to add an alternator in place of the power steering pump that had been on the Mercedes engine. This added additional charging power for the extra battery bank that Luke decided to include. There seemed to be nothing wrong with having a freezer for making ice cubes when one wished for Margaritas at sunset.

Luke set out all four of his best fishing lures after they cleared the harbor, and they cruised along at a good six-knot pace in an easy swell. They stayed well outside the one-mile limit of Kaho'olawe and commented how barren the island was. No trees or greenery of any kind could be seen. There was a grassroots effort by some native Hawaiians to reclaim the land from the Defense Department, but that was taking time as it was deemed "in the interest of National Security to maintain possession of Kaho'olawe."

About an hour out of Manele Bay, they hooked up a small aku, a type of tuna, and Luke let Teruyo bring it in. It was her first fish. He used his new knife from James at the Rusty Harpoon and cleaned it on the stern as they motored on towards La Perouse Bay.

Luke suggested, "Now that we are clearly away from the cliffs of Manele Bay, why don't you try and reach Honolulu again."

She gave them a try; there was still no response.

"Luke, I'm worried. What should we do?"

"We're not far from Ma'alaea Harbor on Maui. I'm sure there is a phone there we could try calling them again. Let's turn to port and head in there. If we can't reach them, do you want to call your grandfather's company in Japan and check in there?"

"I suppose you're right, but I am hoping we can still make La Perouse Bay and head on to the Big Island."

"Well, this ain't right, so we better try

and find Shindo to keep in his good graces," Luke replied.

After docking in the harbor, Teruyo used the pay telephone at the head of the dock to call the team in Honolulu—no answer. Next, she placed a call to her mother's home in Japan. Because of the six-hour time difference from Hawaii to Japan, it was too early to call her grandfather's company; besides she didn't know whom to ask for. She didn't wish to upset her mother, but this was now a way of life for her family, and her mother would know who to get in touch with. She certainly didn't want to talk with her grandfather. He wouldn't think too kindly of her sailing alone with a man around the Hawaiian Islands, especially a non-Japanese man.

"Hello, Mom. How are you? Sorry it's so early. I'm doing great... yes..."

Luke could tell her mother must not be fully awake, and this could get a bit personal, so he went back to *Tranquilo* to check on the dock lines and make himself busy.

"Yes, Mom, I'm positive I'm OK. In fact, I'm having the best time. You see, I met this guy, and he has a boat, and well... we are sailing around the islands together. I really like him, and you would too... Yes, we arranged everything with Shindo... No, I'm not trying to lose them again; in fact, that is why I felt I needed to call you right away. We have not been able to contact Shindo by phone or via the radio frequencies we've been using, and I felt we should try and find out what happened to them so they wouldn't think it was my fault for not contacting them as we were supposed to… No Mom, really, I'm great. I just need to know how to get in touch with Shindo so we can proceed with our plans… Luke, his name is Luke, and he is really treating me great and is very, very nice… OK, here is the number where I'm at and I will wait here for them to call. Please don't say anything to Grandfather yet. I'm sure we are just having a communication problem… Yes, I'll let you know as soon as I find out… No we don't have a phone; we are sailing on Luke's yacht… Yes it is very nice; he has done a lot of work on it himself, and we are having such a wonderful time… OK, I will. I love you. Bye."

Teruyo walked back down the dock to *Tranquilo* where Luke was waiting in the shade of the bimini.

"Well, what did you find out?"

"As far as my mom knows, everything is OK, but it was just after 5:00 a.m. there. She is going to contact her security team and someone will call me back here soon. Mom says to say hello; she thinks Luke is a nice name. I could tell she is a little concerned about me being alone with you, though. She was worried about my breakup a few months ago and wished I would have just come right back to Japan immediately. However, I didn't want a bunch of relatives fussing over me just then."

The pay phone started ringing, and Teruyo ran back to answer it.

"Hello... yes it is," she said and then started speaking in Japanese.

Luke stayed in the shade of the bimini but could tell something was wrong. Her shoulders drooped, and she became nervous in the way she kept changing hands with the receiver and moving about in the confines of the phone booth. He jumped to the dock and hurried over to her.

She hung up the phone just as he arrived and said, "Luke, we need to get out of here!"

Teruyo started the diesel engine as Luke stood by with the dock lines. When she was ready, he cast off and jumped aboard. She eased *Tranquilo* away from the dock, turned to port and quickly headed out of the harbor.

Luke waited for her to talk. She was tense. "There's a problem in Honolulu. One of my grandfather's closest associates was murdered yesterday. The security team in Honolulu was coordinating his safety as well and they are not responding to the offices in Japan. A new team is en route as we speak, but they advised me to go into hiding right away and to contact them later this afternoon. I have a new frequency to call them, and they are going to try to put the pieces together. Oh Luke, I hope Shindo and the team are all right. They are so dedicated. If anything happened to him, I...I just..." And for the first time, Luke saw tears in her eyes.

Luke took over the helm and let her sit down. This was all happening very fast, and they needed to get a grip and try to figure things out rationally.

"Hey, remember I'd just spoken to Shindo a couple of days ago on the beach, and we'd seen him at a distance in Lahaina on Front Street. Most likely he was still on Maui when this all happened. He might still be on Maui for all we know. Today is Monday, and you say your grandfather's friend was killed yesterday? I bet Shindo would not have gone to Honolulu knowing we were just across the channel at Manele Bay."

"Oh Luke, I hope so. But what if he did? What if he..."

"Hey, let's not think that. We have to keep focused on your safety right now. What else did they say? Did you tell them about us?"

"Only that I had been keeping in touch by the single side band radio or by phone, nothing about sailing, or you, or our plans."

"That's good. We ought to keep it that way for now. Let's see, you didn't tell the Honolulu team about La Perouse Bay yet did you?"

"No, only of our location on Lanai."

"And La Perouse Bay wouldn't have been on their map of coded anchorages would it?"

"No, we didn't assign a code for it."

"Alright, let's head there for now, and we can decide what to do after making contact in two hours."

They were only a little over an hour away, so they motored on to La Perouse.

Chapter 13

After setting the anchor in thirty-five feet of crystal clear water, Luke put on his mask and snorkel and jumped in to ensure the anchor was going to hold.

"Hey Baby, get your mask and fins on and get in here!"

Baby? Teruyo was surprised with this new expression. She could see he had his face in the water; something must be exciting. This was a welcome distraction to her worries about the crisis in Honolulu.

She got her snorkeling gear on and jumped into the water. There were two stingrays swimming about the anchor chain, circling in perfect harmony. They were so beautiful, and the coral heads with the tropical fish made for a skin-diver's dream. They joined and swam closer to shore and to the shallower reef where the blues, pinks, and yellows of the different corals seemed to be so vibrant that no artist could have painted it this brilliantly.

"Ouumh...Ouummh..." Luke tried to talk with his snorkel in his mouth. He was looking at his first shark swimming twenty-five feet below them. It was only a three-foot sand shark, totally harmless to humans, but seeing one for the first time and not in a cage, made for some quick twitching of the feet.

"It's OK, Luke. It's just a sand shark. He won't hurt you." Teruyo, the biologist and a much more experienced diver, tried to calm her nervous lover down. She had the experience and the wherewithal to take her snorkel out of her mouth. She didn't mean to laugh, but this was funny. If she'd had a dollar on her, she would have made a bet right then that Luke must have watched the movie "*Jaws*" too many times.

"Ouummph...Ouummph... Oh, I guess this might help some." He removed his mouthpiece. "You sure they don't have any big brothers swimming close by?"

"Oh come on, silly. I bet you are trying to get me all worked up so you can pretend to rescue me from the dangers of the deep. Let's go have a beer."

"Oh, well, alright... I wasn't really scared," he claimed.

They swam back to the boat, climbed up the swim ladder, and rinsed off with fresh water from a rinse hose he'd installed in the aft lazarete.

"Did you call me *Baby*?" Teruyo asked.

"Yeah, I guess I did. Do you mind?"

"It caught me by surprise, but I like it."

From the single side band radio down in the cabin came, "WH6-BXC, WH6-BXC...this is Hilo-Niner-Xray, over." Someone was calling Luke's radio call sign. Luke jumped down into the nav-station and grabbed his microphone, "Go ahead Hilo-Niner-Xray, this is WH6-BXC, over."

"WH6-BXC, are you both in good health, over?" It sounded like Shindo.

"Roger Roger Hilo-Niner-Xray, we are fine and standing by. Would you like to talk with number 1, over?"

"Negative. Are you still planning on arriving at Lincoln 6 this week, over?" Luke had to look at the map Teruyo used when communicating with the security team. Lincoln 6 was the code designation for Kona Bay on the Big Island.

Teruyo recognized Shindo's voice and took the microphone. "Hilo-Niner-Xray, good to hear your voice. What do you advise, over?"

"Please proceed to Madison 4, repeat, Madison 4... I'll meet you there tomorrow at noon, over."

Madison 4 was a yacht club on the north shore of Oahu, Kaneohe Yacht Club.

Teruyo replied, "Roger that, WH6-BXC out." To Luke she said, "Can we make it by noon?"

"I, uh, guess so. It means sailing all night, and we would have to time our approach to the Kaneohe Bay for morning. I went to that club to look at a boat before *Tranquilo* came to the Ala Wai, and it is in a very well protected harbor, but a long way from the entrance to the bay. I'll get out the chart, and let's plot out our course." After locating the chart, he said, "Let's see here. We'll run along the south coast of Maui and cross the Pailolo Channel and head straight for the north shore of Oahu. Figures to be about one hundred thirty-five nautical miles, and if we average six knots that should put us close to the entrance of Kaneohe Bay in, say twenty-two hours. Yep, no problem, even if we don't have any wind, we can motor there the whole way. Hand me my cruising guide in the cockpit."

"Oh Luke, I'm so glad Shindo sounded OK, but I wonder why he wants to meet us way over there?"

"Something must be wrong, and he's taking some precautions. We'd better leave now so we'll have plenty of time for getting there with some room to spare in case we have any trouble. We'll need to get our slickers ready for tonight and rotate a couple of watches alone so we can make it. Let's keep the radio tuned to this frequency if Shindo needs to contact us... we'll be alright."

Teruyo started the coffeepot and began getting ready snacks and food she anticipated they would need while Luke fired up the engine and did a thorough check of all the systems. Still no signs of water leaking anywhere, and the batteries were still showing fully charged. His water tanks were just topped off the previous night in Manele Bay, and the fuel gauges still read full. When all below was secure, Teruyo eased *Tranquilo* slowly forward so Luke could retrieve the chain and anchor. At 1335, they left La Perouse Bay.

Right away they caught a nice sea breeze, set all the sails full, and were able to get up to five-knots without the engine running. *Tranquilo* was sailing well, and Teruyo frequently kept trimming the main and the genoa, like she was in racing mode to ensure the greatest speed as Luke drove. When they hit the valley separating Haleakala and the West Maui Mountains, the trade winds kicked in and boosted them up to seven-knots for a while, but it was back to the sea breeze as they came into the lee of the West Maui Mountains.

Luke tried to break the silence and intensity of the mood by saying, "The lush green sugar cane fields are sure a contrast to the barren landscape of Kaho'olawe, aren't they?"

"Yes, they really are. I'm sorry Luke. I guess I've been lost in thoughts of what could happen."

"I figured you were. You know these people. What are you expecting?"

"They instructed us that we have certain levels of alerts for different types of incidents, and I'm betting we are being asked to meet Shindo to decide on how best to deal with me. Oh Luke, I can't stand the thought of leaving you right now. This is so wonderful, and I don't want my grandfather's business to interfere with you and me. What we have shared these few days has made me so happy and I'm really... I don't know what to say, but I just don't want to be taken away from you."

"Baby, I feel the same way. I've wanted to tell you how I feel, but knowing that just a few months ago you'd had your heart broken, I've felt the timing might be wrong for anything heavy." Luke paused and when Teruyo shifted her gaze from the sugar cane fields of Maui back to him, he looked her in the eyes and said, "Teruyo, you're the most amazing woman I've ever known. I just want you to know that, and as crazy as this whole involvement with you and this bizarre turn of events is, I look at you sitting there and my heart starts to melt."

"Oh, Luke!" Teruyo exclaimed as she bounded up from her seat next to the genoa winch and embraced him. "This is exactly what I've been feeling. I've been afraid to mention strong feelings, fearing it would scare you off. I've never been this excited, ever. Not even with my last relationship."

"This is happening really fast, but I've never been as overwhelmed by a lady as I am with you. I've tried to rationalize that it's related to us having such a great trip so far, and that my boat is working so well. Yeah, that surely is part of it, but Teruyo, I... I am so... I mean... I just want you to know..." He stopped short of saying how he thought he really felt.

They kissed and hugged with passion and fire that was real and growing.

Teruyo gasped from their long kiss, "We haven't even known each other one week, and I'm sure of it as well. I can't believe how incredibly fun and amazing you are."

"Are you thinking Shindo may want you to leave?"

"That's just what has been on my mind for the last hour. I don't know what to expect, but I have a feeling the alert level is higher with whatever is going on, or he wouldn't want us to meet where he has asked on such short notice."

"Yeah, that's what I'm thinking too. Something's up, and like I promised him, I will protect you. I guess we'll need to work with him to ensure your safety, which is their business."

"But I don't want this to end."

"Maybe it won't have to, but it's best for us to meet him as we planned and figure out what he wants to do. Like you said the first day we met, they are very good at what they do, and we need to ensure your safety above all. Things have a way of working out, and we'll find a way to get through this. Maybe Shindo already has a plan in mind where we can still be together and your safety won't be jeopardized."

"Oh, I hope so. The last place I want to go is Japan. I'm sure that's what my grandfather is going to order Shindo to do. He's not going to like one bit hearing about us sailing around the islands together."

Luke smiled, "You know, if you were my little granddaughter and I heard about you sailing around with someone like me, I'd come to the islands *myself* and take you back home!"

"Once he gets to know you, he'll like you. It's just with him being so traditional, it's going to be a big obstacle to overcome."

"You think I'd have to consider getting a haircut and shave?" Luke added, trying to bring a little levity to the conversation. She grinned.

"That would help, but I don't want you to change a thing about yourself. He may be a powerful man in Japan, but he doesn't rule me! I've only gone along with this security protection for the last few months because of my cousin's murder and how it really scared my mother. I now understand the real dangers of being in this family and the craziness that goes along with greed, but I'm not going to live my life in a bubble! So don't even think about cutting your hair or shaving your beard unless it is something you want to do."

"Well, let's not worry ourselves into a frenzy until we talk with Shindo. Then we can decide on what to do next. How about you drive for a little while and I'll start the generator and cook us up a big pot of rice while we charge the reefer and freezer?"

"I'm getting hungry too, and it would be better to fix a little dinner before we leave the lee of Maui," Teruyo replied.

Knowing they would be moving into some rough channel sailing, Luke wanted to prepare food that would easily digest, so he started the generator to charge the batteries and the refrigeration systems and put on a pot of rice. Not knowing what they were, he added some of the Oriental surprises Teruyo purchased from the Japanese department store for flavoring and it made for a nice warm meal they enjoyed as they sailed past Lahaina and Ka'anapali Beach towards Oahu.

When they entered the Pailolo Channel just past Black Rock, they were again hit with channel conditions, so Luke reefed the main sail and genoa, then stowed the mizzen so they could continue on course without being overpowered. They were making excellent time by sailing well as a team and staying focused on their destination. Luke didn't set the fishing lines because they didn't need the distraction, plus it would be dark in a few hours anyway.

After leaving Maui behind, they changed course a few degrees to port and reached off into the easy open ocean swells. This was more of a rolling motion rather than beating straight into the wind and waves that the mountain-funneled winds brought with channel crossings. The easier ride and the setting sun helped relax them from the tensions and anticipation of their next meeting with Shindo. Luke lowered the bimini top to give a better view of the stars, and they sailed embraced in the cockpit bound for Kaneohe Bay.

Chapter 14

They eased into the courtesy dock at the Kaneohe Yacht Club at 1015 the next morning. The overnight sail to Kaneohe Bay was beautiful and just a little faster than Luke had anticipated. Teruyo slept from around eleven until three in the morning, then she relieved Luke and he slept until sunrise. He was grateful they had good weather for navigating the entrance through the barrier reef and on into the yacht club. The range markers, which guided them through the channels, were difficult to read, and it took a team effort with Teruyo reading the charts and the depth sounder to keep them off the coral.

Teruyo gently guided *Tranquilo* to a stop as Luke set the dock lines. They had contacted the Dock Master of the club over the radio after they had cleared the barrier reef, and he welcomed them to come in. He was at the courtesy dock and greeted them with "Aloha" while helping to secure the lines. Luke could tell the Dock Master admired his boat, but when he noticed Teruyo, all of his attention turned to her. She was a very beautiful lady, and her smile along with her skills with the boat could easily perk any man's interest. She jumped right away to the dock and thanked him for his help and the invitation to his club.

"Thank you for letting us use your facilities. This is very nice."

"You're more than welcome. How long do you need to stay?"

"Actually, we just sailed from the southeast corner of Maui and we are tired and could use a good wash down." Teruyo grinned, inferring a hot shower as well as washing down the boat. "I need to meet with a business associate whom we spoke with over the radio. We asked him to meet us here. Is that OK?"

"Sure, you'll need to let him in because the locked gate controls access to the club. We have nice showers and a pool you are welcome to use."

"Oh, that sounds great. Can we let you know how long we would like to stay after my meeting?"

"No problem, you can have up to two weeks a year if you need, you know."

Luke was observing the conversation, as he secured *Tranquilo* to the dock. He stepped in and introduced himself, showing his Hawaii Yacht Club membership card and his ID. The Dock Master was very friendly and went to the office and got them keys to the showers and a magnetic card to open the front gate.

Not knowing how things would turn out, Luke started washing down the boat while

Teruyo checked that everything down below in the cabin was tidy and clean. They had talked during the night that in the event they would need to leave abruptly, they wanted to take advantage of the fresh water for cleaning off the salt and filling the water tanks. They also wanted to do laundry and maybe get to the market if possible as well, but they would just have to wait to see how their meeting with Shindo turned out.

At exactly noon, Shindo arrived at the gate and the freshly showered couple was there to meet him and invite him into the club. He was alone.

Revealing sincere affection, Teruyo smiled and said, "Shindo, it's so good to see you. I feared something happened to you when I got the call from the security department in Japan."

With a slight bow to both of them, Shindo replied, "And it is good to see you, too, Teruyo-san. My how the sun and a few days of sailing have given you a nice tan. Thank you, Mr. Davis, for bringing Teruyo all the way here for this meeting. I assumed it would be no problem, but after our radio contact, I realized it is not as simple as flying. Is there someplace we can talk in private?"

Luke replied, "I'm glad we made it with no problems. Let's talk on my boat. Teruyo caught a nice tuna yesterday, and I thought I'd fix us some lunch. And please call me Luke from now on."

They went to *Tranquilo* and down into the salon. Luke hadn't bothered to put up the awning, and as Kaneohe Bay is on the windward side of Oahu, the breeze was circulating nicely through the boat so it was very comfortable down below. Teruyo had already started a pot of rice, and Luke tried his hand at cutting some sashimi strips with wasabi and soy sauce. Shindo was pleased they were courteous enough to offer a Japanese-style lunch.

"Late Saturday night, Mitsuki Motokuro was murdered, and when the security team responded, they too were shot and killed. He was a close friend and associate of your grandfather. Your grandfather had invited Mr. Motokuro to stay as a guest in Honolulu in his condominium under our protection. When I was unable to make my evening contact with our team via phone from Maui, and you were at Manele Bay, I flew back immediately. I found our team member missing at the office where we maintained our 24-hour radio and phone service. Nothing was out of the ordinary, except that the office is to be manned at all times. We still have not found the missing operator, and I fear whoever is behind this knew of that office and may have been there.

This causes me concern for your safety because communication records with you may have been examined. We also need to consider the operator may have divulged your whereabouts. I have personally informed your grandfather of the situation, even as of two hours ago, when we saw you arrive here at the yacht club."

Teruyo replied, "You saw us arrive? Why didn't you come to see us then?"

"I have four other men observing us now. We were watching for any sign you were being followed or of the possibility someone may have heard our radio contact of last night."

"How did my grandfather respond when you told him about Luke and me?"

Shindo paused, then with a sigh, replied, "There was a long pause after I told him why I'd been to Maui, and another after I explained the security arrangements you, Luke, and I have. He did not say anything but only told me to insure your safety and to ask you to return to the family home in Kobe as soon as possible."

"So he is giving me a choice in the matter?"

"You and I discussed last week how he would react if he ever found out about your sailing with Luke. I stressed to him then, and again two hours ago when I saw you arrive safely, that Luke was a responsible person and was complying with our agreed procedures up to this point. I even emphasized to him how you took the initiative to call your mother in Japan after not being able to make contact with us here."

Luke was listening to all of this as he cooked the fish and prepared a salad. He suggested, "Shindo, if you are worried our communication procedures have possibly been compromised, why don't we consider just changing our destination codes to the map of the islands?"

"I have observed you together in Lahaina and at Ka'anapali Beach, and I see you are most attracted to each other. It is very obvious to me that you two would want to continue with your 'charter' and I have taken that possibility into consideration. I have a lot keeping me very busy at this time. I'm trying to find who is behind these murders, and actually, I don't have the staff available to be watching you and at the same time investigate what happened there. The Honolulu police have full authority and are investigating it very thoroughly, but we have resources and means they are not privileged to have. From a security standpoint, I want to get to the bottom of this as fast as we can."

Luke asked, "At this point, do you have any connection with Mr. Motokura's death and Teruyo's safety?"

"No, only the ties between the disappearance of the operator at our office and the communication codes. Other than that, I have no reason to believe any connection."

Luke finished preparing lunch and served Shindo first, then Teruyo. "What would you care to drink?"

Shindo gave a slight bow, "Your water is always very good. This is most appreciated."

Teruyo could see Shindo valued being respected by Luke. She continued the conversation, "Shindo, I want you to know that Luke and I have acquired very strong feelings for each other. I know this may appear out of the ordinary because of the suddenness, but in the short time we've shared, we've found so much happiness that we both don't want any interruption in our time, if at all possible."

"Yes, I could see that when I observed you two in Maui. Luke, this lunch is wonderful! Teruyo, *you* caught this fish?"

"Well, Luke let me bring it in. He has learned a lot about fishing by spending a great deal of time with a local fisherman."

"Yes, I saw the big fish you brought in and sold at Ka'anapali Beach."

Luke said, "You were there?"

"Oh, yes. That was a very impressive fish. Now what to do about you two?"

Luke added, "If I may, I'd like to impress upon you that what Teruyo stated about us developing strong feelings goes for me too. I'd really like you to know that her safety is most important, but I'd do anything to keep us together."

Shindo replied, "Knowing that you have done all we have asked to this point, and that I do believe in your sincerity, I guess we could change our codes and frequencies so we can stay in contact. Your call letters need to be changed as well. I realize your government assigns them to you, but it is a possible link whoever is behind this may have to Teruyo."

"OK, good point. How about for now we use my friend Gus's call letters, WH9-DZK?" Luke offered.

Shindo agreed, and they both wrote that down along with the new radio frequencies they'd use. Then they changed the destination codes on their maps of the islands. Shindo showed them a new hand-held radio he would be carrying from now on, which he would use in addition to setting up a new base station with a powerful antenna. He also gave them a new phone number for them to call when they had access to a telephone.

"Although everything seems safe here at this location, I'd prefer if you would leave Oahu today."

"That's fine with us, though we could use some supplies from a market if we are going to be in hiding for an extended period."

"There is one not far from here. I will drive you there and help you with anything you need."

On the drive to the market, Luke said, "Last night on our sail here before Teruyo went below to get some rest, we talked about some contingencies in the event we ran into some security concerns. We both agreed we would even consider sailing outside of the state, maybe south to Tahiti or further. I was able to buy charts of the Society Islands from a family who needed money to get back to the mainland, so all we need would be enough supplies. Would that be a possibility, as far as you are concerned, if we chose to head south?"

"Luke, I would like to respect your wishes as long as they don't directly conflict with Mr. Tanaka's. You must realize he would never approve of a plan such as that. In fact, though he did not state it, he is most assuredly unhappy with Teruyo's situation at this moment. We first have to see what kind of element we are dealing with regarding these murders. For now, it is wise to be prepared for extended hiding, but please assure me you will not try to flee out of the range of my ability to come to Teruyo's assistance."

"You have my word; we will do nothing of the sort without your approval. I'm a retired stockbroker, not a security specialist."

Chapter 15

They stopped at a bank so Luke could withdraw plenty of cash for shopping as well as for future needs, and they shopped at the market like they were stocking *Tranquilo* for a trip around the world. Teruyo wanted to mail a letter to her mother she'd written while on her watch the night before and fill her in on more of the specifics about their trip and about Luke. She hoped if her mother was at ease with this situation then maybe she could help break the news to her grandfather. Luke also called his friend Gus and told him of the recent security developments and that he needed to "borrow" his call sign for a few weeks.

Luke topped off his fuel tanks and refilled his *Gerry jugs* (spare fuel cans) with diesel, and he filled another gas can with gasoline for the dinghy motor. By the time everything was stowed in the proper cabinets and lazaretes, it was five in the evening. Shindo was a great help, and the other members of the security team who were watching from a distance, assured him that no one was following them or attempted to observe them at any time.

After everything was secured, Luke said, "We'd better be off while there is still good light to get through the channels and out to sea. We'll sail all night and shoot to make Hanalei Bay on Kauai by morning."

"I'm sorry to have to ask you to leave Oahu with so little sleep, but we must get back to the investigation as soon as possible. Without direct surveillance from our team, I feel it would be safer if you were away from here until we put an end to this threat."

"No big deal. We will sleep in three to four-hour shifts and have plenty of time to recuperate once anchored in Hanalei. I hear it's one of the most beautiful bays in Hawaii. Even though there is still a chance of a north swell coming up, at least there isn't one right now."

Luke started the engine and let it warm up as he prepared to cast off the dock lines. Teruyo approached Shindo as he stood next to the bow of Tranquilo. "Shindo, I'm truly grateful to you for providing for my safety as well as your understanding of my desire to remain with Luke. I'm very sorry if this puts extra pressure or difficulty on doing your job. I have never felt this way about anyone and I really want to stay with him."

"Let me worry about things here and dealing with your grandfather. You two go and be happy and take care of each other, but stay alert."

Teruyo gave the big man a hug and said, "Thank you so much, and you take care of yourself too." Then she jumped back up on the deck and assumed her position at the helm.

Luke began gathering his dock lines and when he came to the bow where Shindo stood, they shook hands. He also thanked Shindo for approving this arrangement. Shindo replied, "Luke, I believe in your ability to protect Teruyo, and you have demonstrated your concern for her wellbeing by working with me. I saw this beautiful girl hurt very badly a few months ago and now I see her happier than she has ever been. I sincerely hope you are what you seem." And with that, he turned and left the dock.

This left Luke with the feeling he had when Shindo left him on the beach at Black Rock. *Better never cross this fellow.*

"Luke, is everything alright?" Teruyo asked.

"Yeah, back her up," Luke replied as he uncleated the bowline and gave *Tranquilo* a shove off the dock.

They had returned the keys to the Dock Master and thanked him for his hospitality. He said he was sorry they had to leave so soon, and Luke could tell it was Teruyo he was most disappointed to see leaving. So as not to indicate their destination, he told the Dock Master they needed to get back to the Ala Wai Yacht Harbor and clear up some business.

The afternoon winds were stronger than

those of the morning, making getting out through the channel to open ocean more difficult than coming in. Teruyo did an excellent job of driving *Tranquilo* while Luke kept an eye on the reefs and the channel markers. They eased into the exit of the bay and sailed past "Chinaman's Hat" an extinct volcanic cone that resembles the old-style straw hat associated with the Chinese laborers who immigrated to Hawaii to work in the sugar cane fields. The trade winds were blowing a steady fifteen knots so all the sails were hoisted, and they soon fell off to port, heading northwest on a beam reach. The beautiful Ko'olau Mountain Range was off their portside and was a gorgeous setting for the next three hours as they sailed along the windward side of Oahu.

They were both tired, but too full of anticipation for another channel crossing to be able to sleep. Teruyo fixed a light meal, which they ate in the cockpit just as the sun was setting. Oh how nice it was to have the autopilot steering so they could enjoy each other's company. As they rounded Kahuku Point on Oahu and entered the Kauai Channel, they now had one hundred and twenty three miles to Hanalei Bay. They were easing along at six-knots, in a gentle swell. With no tacking or change of course necessary, all they needed to be concerned with was maintaining their course and watching for other traffic.

As darkness arrived and the stars came out in all of their brilliance, another light flashed intermittently on the horizon. It came from the Kilauea Lighthouse, the tallest one of its kind in the world, guiding them to the north shore of Kauai. The gentle roll of the boat and the fact that he had the least amount of sleep caused Luke to fall asleep in Teruyo's arms. She would have the first watch of the night.

Chapter 16

They arrived at the entrance of Hanalei Bay in the afternoon after another beautiful night and morning passage. Luke had set the fishing lines off the stern at sunrise, but there were no anxious takers this day. Luke and Teruyo were doing fairly well for the limited sleep they'd had. The feeling of arriving at one of the most beautiful bays in the world, let alone the Hawaiian Islands, was just too great to allow for another nap.

Kauai, known as the "Garden Isle," boasts one of the most lush and diverse landscapes of any of the islands. With one of the wettest spots on earth, "The Grand Canyon of the Pacific," and stunning sea cliffs along the Na Pali coast, Kauai is one of the most anticipated destinations for cruisers and tourists from around the world. The North Shore is the most beautiful area and boasts an annual rainfall up to 400 inches a year. Hanalei Bay is where the movie classic "South Pacific" was filmed and some say was the inspiration for the popular 60's song "Puff the Magic Dragon." Kauai, the oldest of Hawaii's major islands, was formed 5 million years ago from a single shield volcano that has become deeply eroded with time and volcanic action.

As Luke and Teruyo navigated the entrance to Hanalei Bay, the misty clouds that hung in the mountains in contrast to the bright sunny afternoon behind them, made for double rainbows ending right in the bay. They knew this was going to be a magical place.

"I wonder if we'll see Puff," Luke teased.

"Oh Luke, I've never seen such a beautiful place."

There was only one other sailboat at anchor in the huge bay. According to Luke's cruising guide, this was a bit early in the year to be in Hanalei Bay as late winter north swells could still make for a rough anchorage, but today it was calm.

They picked a spot to anchor quite a ways from the other boat, not meaning to be unsociable, but looking forward to as much privacy as possible. They had all they would need to just stay to themselves for a long time, and that was what they wanted. Teruyo contacted a security team member on the ham radio frequency. They evidently already had set up a new station as the signal came through loud and clear, and it wasn't Shindo who took the call. Luke couldn't wait to get the anchor set, take a shower, and whisk Teruyo off to the aft cabin.

The anchor set nicely in fifteen feet of the whitest sand he had ever seen. After diving on the anchor and insuring the proper amount of chain was laid out, they worked quickly to hang the awning, as an afternoon rain shower was already treating them to a fresh water wash-down. They wanted to have the ability to keep the hatches open even when it rained, so Luke's intentions for Teruyo would have to wait until all was settled.

The next two days were almost entirely spent below decks of *Tranquilo*. The two lovers enjoyed their quiet and secluded nest in the aft cabin, leaving only to change music or to fix something to eat. Luke had always been on the lookout for a good assortment of paperback books for casual reading and his library was coming in handy as they each found good books to entertain them during the periods between the long talks they shared. He also purchased sheet music to help him with learning new songs on his guitar, so he worked on building the calluses on the tips of his fingers and practicing new tunes. The afternoon rains that moved down the valley and into Hanalei Bay, made for being outside the shelter of the awning or the cabin, less preferred than the confines below. Luke was busy relaxing; no projects needed to be There was a slight surf break on shore addressed and they had no demands from anything or anyone. They hadn't even assembled and inflated the dinghy yet.

On their second morning in Hanalei Bay, they swam to shore and walked hand-in-hand along the beautiful beach. They literally had the whole bay to themselves. There was a dinghy on shore, most likely from the other boat at anchor, but they were yet to see any sign of the owner or crew. Spring was a very slow time for tourists or cruisers to this area, as school was not out on the mainland, and it was a bit early for the cruisers to arrive from their normal migrations from the South Pacific or from the mainland.

A slight north swell arrived during the night, but it's only effect on *Tranquilo* was a gentle rise and fall that was not even felt below in the cabin. There was a small surf break on shore, and it made for some potentially good body surfing. Luke tried body surfing early in his first week in Hawaii and came away more bruised and battered than he felt merited the thrill. His friend Gus took him board surfing outside of the Ala Wai Harbor, however it only took one fall off the board and subsequent scrape on some coral heads to turn him off to that as well.

After swimming back to *Tranquilo*, they showered together, which was becoming a frequent practice. This again led to making love and further passion that intensified with each day. They were able to extend way beyond each other's past pleasures to a point where they were now both keenly aware that this relationship was developing far outside each other's wildest dreams.

Hardly able to speak from gasping for breath as they'd both just reached their peak, Luke looked into Teruyo's wide-open eyes and said, "Teruyo, I love you."

"Oh Luke, I love you too," she replied as they continued to look into each other's eyes, still bound in their embrace. "You've just made me the happiest woman in the world by saying that!"

"I'm sorry I haven't said it sooner."

"Oh, me too. I was scared you'd feel pressured."

"Baby, this past week has been the happiest in my life. I've never thought I'd allow myself to fall in love again, and as crazy as it seems, I really am." He paused, holding her tightly and thinking about where to go next. "It's about time to explain some painful parts of my past, and I only bring it up because you're going to need to fully understand why I've been so reluctant to accept I'm really feeling this way about you."

Still holding her man, not wanting him to let go, she replied, "Luke, I have skeletons in my closet, too. I sense you've been holding back like I have, but don't feel you have to bare it all right now. We have all of the time in the world to get to fully know each other."

Pulling away, Luke became very serious, "I told you that when I was in Nam, that my wife filed for a divorce. When I found out that she had taken up with another guy, I didn't hesitate to take care of the paperwork as quickly as possible. What I haven't told you is just how deeply hurt I was and for how long I've been bitter."

Pausing, then sitting up and resting his shoulders and head on a pillow he'd propped up against the aft bulkhead, he continued, "I really loved her, and the most painful thing I'd ever experienced was reading the words in that letter saying she'd left me. I'd almost shot myself in a drunken rage two nights after receiving that letter, but my crew chief Willie was able to talk me down and finally get my pistol away from me until I sobered up.

"Shortly after that, we were returning from dropping a squad of troops at a hot LZ, when my chopper was shot down, and the Viet Cong captured us. We were taken to some underground tunnels and beaten to the point of giving up hope for survival. My life during those six days meant nothing to me... I wanted it to end." Tears began welling up in Luke's eyes.

"Don't go on, Luke. We don't need to

talk about this now." Teruyo was also tearing up, totally taken aback about this part of his past.

"No, you need to understand this. I've been agonizing over this the past few nights while on my watches sailing over from Maui, then from Oahu. You see, I've been denying myself the ability to love again because I swore I'd never put myself in a position to be hurt like that again. The beatings and torture were about the final straw to me not caring if I lived or died.

The only thing that kept me alive during our capture was to be there for Willy. During the sixth night when we were forced to march through the jungle, I was able to work lose the leather bindings on my wrists and overpower one of the guards. I broke his neck and then killed the other two guards with his weapon. Willy and I crawled through the jungle for four days and luckily found our way back to a sector where a Marine patrol found us and got us airlifted back to Da Nang and to a hospital. After a week there, we were shipped on to Tripler Hospital in Oahu and later honorably discharged. All during that recovery and reliving the ordeal as many times as I have, I swore over and over I'd *never* put myself in a position to fall in love again.

"I have used and misused women ever since. Knowing there could never be any possibility of getting too close, I have gotten what I've wanted and never allowed anything to develop. You're the first woman I have felt this way with, and believe me, it never crossed my mind from the beginning this could happen."

"Luke... Oh Luke, I'm so sorry. I would never have suspected you had so much pain and lived with her betrayal so long."

"It's important you understand this... I haven't been taking from you this last week. I've really been totally overcome with you from the beginning, and the more we are together and the love we are sharing, I've finally realized this is real... not just a fling. I'm sorry I haven't been able to tell you sooner."

"Hon, I love you," she whispered as she laid her head on his chest. "I've also been scared to admit it because just a few months ago, I was saying the same thing to Jamie, my former fiancé back in Rhode Island." Teruyo had sat up and covered herself with the sheet, as intense as Luke had ever seen her. She continued, "You know what? I don't care that it has only been a few months since I left him. I know in my heart what you and I have is real. I've felt it since we made love on the deck under the stars that night in Hale Lono and I'm so grateful we're able to still be together. Shindo was wonderful to let us work this out."

"Yeah, I'm not sure just how I'd have dealt with you having to leave."

"Could we have gotten back together?"

"No doubt about it, Sugar. This is too special to give up. I did mean what I said to Shindo that whatever he felt was best, I'd agree too. But I was hoping if we were separated, we could get back together soon. It's scary knowing you could be in danger, and that's my biggest concern."

"These past two days in Hanalei, I've almost forgotten about any dangers."

"I've been aware of our surroundings and any possibilities of danger, but so far, this seems to be just the perfect place to be."

"How long do you think we can hide out here?"

"I'd say until there gets to be too many boats or too many tourists, and then it's off for new waters."

"Oh Hon, I'm so happy."

"I love you, Baby"

"I love you, too."

And they cuddled back down together again.

Chapter 17

"Ahoy, *Tranquilo*!" a voice yelled from the starboard side.

It was early evening, not quite dark. Teruyo was cooking dinner in the galley and Luke was napping in the salon. He awoke and bounded up the companionway to see a smiling man rowing up in a dinghy next to *Tranquilo*.

"Aloha," replied Luke.

"Just on my way back from work and thought I'd check to see if you guys were alright. I live on the sloop over there and wanted to let you know I'm there in the evenings if you need anything."

"That's awful nice of you. Would you like to come aboard for a spell?"

"Great! Let me tie up to your stern."

Luke lowered his swim ladder for the fellow to climb up. They shook hands after he made it to the deck and Luke had secured the painter (bowline) of his dinghy.

"Hi, I'm Jim Robinson."

"Luke Davis. Welcome aboard *Tranquilo*." Teruyo curiously looked up the companionway. "This is my lady, Teruyo."

"Aloha. I'm Jim from the boat anchored over there."

Not having been introduced quite that

way ever before, she replied with a grin, "Aloha, Jim, nice to meet you. Would you like a beer or something else to drink?"

"Well now, that would be great. I just got off work, and a beer is the first thing I grab when I get home to my boat."

Luke asked, "Where do you work?"

"I picked up a remodeling job on a condo not far from here. The owners want it painted and some trim work finished before they come to spend the summer in a month. I've really lucked out because the bay has been fairly calm this spring. Not too much of a north swell lately. Usually I try to find work close to where I can anchor, and this job came a little early in the season for this bay."

"So you have been here before?"

"Yeah, I've been living aboard for eight years, mostly around Kauai."

Teruyo brought up two cold beers from the reefer, eliciting a surprised exclamation from Jim, "Oh my, that's a cold one! You have refrigeration?"

Luke replied, "Yeah, it seems to do well. We can power it off the generator or the main engine. These past two days we have only used the generator. Been really peaceful here."

"I've learned to live with warm beer for so long; this really is a treat. Thank you."

"Our pleasure. Say, what's behind those condos and beachfront homes?"

"Well the little town of Hanalei is quaint. There is a small market and of course a Post Office. On up the road you can find some good restaurants next to the resorts and on down to the towns of Kapa'a and Lihue. Do you need anything?"

"No, not now. We haven't even inflated our dinghy yet. Been content to stay in and relax."

They talked about Luke and Teruyo's recent crossings, and Luke tried sound like they'd been cruising for a long time. Teruyo invited Jim to stay for dinner, and he readily accepted. Jim was most taken with the beauty and amenities of Luke's yacht. He really appreciated the quality and the attention to detail that Luke had given *Tranquilo*.

After dinner they returned to the cockpit and continued to talk about Kauai and some of the formalities like the disposal of trash, stowing one's dinghy on the beach, and other good information to keep in the good graces of the locals. Jim encouraged them to go exploring up the Hanalei River in their dinghy and he also noted some quality restaurants along the north shore.

"There is a great anchorage just to the west of here called "Tunnels." It's easy to find: just follow the reef and when you see a pinnacle that rises right from the water's edge, you'll know you are there. One of the most beautiful snorkeling sites I've ever been to. Wait until there is no north swell though, or it'll rock you silly."

"Thanks. We love to dive."

After dinner, Jim thanked them for their hospitality and the wonderful meal. "That was real nice of you to invite me up and include dinner. In a couple of weeks when some of the other cruisers start filtering in, we'll be having potluck suppers on the beach, and maybe I'll get a chance to return the favor."

Teruyo replied, "Stop by anytime. It was a pleasure meeting you."

"Aloha," Jim said as he rowed off to his boat.

"What a nice guy," Luke stated.

"Yes, a real earthy and honest kind of fellow."

"Maybe we should get motivated and assemble the dinghy tomorrow to go exploring."

"Oh, alright. I wouldn't mind having dinner at that Italian restaurant he spoke about."

"That's going to cost you extra," Luke said with an air of authority.

Teruyo cocked an eyebrow and gave a sultry smile.

The next morning they assembled the dinghy and mounted the outboard motor, then headed for the Hanalei River to do some exploring. With all of the rain coming down in the valley, the water eventually ran into Hanalei Bay, but at this time, the tide was low so they had to carry the dinghy over a sandbar to get into the river. As they cautiously motored up the river, they felt they had entered a new world.

Luke asked, "Ever seen the movie *African Queen* with Humphrey Bogart and Katherine Hepburn?"

"Yes, you want me to start calling you 'Charlie'?"

"Of all the gin-joints in the entire world, why did you have to come to mine?" Luke tried his best Bogart impression.

"Wrong movie, Humphrey. That was *Casablanca*, I believe."

"Oh, well anyway, doesn't this remind you of them steaming up river through the jungle?"

"Yes, it does. It's so beautiful. Look at that little house!" Teruyo exclaimed and pointed to the most beautiful little farmhouse as they rounded a bend in the river. It had a barn with some horses grazing in a pasture out back. "Oh, wouldn't you love to live there?"

"You didn't impress me as a country girl."

"I guess I really wouldn't. It's just so picturesque. And these beautiful flowers all along the river, it's just like a Garden of Eden."

"Ya wanna bite of apple?"

"Stop it," Teruyo replied with a grin.

They found some beautiful flowers growing right out to the river's edge and picked some for the cabins on *Tranquilo*: Torch Ginger, Heliconia, Hibiscus, Anthuriums, and Plumeria. This was as close to a jungle paradise as they had ever been in, and they wanted to absorb all of the fragrances and beautiful scenery. It was quite a distance up stream before they came to a one-lane bridge. They decided to turn back and gently float back with the slow-moving current.

"Did you know Hawaii has no snakes?" Teruyo asked as she started to dangle her legs over the side of the dinghy.

"Why, are you afraid of snakes?"

"Not really," she replied, dabbling her feet in the cool river water.

Luke grabbed Teruyo suddenly, startling her, and pulled her back into his arms. "But they have crocodiles!" They laughed and lay together in the dinghy as the river took them on back to the bay.

It was still a beautifully sunny and warm morning, so after taking the flowers to *Tranquilo* and arranging them in makeshift vases, they motored to the beach where Jim kept his dinghy when he was off to work. They headed into the town of Hanalei, which was just a short three-block walk, and they found the market and Post Office in a little strip mall. Teruyo stopped at a pay phone and placed a call to Honolulu to let the security agent know everything was going fine.

"Has Shindo found out anything in his investigation yet?" she asked the agent.

"I don't have any new information, but I will let him know you called and inquired."

Luke asked her, "What did he have to say?"

"He was just going to pass on to Shindo we are fine and he appeared to know nothing of the investigation."

Luke pointed to a Mexican restaurant. "Want a Margarita?"

"You sailors are all alike: offer a lady a Margarita and try to take advantage of them! I know your type."

They had a nice lunch and headed back out hand-in-hand to check out Hanalei. "What beautiful little well-kept homes," Teruyo exclaimed. "I wonder what everyone does for a living to be able to live and work here."

"Probably, from the looks of things, they're local retired people. Not many swing sets or other indications of families with children."

Just as Luke finished speaking, they

noticed an elderly Japanese lady tending to her flowers in her front yard. Teruyo walked up to her and said, "Aloha, what a beautiful garden you have."

With a slight bow and a wonderful smile, the woman replied, "Oh, thank you so much. These are orchids my late husband bred and I keep them up in his memory."

"They are magnificent."

"Thank you, aloha."

"I like this place," Teruyo said as they strolled back to the beach. They were in such a peaceful, mellow mood, but the afternoon showers were looming and they wanted to get back to their nest before getting wet.

Luke had one project he was interested in tackling. With all of the rain that consistently fell each afternoon, he wanted to set up a means to capture some fresh water for his water tanks on *Tranquilo*. He had read in one of his cruising books how to rig a water catcher, so with some spare garden hose and some fittings, all he needed to do was to cut a small hole in the awning and devise a way to attach the hose to the hole and lead it to each of the water tank fill ports on the deck. He attached the fitting to the awning with some patching material from his dinghy, then devised a way to attach the oars to hold it up in two places, making a "cup" shape to collect the rainwater. Working in the rain all afternoon,

Luke had received a good long shower for himself, but he did devise a rain catcher to fill his tanks with fresh, pure rainwater.

Chapter 18

Two days later, Jim stopped by *Tranquilo* in the morning to say he'd finished his job and was sailing over to the harbor at Kapa'a. He said he'd be back in a month and hoped to run into them again.

That evening they decided to go to shore and hail a taxi to take them to the Italian restaurant that Jim had recommended. It hadn't rained all day so Teruyo suggested they dress up a bit for their evening out. Of course this meant bringing extra clothes in a backpack, but that was no problem as this was just part of adjusting to 'living off the hook.'

Getting a cab was not like being in downtown Chicago. Luke had to call from the Mexican restaurant and they waited over Margaritas for about a half-hour until it arrived. The Italian restaurant was very nice, and Luke was glad Teruyo suggested dressing up from their very casual boat-life attire. Luke made arrangements with the taxi driver to pick them up two and a half hours later so they would have plenty of time to enjoy the meal and relax.

The meal was fabulous, as good as any Italian meal in Chicago. The setting was spectacular with a view not far from the lighthouse, which had guided them on their crossing from Oahu. They talked and enjoyed each other's company in the almost empty restaurant, which during the high season would have been packed with an hour wait to be seated. Luke ordered a nice bottle of Chianti to go along with his Veal Parmesan and her Beef Medallions with Scampi, but since Teruyo only sipped at her one glass, he developed a pretty warm glow from almost finishing the whole bottle by himself.

The time passed quickly, and Luke was anxious to get home to some romantic candlelight in the aft cabin. Their taxi driver came into the restaurant to see about his fare. He was more than patient as this was his only income for the night anyway. Upon dropping them off at the beach, Luke gave him a nice tip and they didn't even bother with changing back to their boat clothes; they headed straight for the dinghy like two mischievous lovebirds hurrying to get to their nest.

All of a sudden, Teruyo screamed as she was grabbed from behind with a forearm around her throat, and a hand locking her right wrist behind her back. Luke was clubbed with the butt of a pistol from behind, causing him to fall forward, but it was not a sufficient enough blow to knock him unconscious When he regained his footing, he was staring down the barrel of a semi-automatic pistol being held by a very short, muscular Asian man. Luke saw that Teruyo was struggling to get free. She was able to somehow kick her assailant's right knee with her bare foot. The sound of his kneecap shattering and his immediate scream in pain was astonishing.

Luke's assailant was distracted by the scream from his partner, and Luke immediately grabbed his right wrist, which was holding the pistol, and pushed it off to their side. A shot rang out, but Luke didn't let go. He thrust his right fist into the man's throat, collapsing his esophagus and cutting off his air supply. The assailant fell to the sand, dropping the pistol and grasping his throat with both hands like someone choking desperately for air. Luke compounded his breathing problem by thrusting his right fist with all of his strength into the fallen man's sternum, forcing out any air that remained in his lungs. The thug went into convulsions, as his body had no means to supply oxygen to its blood stream.

Luke turned his attention back to Teruyo and at that moment, he saw her flip her assailant onto his back. He immediately bounced up and tried to whack Teruyo with a blow toward her head. She fended it off with her forearms, but the force still knocked her down. Luke had been a linebacker on his high school football team and he dove right for her assailant's broken right knee, tackling him to the ground as the whole knee was now separated out from under him. He cried out in tremendous pain. Teruyo grabbed his wrist, and bent it back, forcing his face into the sand. Luke jammed his knee into the back of the man's neck. When they saw they had him neutralized, they scanned the area to ensure there were no other dangers. Luke's downed assailant was still convulsing, but slowly regaining his ability to breath.

"Hold this one down while I take care of that one." Luke got up and ran over to his thug, slamming his fist square into his jaw, knocking him unconscious and not caring at all if he'd killed him.

Hc returned to Teruyo, "Are you OK?"

"I'm fine," she gasped, trying to regain her breath. The adrenaline was flowing through their bodies like never before. "Are you OK?"

"Yeah, let's drag your boy here over to the water and see if he wants a drink!"

"Luke, shouldn't we call the police?"

"That gunshot probably raised some attention; I want to first see who these guys work for. Come on help me drag him to the water."

They got him to the water's edge, where he continued groaning in agony from the broken knee. Teruyo expertly kept pressure on his wrist to keep him under control. Luke grabbed him by his ears, almost ripping them

176

off, and raised his head to look into his eyes. "What are you after?"

The assailant said nothing, returning Luke's glare with one of utter defiance. Luke shoved the thug's head below water and held it with a knee in the back of his neck. He struggled, but with the hold Teruyo had on him and with all of Luke's 180 pounds coming down on his neck, he couldn't move.

"That's enough Luke! We can't kill him!" Teruyo cried.

As his body starved for oxygen and the adrenalin kicked in to his entire muscular system, the muscles began to tighten and he thrashed with all of the power he could gather. As his mind was also deprived of the flow of oxygen, he began to fall into a semi-conscious state. Luke grabbed him by the ears, again inflicting a great deal of pain and raised his head out of the water to face him. Luke punched him in the sternum, knocking the water out of his lungs, which helped to restore the flow of oxygen to his system. After coughing and vomiting out the sand and salt water he'd inhaled and regaining his ability to breathe, his eyes reopened, no longer holding the look of defiance but, instead, of horror. Luke, almost nose-to-nose with him, yelled like a Drill Sergeant to a new recruit on the first day of Boot Camp, "Are you ready to talk or do you want another drink?"

"We kidnap the girl and kill you," the assailant cried as he gasped for air.

"Who are you working for?" Luke asked with gritted teeth.

After continued gasps for more air, "I...I don't know."

Luke shoved his head under water again. Teruyo continued to maintain her grip on the assailant, however she pleaded with Luke, "No, Luke, don't kill him! Let the police take care of this!"

"I'll have him talking soon. This is what the bastards did to me and Willy in Nam and I'm going to show 'em what it's like!"

He brought his head up by the ears again, this time giving him extra time to cough out the sand and salt water. "One last time, who are you working for? We can keep this up all night. You're going to keep drinking salt water and eatin' sand until you talk."

The thug's eyes looked like they could pop right out of their sockets from fear. He pleaded between gasps, "Suh Byung-min... He...he kill us if he find out we talk."

"Where do I find him?"

"Hotel Kohiko in Honolulu, room 2332. That all I know," the thug gasped.

"What else? Why did they want the girl?"

"I don't know. I don't know!" he cried.

Back into the water his head went. He

was again fighting for his life but unable to break free from the force of Luke's knee to his neck.

"No more Luke! He told you all he knows. Luke! Luke, we're not in Vietnam!" Teruyo yelled.

"Go check on his buddy and grab the pistol if you can find it."

Luke took over holding the man's wrist but was even more forceful by pulling back on the arm to where a little more tension would dislocate the shoulder. The man stopped fighting, and Luke knew he had drowned to the point of unconsciousness. He pulled his head out of the water and kicked him in the lower back, forcing out the water that he had inhaled. Teruyo returned with the pistol as Luke gave him the blow to the back. She screamed, "Stop it Luke! You're going to kill him!"

The man started coughing and gasped for air again. "Just giving him another chance to keep talking."

Teruyo didn't like what was transpiring right in front of her. Luke was so brutal; she couldn't have imagined anything so inhumane coming from him. "Luke, let me go get help."

"No wait! Go to the boat and call Shindo. I'll watch these two and if the police do come, I'll turn them over. Shindo might want at them first. Go. Take the dinghy and come back as soon as you give all the information to Shindo. Tell him about this Suh Byung-min fellow and the address…what was it?"

"Hotel Kohiko, room 2332. Luke, please don't kill them," she pleaded. "If you murder them, the police will take you away from me!"

"If we don't find who is behind this, we might not have a very long life together anyway. Now, go on. Do as I say! Call Shindo and see what he wants to do."

Luke gave a good kick to the man's ribs to keep him down. He helped Teruyo drag the dinghy into the water and started the engine for her.

"Go on now, quickly. I'll be right here. Oh, bring back some rope. There is some in the port stern lazarete."

She sped off as fast as the little outboard would take her.

Chapter 19

Luke stood guard over the two injured assailants like a cat over a mouse. Every once in a while, one would start to regain consciousness, and Luke would kick or punch him a couple of times until he moved no more. He was still furious over the thought of them trying to kill him and take Teruyo. Luke had no remorse for the pain he inflicted upon these two and he barely felt the swelling in his own hands and feet from the blows he'd landed.

Surprisingly, no one responded to the gunshot or the yelling on the beach or even happened to walk by. It was actually a beautiful moonlit evening, with just enough light to notice any movement by his captives, but not enough to be very noticeable from the homes along the bay. Teruyo had given Luke the pistol, and it took him some time to figure out how to work the safety. Luke was raised with shotguns, rifles, and revolvers on the farm, but other than the Army-issue Colt 45 he'd been given after becoming a helicopter pilot, he'd had no experience with semi-automatic pistols.

After what seemed like forever, but was really only ten minutes, Teruyo motored back to the beach. Luke checked to ensure the thugs were still out then helped her bring the dinghy to up the beach.

"Were you able to reach Shindo?" Luke asked.

"Yeah, I talked directly to him," she gasped between breaths. "He will be here shortly. He is bringing one of Grandfather's helicopters over to a helipad close by, and a car will be there to meet them. He is sending another team over to the Hotel Kohiko to try to find Suh Byung-min. He told us if the police do show up, to just tell them everything, except about this Suh Byung-min or why this happened. He has had no cooperation so far from the Honolulu Police, so he is excited to have the lead on Suh Byung-min."

"Let's tie these guys up and wait. Are you familiar with guns?"

"No, not at all."

Rather than having Teruyo hold the pistol while he tied them up, Luke laid it in the dinghy. The thugs were both still out cold, so securing their wrists with the rope Teruyo brought was no problem. Luke made sure they would not work themselves loose, as he had done in the jungles of Southeast Asia twelve years earlier.

After all was secure, they sat down in the sand, facing their captives, resting their backs on the soft tubes of the inflatable dinghy. The flow of adrenalin was easing somewhat, but their minds raced with questions and fear over what would come next.

"Luke, I'm scared."

Luke felt like his whole world came crashing down with her confession. "Let's try and stay calm. We can figure this out...hey, through all the fighting, I didn't tell you how fantastic and brave you were. You were unbelievable! How'd you break that dipshit's knee like that?"

"I didn't know your guy had a gun. I'd never have fought if I had known that. How'd you get that gun away from him anyway?"

"I guess he couldn't shoot and deal with his sore throat at the same time."

"Sore throat?"

"Yeah, an old boot camp karate lesson from my Drill Sergeant. I'll forever be grateful to him for that one," Luke said as he demonstrated with a quick flick of his knuckles at his throat.

"Oh, yeah, I know that one too."

"You were so great! You should have seen the look on my guy's face when we heard your boy's kneecap break. It was just freaky enough he moved to my left to see what that was and I had my chance to get inside of him before he could swing the gun back on me."

"I'm so sorry I kept yelling at you. I thought you were going to kill them."

"I guess I got a little crazy over there,"

Luke looked back to the spot where he kept dunking Teruyo's assailant. "I'll never forget the VC doing that to Willy and me to get us to talk. If we'd have known anything important back then, we may have had a lot of our boys killed. But as it turned out, the only information we gave them was of little or no use. Willy and I have lived with the guilt of breaking down under their torture ever since. I'm just grateful to God we didn't have anything important to divulge, and that we were able to kill the sons-o-bitches and get home."

"Luke, I'm so sorry."

"I am too, Baby. I really hope I did the right thing there. At this moment, I feel I did. We need to know who is behind this and we need to know *now* so they can be stopped. Sometimes our laws are too protective of the rights of the bad guys. That's why Shindo wants to talk to them."

"Let me see your hands. They're so swollen."

Luke was not aware of his hands and feet. Teruyo took a t-shirt out of the backpack, dampened it with saltwater, and wrapped it around Luke's hands. Still the attackers didn't move, and Luke never let his eyes off of them for a moment.

Some car headlights appeared about an hour after Teruyo made it back from calling

Shindo over the radio. Luke and Teruyo stood and were instantly alerted by sharp pain and stiffness throughout their bodies that they'd just been in a good fight. They had both used every bit of strength they had to subdue these two and get what information out of them that they could, and their muscles and joints were tightening up from sitting in the damp sand.

It was Shindo and four other men, one staying behind with the car. Shindo was an easy man to distinguish, even in the low light of the early morning hours. Luke signaled them using a small flashlight that he always carried in his backpack. The men came running with sprinters' speed and a combat readiness about them as they searched the area for any other dangers. Two of the men fanned out to about twenty feet from Luke and Teruyo, and Shindo came right up to them. "Teruyo, are you alright?"

"Yes, thanks for coming so quickly."

"Has anyone spotted you here yet?"

Luke replied, "No. No one has been by since this started."

Shindo surveyed the situation, carefully bending down to examine the captives. "Very good. I'll take them with us. You sure don't mess around!" he exclaimed as he stood up and looked at Luke.

"Yeah, if I were you, I'd never mess with this little lady either." Luke smiled and looked at Teruyo.

Shindo noticed the t-shirt wrapped around Luke's hands and knew this wasn't all Teruyo's doing. "Can I help you with your hands?"

"No. I'll be all right. Let me help you get them to your car."

"No, please. You've done enough. Go to your boat and leave as soon as you can. Is there some place you can hide?"

"How about Tahiti?"

Shindo was in no mood for joking, even though Luke was serious. "Let me talk to these men and see if we can locate Suh Byung-min. I'll be in touch as soon as we find out anything. Do you know of another anchorage where you will not be seen?"

"I'll find a place and let you know."

Shindo turned to Teruyo, "If I was not trying to take these men illegally as I am, you would have to come with me. But I cannot risk the police finding you involved with me as I do this. I trust you still wish to be with Luke?"

"Yes, he'll take care of me, as you can see." She smiled as she glanced towards their attackers.

"I will contact you on that same frequency as soon as I determine our next plan, and please contact me as soon as you find a place to hide. It is most important you are able to hide!" He emphasized.

Luke and Teruyo drug the dinghy to the water. She started the motor and pushed off from the beach as Luke's hands were so swollen, they were almost useless.

Chapter 20

Luke's hands and feet were a mess, and he was not sure if any bones were broken. He was able to move his fingers and toes but with much pain, so they iced them down and the swelling was subsiding some. Teruyo was fussing over Luke "like a mother hen," as he'd said, changing the bandages and making sure he kept them wrapped in ice.

Tunnels was not listed on the nautical chart or in Luke's cruising guide. All they had to rely upon was the directions a few nights earlier from Jim, the other sailor in Hanalei Bay. They'd had no sleep yet, because of too much adrenaline from the ordeal plus they wanted to leave Hanalei Bay at first light. It took less than two hours to haul anchor and relocate to Tunnels. Fortunately, there was no north swell coming in so the anchorage was calm and well protected, however, Luke was so tired he felt he could sleep through a hurricane if one came up. They'd even left the awning up and Teruyo handled the anchoring duties as well as diving to ensure it was set. Now that *Tranquilo* was secure in her new anchorage, sleep would come easy.

This was a perfect spot in which to hide. They were just around the bend from Hanalei

Bay, so it didn't take long to get there. Teruyo was taking charge of getting everything in order, but Luke was still capable of driving, evaluating the anchorage, and deciding where to drop the hook. They were working well as a team.

The pinnacle that Jim had described was a beautiful geologic feature that probably had similarities to those in Tahiti and Fiji. The water was crystal clear, but unlike Hanalei Bay, magnificent coral and abundant sea life surrounded them. There had even been a pod of dolphins to greet them as they steered into the anchorage. When all was secure, Teruyo started making a warm breakfast, and Luke, who was exhausted, lay in the salon listening to marine weather and scanning the pages of his cruising guide for their next destination if they needed to pull up in a hurry.

"How about some sausage and eggs? That should help you sleep."

"Baby, that sounds great. Like I'd need any help getting to sleep, though."

"I don't want you to worry about a thing. We'll be fine here, and I'll keep an anchor watch so you can rest easy."

"What about you? You need rest too. Just let me have four hours, then I'll relieve you."

"Actually, I'm fine. Still stiff and sore, but I'm doing OK. Besides, I'd rather not get too off schedule, and if I need a nap, I'll come on down. If Shindo calls, I want to be able to answer right away."

"Don't forget to call in after we eat."

Luke was out almost before he finished his last bite. Teruyo took a pillow, towel and a book up to the cockpit and made herself a comfortable "watch perch" in the shade of the awning. She only observed two fishing boats heading west about a mile off shore. Other than that, there was no sign of any other boats or people. Once again, they had anchored in a fantastic place, but it was hard to find a distraction from thoughts of the previous night. She couldn't help but wonder how all this would pan out. Negative thoughts kept coming back of her and Luke being separated *"for her own safety."* Then she would look at that pinnacle and dream of sailing on south to Tahiti and beyond. How could they ever be found if they kept moving until this mess was solved? She figured she would have to do a major sales pitch to make that fantasy happen.

Just after noon, she heard a familiar voice calling over the single side band radio, "WH9-DZK, WH9-DZK... this is Whisky-Tango-Charley, over." It was Shindo with his new call sign.

Teruyo jumped down to the nav-station and responded, "Whisky-Tango-Charley, this is Whisky-Hotel-Niner-Delta-Zulu-Kilo, I read you loud and clear, over."

"We arranged a meeting at the hotel this morning and are continuing our negotiations most successfully. There appear to be no further members to attend to at this time, but their home office may wish to send more delegates. Do you copy, over?"

"Yes, we copy. Do we need to send you any further documents, over?"

"No, our home office certainly wishes to have a package, but we convinced them for now no further help would be needed, over."

Thank you so much, that's the best news we could have had, over."

"Whisky-Tango-Charley out."

"WH9-DZK, out."

Teruyo had been granted her wish: she could stay with Luke. She jumped up and whispered loudly, "Yes!" Then she turned to see Luke standing in the entrance to the aft cabin, sleepy-eyed, but smiling.

"So is this charter continuing a little longer, Ma'am?"

Teruyo ran to Luke's waiting arms, "Oh Hon, did you hear that?"

"Yeah, as best as I could cipher ole Suh Byung-min is having a little conversation with your good buddy Shindo."

"Yeah. I guess he's determined there is no threat to us right now. Isn't that great?"

"Yeah, Baby, that's the best news I've

191

had all day. Now, let's go to bed."

"Let me see those bandages first. I've got to take care of you till you get all better."

Although his hands and feet were sore, he didn't think anything was broken, now that the swelling had gone down. "I'm going to be all right. Maybe a little more sleep and I'll be back to normal."

"If you sleep too much now, you'll be up all night. Why not try and stay awake the rest of the evening and we can try and sleep through the night?"

"Yeah, you're probably right. Besides, I'm hungry."

"Hungry? You just had a big breakfast!"

"Well that was five hours ago. Remember I'm your patient. How does the ole saying go, 'Starve a cold, and feed a warrior'?"

"Oh yeah, something like that." She grinned.

During lunch, Teruyo told Luke how magnificent the coral and fish were in the tight little reef. They decided to give snorkeling a try, and hopefully the swimming would be good for their stiff joints and muscles.

Once in the water, they were welcomed with the most beautiful snorkeling area yet with magnificent coral formations. The fish were just as curious of them as they were of the fish. Teruyo was able to see species she had seen only in books and was able to identify not only some of the most common Hawaiian reef fish she had observed previously in Honolua Bay, such as both Yellow and Achilles Tangs, several Trigger fish, Saddle Wrasses, and a variety of Butterfly fish which darted and danced to a silent serenade, but also a Zebra eel, a Scorpion fish, a Porcupine fish, and a Harlequin shrimp. They both saw a small octopus, which undulated over the rock formations where its skin began to transform, completely camouflaging itself with color and texture, until it eventually melted into a small crevice and disappeared.

"That was so amazing how its whole body was able to slither into that tiny hole," Luke commented when they had come up for a breath of air.

They stayed in the water for the better part of an hour, until they began to get chilled. Luke had totally forgotten about his injuries until it came time to lift himself up the swim ladder. There was still a great deal of pain, but the swim had done him a world of good.

After rinsing down with a fresh water shower and drying off in the cockpit, Teruyo brought Luke a cold beer and they lay in the sun on the foredeck to warm up. She said, "Well, my warrior, that was just about the best swim I've ever had."

"Yeah, I'd never imagined anything so beautiful, so many different types of fish and coral!"

"I don't see how we could ever tire of exploring like this."

"Me neither. And to think, if you hadn't whacked that thug on the knee just right, I'd be dead right now and who knows where you'd be."

"Now why did you have to bring that up?"

"Baby, this is a paradox that we need to talk about. We are anchored right now in the most beautiful setting, in love, and so full of contentment. And yet, we have to be looking over our shoulders, never sure how we can control our own future. When you said how we couldn't ever tire of living like this, it just triggered the thought that we still have to face a major decision real soon about what will happen between us."

"What are you trying to tell me? Is this too complicated for you? Don't you think I'm scared enough already?" Teruyo cried.

"I know you're scared. Hell, I'm scared! I'm scared of facing another encounter like that, but most of all, I'm scared of losing you!" Luke emphasized a bit too loudly.

"Well, I didn't choose this whole mess. In fact, I didn't come looking for love either; it just happened! Don't you think I'm just as fragile as you when it comes to the thought of us losing each other?" Teruyo shouted back.

They both stopped. It struck them at the same instant that this was the first time they had not been on the same wavelength. Teruyo had been immersed in the overwhelming magnificence of their experience snorkeling, and Luke ruined it by bringing up thoughts of them being torn apart.

"OK, you're right," Teruyo conceded. "We are facing a big paradox right now. What do you propose we do? Do you want to make a decision right now? Why do we need to ruin this beautiful afternoon by dealing with this right now?"

"Whoa, Baby. I'm sorry. I didn't mean to ruin the afternoon. I shouldn't have brought it up. Let's drop it, and we'll deal with it later," Luke said, feeling really bad. "I don't know why those thoughts came up. I'm really sorry."

"I'm so in love with you, Luke. Nothing is more important to me than being with you. I can't believe anything could tear us apart. Maybe I'm feeling too invincible since we just got out of a big jam and Shindo just gave us the OK to stay here for now. Maybe you are right to question our next move, but I'm just so happy and..." Teruyo began sobbing uncontrollably for the first time in their short relationship.

He held her close to his chest and for the first time, realized just how fragile their time together could be. Sure they had both been privately worried, especially with the events of the past fifteen hours, but she was doing her best to help him with his injuries and take care of moving the boat. He'd forgotten that she hadn't had any sleep yet.

"Hon, it's alright. I'm so sorry I brought it up. We need to get some rest and think more clearly after getting more input from Shindo. We don't need to worry about this now. I'm sorry... I love you, Baby."

She looked up from his chest and with tears running down her cheeks, said, "I do love you, Luke."

Chapter 21

Luke slept just over nine hours, and Teruyo was still sleeping when he awoke to make coffee. After going topside, checking on their position in the anchorage, and finding everything as it should be, he went below for his first cup of coffee. He heard Teruyo stirring and went to look in on her. She looked at him with a sly little smile and back to bed he went. They made love like it was their first time.

Last evening after their spat, Luke had started the generator to charge the reefers and cooked a pot of rice in the electric rice cooker. Teruyo helped fix some tea and tuna to go along with the rice, but they hardly spoke while fixing dinner and eating. Both were lost in their thoughts and a little ashamed for "going off" on each other. That was the first night staying together they hadn't made love.

"I love you, Babe."

"Oh, I love you, Luke."

"What do ya say we go for a swim whenever you feel like getting up?"

"I'm hungry."

"Hmm, care for some banana pancakes and sausage?"

"Yeah, why don't you summon the chef, give our order, and stay here with me?"

"What kind of ship do you think you chartered? The Queen Mary?" Luke replied with a laugh.

"I'm feeling so lazy. I think your boat has me "tranquilo.""

"That was the plan!"

Luke got up and fixed a huge breakfast, the best they'd eaten so far, excluding the ones at *Eggs & Things*. They were content to hang out in the cockpit in the shade of the awning as their stomachs digested and continue to take in the serenity of the incredible anchorage. It was another sunny morning and they could see the wind line off shore, the trade winds barely blowing ten knots.

"How about going sailing?" Luke offered.

"Yeah, it's a perfect day. You want to look for another anchorage or return here?"

"I don't know. Let's just see what's on west of here. The cruising guide indicates some beautiful sailing along the Na Pali coast but no protected anchorages. But then they didn't show this one either. We'll just see what the day brings."

"I think that's just what we need. See what the day brings and enjoy it."

They took their time stowing the awning and the dinghy, and getting everything closed up down below. Luke's hands and feet were better this morning, so he resumed his place on the bow as Teruyo slowly drove forward on the anchor. Luke appreciated having the electric anchor windless for taking away the backbreaking job of hauling up the hundreds of pounds of chain and anchor, especially with his hands still sore.

As they cleared the reef and started making their way out to the wind line, a very large pod of dolphins surrounded *Tranquilo*. There seemed to be a hundred or more. Luke told Teruyo, "Hey, get your snorkeling gear and my underwater camera and see if you can get some good photos. I'll hold us steady here while you check them out."

Teruyo gladly jumped at the chance, and was soon in the water. "Ohmmmmm, Ohmmmmm!" She exclaimed, trying to talk without thinking about her mouthpiece.

"What is it, Honey?" Luke asked, knowing it must be good.

She surfaced and took her snorkel out of her mouth, "Luke you've got to see this! There are so many dolphins. There are mothers with babies and big ones swimming in escort! It's amazing!"

"Stay there and get as many pictures as you can. I'll hold *Tranquilo* steady. You go on. This is your specialty."

She was in marine biology heaven. The dolphins were as curious of her as she was of them, but they didn't let her get too close. She was astonished at how they swam in perfect synchronicity. Each movement made by the mothers was perfectly duplicated by their calves. The "escorts" were swimming just above the "families" and the whole exhibition was such a happy existence. There seemed to be no fear from either of the species, and they continued to stay in the area and swim in curiosity around *Tranquilo*. Teruyo took a whole roll of film from Luke's underwater camera, and then came up to the cockpit to take over the helm and give Luke a chance to swim with them.

He eased himself into the water and was equally entranced with the scene in the clear waters just off the reef. *"Wow."*

After finally getting their fill of this extraordinary encounter, they headed on out to the wind line and set the mainsail. If they had wanted to make the best time for the light-air conditions, they'd have hoisted Luke's colorful spinnaker sail as they were on a run (the wind at their backs). However, the scenery of the Na Pali Coast was breathtaking, so they wanted to just ease along and enjoy the magnificent views of the waterfalls and the contrasting palette the landscape provided. Of course going with the wind one direction means beating and tacking against the wind coming back, so they didn't want to have to go too far too quickly or they would have a long fetch back to Tunnels if they didn't find a more appealing anchorage.

The crackle from the single side band radio broke the mood of the mellow symphony music they were listening to as they slowly ran down the coast just under power of the mainsail alone. "WH9-DZK, WH9-DZK... this is Whisky-Tango-Charley, over."

"Oh, pooh," was Teruyo's remark as she went below to answer.

"Whisky-Tango-Charley, this is Whisky-Hotel-Niner-Delta-Zulu-Kilo, I read you loud and clear, over."

Shindo asked, "Is it possible for you to meet the boss and me for a meeting this evening where we last saw you, over?"

Luke was peering down the companionway hatch and heard the request, "Does he mean Hanalei Bay? If so, yeah, we can make that."

"Roger that. You are talking about our last meeting location as the one where you flew over here, over?" Teruyo answered back.

"That is affirmative. We would like to take you to dinner and introduce your secretary to the boss, over."

"Secretary! Couldn't he come up with something better than that?" Luke frowned.

Teruyo grinned and replied, "Yes. That will be OK. I'll see she wears a new dress for the occasion, over."

Shindo replied, "Very well, we will pick you up at 6:00, over."

"Copy that. WH9-DZK, out."

"Whoa, taking this code talk a little to the extreme aren't we?" Luke smiled as he grabbed Teruyo when she returned to the cockpit.

"Hmm, I wonder how you would look in a dress and makeup."

"Easy Baby, I'm not that kind of guy!" Luke protested with a grin.

"I hate to have to come about, but we better get back to Hanalei and get all cleaned up to meet the boss. I really want to make a good impression."

"Arc we talking about your grand-father?" Luke asked.

"Yes, I'm sure he flew straight here after being informed about recent events."

"Would he be open to go for a sail and see just how well we are doing together?"

"Oh no. We'd never get him on the boat. I'm not sure just how this is going to go."

They brought *Tranquilo* about and tacked on back to Hanalei Bay, arriving in plenty of time to set the anchor, reset the awning and inflate the dinghy. There was a new sailboat now anchored in the bay, a beautiful sloop that had *Pretty Lady* Honolulu, HI on her stern. Luke recognized the boat from the Ala Wai Yacht Harbor, but he didn't know the owners.

Teruyo was visibly nervous as she got dressed. Luke tried to keep the moment light by asking, "Would these earrings go with this dress?" As he held up a dress Teruyo had laid out with a set of her earrings.

"Alright mister, you'd better behave this evening. There is a big difference in culture from Japanese businessmen verses *your* sense of humor. Remember to keep your comments easily understandable and try not to assume that he will be aware of the true direction our relationship has gone. We are going to need to clearly articulate our feelings and how we want to proceed," Teruyo replied, still very serious.

"Baby, I know a couple of times I commented to Shindo about us heading to Tahiti. You and I have dreamed together about cruising the South Pacific, but let me ask you now: are you ready to come with me if I ask your grandfather?"

"Yes, I want to be with you more than anything, whether it's staying in Hawaii if they feel they need to keep a tight rein on us, or sailing around the world. I not only love you, I trust you to take care of me. I do believe in us."

"Alright then. I'll see how things go. I was a shrewd negotiator at this time last year."

"Remember, be humble and respectful," Teruyo added.

Luke gave a slight bow of his head in an

attempt to show he was respectful of Japanese customs.

Chapter 22

They pulled the dinghy high up on the beach at five minutes until 6:00 and were met by Shindo. To Teruyo's surprise and delight, her mother and her sister were there too. She ran to greet them, and the reunion was a very happy one.

"Mom, I can't believe you are here! Hey, Sis!" Teruyo exclaimed as they all hugged.

Her mother commented, "Oh, you look so healthy. Look at you... so tanned and happy."

Teruyo's sister was less than two years younger and also very beautiful. She was a graduate student in a Big Ten college in the Midwest as Luke recalled. She said to her older sister, "So is this the Captain we've heard about?"

Luke had just walked up to the group after finishing locking up the dinghy and replied, offering his hand in greeting, "Hi, I'm Luke."

Teruyo's mother took his hand, noticing how swollen and bruised it was. "Very nice to meet you, Luke. Thanks so much for taking such good care of Teruyo."

"I'm honored to meet you, Mrs.

Boudreaux. This is a nice surprise," Luke said with a small bow of his head.

"Please call me Komiko," she replied.

"And you must be Michi." He shook Teruyo's sister's hand as well.

"Hello. Tell me, how do you navigate your boat at night when you get away from land?" Michi asked.

"Take it easy, Sis. How about getting to know Luke before you start the third degree," Teruyo said, jumping to Luke's rescue. "She can be a bit to the point," Teruyo told Luke.

Komiko added, "Shindo pointed your yacht out to us. It's lovely, even from way back here."

They all looked in the direction of *Tranquilo* as Luke replied, "Thank you, Ma'am. I'm very proud of her. She turned out to be so much more than I ever hoped for in a boat."

Michi couldn't help but insert, "Why do you call it a 'her'? It is a boat, not a girl. Besides it's blue, shouldn't you call it a him?"

"Michi, cut it out!" Teruyo replied with a grin. "Don't mind her Luke. She knows that sailors refer to their boats in the female gender. She's just looking to ruffle you up a little."

"But really, Teruyo, doesn't it offend you when he refers to his boat as 'her'?" Michi asked with her arms crossed.

Luke stepped in, "I don't mean any

disrespect, but a boat like that needs all the love and attention a lady would, so I guess it just keeps me honest."

"Ohoo, good comeback. He's a smoothie, Sis," Michi replied playfully.

Shindo interjected, "Ahem, the car is this way, if you please."

During the drive to the Hotel, Shindo explained that Teruyo's grandfather had rented an entire wing of the Sheraton Kauai, which overlooked the ocean and the entrance to Hanalei Bay. Most of the rooms he rented were for security personnel and administrators from a few of his companies here in Hawaii. He had decided to invite Teruyo's mother and sister along for a vacation, as everyone was very anxious to see Teruyo and meet "the Captain."

"Sis, it's not like we could have called you and told you we were coming," Michi added. "Have you seen any sharks? What do you do when you get in a storm?"

"Gosh, we just got here and I haven't seen you two in six months! Relax a little!" Teruyo laughed.

The last time they had all gotten together was in Rhode Island when the news came of her long-term relationship being broken off. Teruyo had told Luke they were a close family, but usually only coming together for special occasions or emergencies.

"Actually I saw my first shark this past

week when we were snorkeling, but Teruyo calmed me down and said it was not an aggressive type. And as far as storms, we just reduce our sails to the point where we can manage the boat and keep right on sailing." Luke wanted to respond to Michi's challenges without showing any sign of weakness, however she was certainly more spirited than he'd expected.

When they pulled into the drive at the Sheraton Hotel, they were met by a group of Asian men who Luke suspected could be bodyguards, except one: Mr. Tanaka.

Teruyo opened the car door as soon as they stopped and ran to her grandfather like a little child. "Grandfather," she said and they embraced.

"Teruyo-san, you look wonderful! My, how the sailing life must be good for you," he replied.

"Grandfather, I'd like you to meet Luke Davis." Teruyo turned as she spoke and proudly gestured to Luke as he was getting out of the car.

Luke came right over, trying not to look too nervous. "Mr. Tanaka, I am pleased to meet you," he said as he extended his hand and gave a slight bow of respect.

"Mr. Davis, I am most grateful for your bravery in fending off the attackers and saving Teruyo. It is I who am honored to meet you."

Mr. Tanaka took Luke's hand and returned the bow.

"Please Sir, call me Luke."

"Yes, of course," Mr. Tanaka replied with very proper English. "Let us go inside. You must be hungry."

Teruyo said with a smile, "When Shindo called us this morning and asked if we could meet you for dinner, I knew I should prepare quite an appetite or you would feel disrespected."

Mr. Tanaka gave his granddaughter another hug as they walked through the doors. "It's so good to see you, Teruyo. You look so happy and healthy."

Since this was still the off-season for tourists, they practically had the entire Sheraton restaurant to themselves. Certainly the section they had reserved was very adequate for privacy as well as a bountiful feast. Mr. Tanaka introduced the awaiting guests to Teruyo and Luke, and he also included the security team members. The way he showed such respect to the lower-level members of the team as well as the management associates impressed Luke.

Luke could tell there were other security staff on duty trying to discreetly remain in the shadows. This was a very powerful and cautious man, and he wanted total security for his family and those who traveled with him.

Luke got an uneasy feeling that it was not going to be easy to keep Teruyo to himself.

The dinner conversation was light, with many questions about Teruyo and Luke's adventures so far. All of the attendees seemed very interested in the stories of how Luke came to be in Hawaii and the process of finding his boat. They especially enjoyed when Teruyo explained how they had sailed from island to island, finding the wonderful anchorages and seeing all of the abundant sea life.

The food kept coming, with one course after another. Luke had been to some lavish dinner parties in Chicago, New York, and in many extravagant settings, but this was one to top them all. Mr. Tanaka must have assembled a staff to assist the Sheraton with this banquet. The exquisite food kept coming.

After the events of the past few days, Luke was surprised how relaxed and casual everyone was. No one mentioned the investigation of the would-be assassins. Luke and Teruyo were very anxious to know what all of that was about, but they didn't want to ask as yet. There would be time for that later, Luke assumed.

They dined and visited until way past dark, and Luke noticed it was past ten o'clock before some of the associates started excusing themselves. Many of the men smoked, and Mr. Tanaka welcomed Luke to smoke if he wanted.

Mr. Tanaka, having quit many years earlier, seemed pleased to hear when Luke stated he didn't smoke any longer.

When Teruyo, her mother, and sister were deep into a conversation, Mr. Tanaka asked Luke to join him for a breath of air. As they exited through a sliding glass door onto the veranda overlooking the waves breaking on shore below, Mr. Tanaka became extremely serious and asked, "I understand you two are falling in love?"

"Yes Sir," Luke replied. "We weren't looking for this to happen, but it began almost at first sight, and we let it flow... I mean, we just let our feelings continue to grow." Luke stumbled over his words, trying to remember Teruyo's recommendation to articulate properly. "We have a great deal in common and really like each other. I've never met a woman who I really *like* as much as Teruyo. I'm not only attracted to her because she is so beautiful and intelligent, but I really like being with her, and I respect what she believes in."

Still very serious, Mr. Tanaka continued, "I understand. I must say you have an air of confidence about you that I have not seen in any of the men she has introduced to me. Certainly much more than that *bakatare* who hurt her so," Mr. Tanaka replied with a hateful tone that didn't surprise Luke. "I will be honest with you; I am very protective of my granddaughters, and knowing that Teruyo was hurt just a short time ago, I am extremely concerned for her, especially so soon after breaking her near engagement. I was very disturbed when I found out she was traveling with you alone."

"Sir, I fully appreciate what you are saying. I even told her that if she was my granddaughter and I heard about her sailing around Hawaii alone with a fellow, I'd be on the first plane here to talk some sense into her!" Luke emphasized his words seriously. "Mr. Tanaka, this began as a totally innocent charter so Teruyo could go sailing. In fact, after meeting Shindo and listening to her proposal, I was real skeptical with even proceeding, as I didn't want the involvement of her security concerns. It didn't take but a few days together to realize that we were really attracted to each other, and we couldn't pretend it wasn't happening. We've talked at great length and have been very open with each other about our feelings, as our attraction has grown. I had a heartbreaking loss many years ago as well, and I also have those pains to overcome. However, let me assure you, we are being honest with each other and I respect her and sincerely feel I am falling in love with her. We realize we have only been together less than two weeks, but the way our time has been, spending twenty-four hours a day together, we feel we have known each other for much longer."

"Yes, Shindo has kept me apprised of your situation... more than just your whereabouts. I can see by meeting you, and seeing you together you are very happy together. And, I have never seen Teruyo looking so happy and excited. Whatever you are feeding her is very good!" Mr. Tanaka smiled like he'd made a funny joke.

"I'm glad you approve. I was afraid I'd not meet up to your expectations."

"Shindo is the one who you impressed a great deal. You and I will need much longer to get to know each other before I fully trust you," he said reverting back to a serious businesslike tone. "However, your cooperation with complying with Shindo's requests as well as your bravery with saving her life have earned my respect. As you can tell, I need to be consistently careful of who associates with my family. I truly want the most happiness for my granddaughters, but at the same time, I *will* insure their safety. Thank goodness you are with Teruyo and not Michiko. She is the rebellious one. We have a very hard time getting her to be reasonable and allow us to provide security for her safety."

Luke grinned, "I think I see what you mean. Just in the car ride over here from the beach, she nailed me with forty questions!"

Teruyo joined them on the veranda. "My ears were burning. Have you been talking about me?" she asked, putting her arm through her grandfathers', knowing full well they had.

"Luke tells me you are in love?" her grandfather asked her.

"He did?" she exclaimed, not ready for that. "Oh my, I didn't know he was ready to tell you yet. It is true, Grandfather; we are so happy, and he takes very good care of me," she replied. "We are both reluctant to commit to a full dedicated relationship, as it has been only a little over one week since we have been together, but he is the most wonderful man I have ever met, and we do so badly want to stay together and continue to get to know and love each other."

"Does your mother know how you feel about each other yet?" her grandfather asked.

"Yes, I wrote her a letter that she had just received yesterday. And this evening, we have talked some of our love, but because this has happened so fast, I don't want to get her all worried that I'm doing something foolish."

"Shindo had already communicated to me that you two were romantically involved and he was very concerned that you not get swept away by the need to rebound from your past loss. However, Shindo is very perceptive and he assures me that your intentions appear to be most genuine."

Luke took this opportunity to add, "We realize that you sincerely care and want the best for Teruyo, and I want to assure you personally that my intentions are of the deepest respect for Teruyo and your family. If I may speak for Teruyo, we are very grateful you have an open mind to our unusual circumstances."

Mr. Tanaka gave Luke a slight bow, "I accept your sincere acts of respect and proven regard for Teruyo's safety and her feelings. I would like for us to talk tomorrow about future plans and make additional security agreements and arrangements." He then looked at Teruyo, "I know you very well, Teruyo, and I have the utmost admiration for you as an adult as well as my granddaughter. I don't want to interfere with your adventure with Luke, but I feel I *must* give you protection because there are still elements that cause me some concern. We will meet tomorrow and continue to talk about future plans." He then put a hand on each of their shoulders, and said to Teruyo, "I know your mother would like to spend time with you. Could I ask you to be apart for at least one night?"

She looked into Luke's eyes, and he gazed into hers and he said, "That would be best; I need to check on *Tranquilo* anyway."

Mr. Tanaka added, "I'll have one of my men drive you back to the beach, and if you could join us for breakfast in the morning, we can get started with our meeting then."

Teruyo and Luke held hands and walked back into the dining room. Mrs. Boudreaux and Michi were both looking sleepy from the large meal and jet lag from the trip that morning. Teruyo asked, "Do you have room for me to stay with you tonight?"

"Of course! That would be great," Michi replied with a sly grin aimed at Luke. "You mean Captain Luke can spare you for one night?"

"I don't know how I'll survive, but I'll try. It's a good thing the cabin boy doesn't have shore leave tonight," Luke replied, immediately wishing he hadn't made the bad joke reference to historical privileges of being the Captain of a ship a couple of centuries ago. "I guess I'll see you both in the morning. Again, I am honored to meet you."

Teruyo walked with Luke out to an awaiting car with a driver. They kissed goodnight and embraced for a long time. Luke said, "Except for us having to spend the night apart, this seemed to go better than I expected with your grandfather."

"Yeah, I can tell he really likes you. That surprises me a lot for just meeting you, but you are a very special man."

"I love you, Baby."

"Good night, Hon. I love you," she

replied. And they kissed again.

Chapter 23

Although Luke was tired from the long day and the big meal, sleep didn't come easily. He tried a couple of times to go to sleep and couldn't get the events of the evening out of his mind: the surprise of seeing Teruyo's mom and sister, and then his acceptance by Mr. Tanaka. They'd both expected him to act disapproving toward Luke and maybe even demand that she leave him and go back to Japan. Shindo must have convinced him that he was all right. *"I'll need to remember to put Shindo on my Christmas List,"* Luke said to himself.

He started the generator to charge the reefers and mixed himself a scotch over ice to help him relax. It was a beautifully clear evening, and he sat out under the stars thinking of what could become of him and Teruyo, and wondering if he was really ready to make that kind of commitment. Luke hadn't thought of marriage again since his divorce almost twelve years ago. He wondered if that was what her family was hoping for or if they were cool with the arrangement they had for now.

Teruyo had not mentioned marriage to him and he certainly hadn't thought of it until now. Hell, they had only been together just over a week. Oh how his heart raced when he thought of her, though. He knew he was in love. After another drink, he finally dozed off around three in the morning.

The next morning, Luke ran the dinghy up on the beach just before ten o'clock. He had arranged with the driver to pick him up then, and he could see him waiting as he finished securing the dinghy and locking up the motor. This was a different driver than he'd had last night, and was not one for a lot of conversation. After just a "Good Morning" greeting, they rode in silence up the hill to the *Sheraton*.

Teruyo and her sister were out front with smiles to greet him. "Hi ladies, you're looking bright and chipper this morning."

"Hi, Hon," said Teruyo, flinging herself into Luke's arms. "You look so good."

"Did you get any sleep?" Luke asked.

"Not much. Mom, Michi and I stayed up till the wee hours of the morning talking."

"What's the matter, did your cabin boy keep you up all night?" Michi had to add with her mischievous grin.

Luke growled in his best pirate voice, "Arrrrgh, bring me the cabin boy... but bring him naked."

This caught Michi by surprise, and finally, at a loss for words, she said to Teruyo, "Ah, Sis, are you sure about this guy?"

Teruyo replied, "Wait till you see his

hook!"

"Aha, no thanks!" Michi walked away shaking her head, finally having had enough.

"Is everything all right, Baby?" Luke whispered, kissing her on the cheek and continuing to hold her in a tight hug.

"Yeah, everything seems to be fine. Mom really likes you, though she is of course concerned I'm getting in too deep, too fast. Michi thinks you are cute, but would be much more handsome if you would shave and get a haircut." She looked into his eyes and fiddled with his beard. "I haven't spoken to Grandfather since you and I left him last night, but apparently they are meeting here to plan security for his associates as well as us."

"Great! Believe it or not, I'm starved. Where's breakfast?" Luke led her into the main entrance of the hotel.

"Back in the same dining room we were in last night. Michi and I just returned from a walk out on the point, and we saw you get in the dinghy and motor into the beach. We're hungry too, probably got our stomachs stretched out from last night's big feast."

Teruyo's mother was just entering the dining room from the veranda where she was admiring the view. She came right up to Teruyo and Luke and said, "Good morning. How did you sleep?"

"Just fine, Ma'am," Luke said. "I hear

you ladies were up most of the night talking."

"Oh yes. Between the jet lag and all we wanted to catch up on, I'm going to need a nap this afternoon."

"I'm sorry I failed to ask last night... how long are you planning on staying on Kauai?"

"I believe just a couple of days before we will fly to Oahu and spend a week at my father's 'Hawaiian Home.' Michi and I plan on doing some of shopping and a lot of relaxing before she returns to Minnesota."

"This was quite an effort to bring you all together on such short notice."

"Yes, my father leads a very private life, but when he wishes to get the family together, it can happen rather quickly."

They were led to seats at the dining table, and Luke was welcomed by the fragrance of fresh Hawaiian coffee. Mr. Tanaka arrived as they were visiting with Mrs. Boudreaux and Michi about sailing and navigating over the open ocean. Michi was much less feisty this morning, and seemed to have a more open mind to what Luke had to say.

Mr. Tanaka greeted them with a smile and bent over to give Michi and Teruyo each a hug. "Good morning, my lovely ladies," he said, and was rewarded with kisses on each cheek from his granddaughters. Turning to

Luke who'd stood as this unfolded, Mr. Tanaka extended his hand and with a slight bow said in greeting, "Good morning, Luke. How is everything?"

Luke shook hands with him, returning the bow, and replied, "Good morning, Sir. Everything's great."

"Excellent, then lets enjoy this fine buffet and we can discuss some plans for meeting later."

The breakfast buffet was filled with every imaginable food that Luke had ever seen at a brunch buffet and some he was not familiar with. They all chose to eat on the veranda after filling their plates, breaking into small groups rather than the formality of the large table. Of course, Mr. Tanaka had Michi and Teruyo at his sides, and the conversation was kept light as he was genuinely interested with how Michi's studies were going and, of course, more about Teruyo's most recent adventures.

Mr. Tanaka directed a question to Luke. "I understand you were a leading stockbroker for your firm just prior to coming to Hawaii. Do you miss the thrill of making successful trades and coming out on top?"

Not at all surprised that Mr. Tanaka knew down to the dollar just how much Luke had earned, was currently worth, and exactly how every dollar had been earned, he replied,

"No, Sir. I really haven't missed it at all. I have become so immersed in the whole aspect of finding the right boat, getting her ready to cruise, and now enjoying the experience with Teruyo, I can say I don't miss it at all. Looking back on my career, I was very successful at making money, but I failed to lead a balanced life. That is probably why I have taken such a tremendous shift in the direction I'm going."

"Aha, that is good. I'm glad you are able to focus your energy now on surviving in such a confined space as your boat. It must be very challenging for someone who is so used to the everyday luxuries which we have grown so accustomed to."

"Yes, challenging, but adventurous in almost every aspect."

Teruyo was proud of how Luke was handling himself under the scrutiny of her family. She added, "Grandfather, you should see Luke's yacht, *Tranquilo*. He installed a new engine, a new generator, and completely refinished her inside and out. He has also added electronic equipment for better communications as well as mastering how to use them by obtaining the proper licensing. We wouldn't have been able to have such good communications with the security team without Luke's knowledge and his equipment."

Mr. Tanaka evaluated her comments, and then spoke to Luke, "Yes, Shindo assured me you cooperated fully and made it possible for him to guarantee good security for Teruyo."

Luke merely replied with a slight bow to Mr. Tanaka. He felt no need to add anything further. During the night when he couldn't sleep, he felt things were going well and he didn't want to "oversell" himself and possibly appear insecure.

When everyone was finished eating, Mr. Tanaka rose and nodded to an associate. He asked Teruyo and Luke to join him and a few men and they proceeded to a secured meeting room down the hall. Luke noticed two men of an extremely serious nature, standing by the door as they entered, and he assumed they were armed and ready at all times for any trouble. Shindo was already in the room with three others whom Luke assumed were security professionals. He was correct.

Mr. Tanaka spoke first, "Teruyo and Luke, I want you both to know where we stand on the investigation of the murders which occurred last week. First of all, Shindo and his team would not have made the kind of progress they have if it had not been for your bravery and skill in capturing your attackers. The information you obtained was invaluable for our ability to break into the ring of thugs that have been stalking my family and closest associates for quite some time. Kajiki, will you continue?" He nodded towards the man sitting at Shindo's side.

"Mr. Davis, the two men you captured, along with the North Korean they led us to in Honolulu, Suh Byung-min, were able to divulge a great deal of information which has led us to more 'apprehensions.' We assume their objective is to obtain valuable secrets from one of Mr. Tanaka's major electronics firms. The North Koreans have tried many different means to obtain highly classified military secrets for the purpose of having the ability to penetrate Japan's defenses, and this last attempt at murder and kidnapping is just the latest in a long battle we have had with their agents. However we are still not able to verify they were agents of the North Korean government."

Luke asked, "Are you still trying to get more information out of them to confirm that?"

Kajiki paused, glancing at Mr. Tanaka, and then replied, "No, they have... expired."

"Good, I'd hate to run into them again," Luke responded as he rubbed his still bruised hands.

Shindo added with a laugh, "From the condition they were in when we received them from you, I can assure you they certainly would not have been anxious to meet you again either."

Luke continued with another question,

"You said for the time being, you feel you have crippled their ability to come after these secrets. Does this mean you feel you can relax some of your security measures regarding Mr. Tanaka's family?"

Kajiki replied, "We are not positive just how much of the intelligence they gathered on you was forwarded on to higher authorities in North Korea. Although just before he expired, Suh Byung-min did indicate as a newcomer to their surveillance, you were not regarded as an important figure. You were apparently considered only a slight challenge in their plans to capture Teruyo. Certainly, the long-standing distrust between our two countries will continue and there will always be security concerns. However, at this time, we feel the risks are greatly reduced until more intelligence can be obtained to raise our level of concern."

Teruyo asked, "Grandfather, may I have your permission to continue sailing with Luke?"

"As I said to you and Luke last evening, I am most grateful for his ability to work with Shindo and to protect you. I do not wish to limit your happiness in any way, but I do want you to always be mindful of your surroundings and assure me that you will always make the most prudent judgment for your safety when you encounter anything questionable. Before I approve of you to go sailing off together, out of the umbrella of my security team, I would request that you and Luke work with Shindo and Kajiki to improve your ability to protect yourselves and detect potential threats. I don't question your dedication; we just would feel better if you developed more skills and had some additional tools with which to protect yourselves."

Teruyo, on the verge of tears, embraced Mr. Tanaka, exclaiming, "Oh Grandfather, you've made me so happy. I have been so afraid this would separate Luke and me from each other. I assure you that we will gladly accept any additional training or assistance you wish to add to help us remain together."

Teruyo was riding a very emotional roller coaster these past few days, and it looked like the ride was about to level out. Luke added, "Mr. Tanaka, I again wish to assure you, whatever it will take to care for Teruyo, I will gladly work with you. I am also grateful for your faith in us."

"And once again Luke, I am forever grateful to you for your bravery and ability to save Teruyo and lead to the breakup of this threat." Mr. Tanaka said with a bow of respect.

"Sir, don't overlook Shindo for promptly coming to our assistance and his immediate and excellent response in this whole investigation."

Mr. Tanaka looked at Shindo. "Yes, my trusted friend. I am most grateful to you as well," and showing the ultimate sign of respect, they embraced.

Chapter 24

The remainder of the day for Teruyo and Luke was spent with Shindo and Kajiki. Luke learned Kajiki was the head of security for Tanaka Industries and a former agent with the Japanese Secret Service. He had many contacts with intelligence agencies all around the world as well as the experience of dealing with these types of issues.

They had some sophisticated electronic equipment that would aid Luke and Teruyo's ability to stay in contact with the security team as well as boosting *Tranquilo's* communication ability. Luke's Gulfstar came with a satellite navigation receiver, which was the newest technology available to the public for getting latitude and longitude position fixes at sea. However Kajiki would give them another receiver to replace Luke's as the new one was limited for military use only and much more accurate but had the cosmetic look of an over-the-counter model now being sold to the public.

Next they talked about weapons. Luke had always wanted to sail the South Pacific, but weapons were prohibited in most island nations. If weapons were found, the owner of a yacht could be imprisoned as well as lose his yacht. Luke never considered violating these laws.

Kajiki opened two suitcases containing what appeared to be spear guns, but actually could also fire a ten-round magazine of high-powered bullets, very similar to the M-16 caliber Luke had used in Vietnam. They also had a high-powered flare gun pistol, almost identical in appearance to the one Luke had on board *Tranquilo* for launching flares in the event of an emergency. This "emergency pistol" however, could also fire very powerful shotgun-type shells and it came with a variety of different shell-type loads for different situations.

All of this weaponry was disguised to look just like emergency or sport fishing equipment, and Kajiki assured them that it would never be questioned by any police or customs agency. Luke was apprehensive but very impressed with the quality of the workmanship of these units. He was worried about how to conceal the ammunition so even trained bomb-sniffing dogs could not detect it. Again Kajiki had an answer. He wanted to take the liberty of modifying the binnacle, which held the steering wheel and the compass on *Tranquilo*. Even without having been on Luke's boat, he knew where the quickest access to a weapon needed to be—the cockpit—and how to modify the binnacle so it could store the weapons and ammunitions. He asked Luke's permission to arrange to have a new binnacle installed the next week in Honolulu. Luke agreed, and they also made arrangements to train at a private indoor firing range on the use of these weapons.

The next area of discussion was the destinations to which they hoped to sail. Luke stated, "Frankly, I didn't expect I'd be making these plans yet. I never dreamed of finding a lady like Teruyo who has so much sailing experience as well as the compatibility to even be planning extended cruising. We will need to give that a lot of thought together."

Teruyo added, "We had only discussed sailing together for a couple of weeks here in the Hawaiian Islands. Now we are dreaming of Tahiti and Fiji and possibly beyond."

"We will want to know your where-abouts and future plans, so we can have a person or team in close proximity if a higher state of alert warrants," explained Shindo. "I have been most happy with the communication we developed and would hope to continue with coded communication, while still giving you the freedom to explore and be alone."

"The great advantage of having both the single side band and the ham radios is that we can almost always find frequencies with which to reach you," Luke replied. I'll purchase another set of charts of all of the possibilities where we might venture, and code them for you to keep. Just remember, when we are speaking over the ham radio frequencies, we are not permitted to do business-type communications, so we will need to talk in code which will be perceived as just casual communications."

Shindo answered, "Yes, and could you also write some code phrases which we can familiarize ourselves with that we can use for those frequencies too?"

"We'll get right on it."

"Next we need to address hand-to-hand self-defense. Mr. Davis, in which martial arts disciplines are you trained?" asked Kajiki.

"Just my military training from thirteen years ago. Other than trading stocks, I've been one to keep myself out of fighting for most of my life," Luke emphasized.

Shindo asked, "How were you able to overpower your attackers on the beach? These were highly trained assassins."

Luke explained, "It was more a combination of luck, Teruyo's skills, and just being really, really mad. She didn't see the fellow holding a gun on me, and when she broke her attacker's knee, my guy was distracted enough that I landed a lucky blow to the throat that almost killed him. We worked together after that to detain and interrogate the other one."

Kajiki said, "If you could give Shindo a week, he can teach you enough to really take care of each other, although I know Teruyo already has the skills she needs. Another week to brush up and learn new techniques may prove to be most helpful."

Luke looked at Shindo and asked, "For my own protection could you teach me some things that Teruyo doesn't know in the event she gets really mad at me?" They all laughed at that.

Shindo responded with a grin, "I'm afraid I would need much more than a week to help you with that problem, Luke."

Teruyo added, "Captain, oh my Captain. Fear not of me... unless you misbehave." Again a little laughter helped solidify the group and the importance of working together.

They made arrangements to meet back at the Kaneohe Yacht Club where they would stay for a week or two and "fix the binnacle" and work with Shindo. It was late afternoon by the time they felt they had covered all of the important issues, so Luke and Teruyo departed in search of her mother and sister.

They found Michi sunbathing by the pool, and she explained their mother had been napping since shortly after brunch. "So what do you think of our little family?" she asked Luke.

"Honestly this is all a little overwhelming, but most of all I really like you all and appreciate how well you are able to deal with all of this," Luke replied.

"Yeah, it's been a wild ride this past year since we all have the bodyguards. Grandfather really has his hands full looking out for us. He'd much rather we all live at his home in Kobe, but Teruyo and I are just too free-spirited for that."

"Hey Mich, why don't we get a car and see the island tomorrow?" Teruyo asked.

"Yeah, that sounds great. I hear it's really beautiful."

Luke added, "If you like, you could join us for the sail back to Oahu in a couple of days. We've been asked to work with Kajiki and Shindo there for a week or so."

"Uh, no thanks. Boats are Teruyo's thing, not mine."

Teruyo said, "Oh Mich, his boat is so wonderful, and we won't have much time together this year. There is plenty of room, and it would be a fun adventure for you. It's kind of like camping."

"I'll think about it, but don't count on it."

Luke interjected, "I'm feeling like heading down to *Tranquilo* now to check on things. Why don't you both come, and you can see her for yourself."

"Oh, alright. Maybe Mom would like to

come," Michi suggested.

"Yes, let's wake her up! Plus, if she sleeps all day, she'll just be up all night." Teruyo said excitedly.

Chapter 25

On their fourth day at sea sailing south from Hawaii towards Tahiti, Luke and Teruyo were enjoying dinner in the cockpit while the autopilot steered *Tranquilo*. Luke had just fixed a dinner of rice and fresh tuna that Teruyo had caught that morning while standing her watch. They were sitting next to each other on the port side of the cockpit when from nowhere surfaced a whale not more than a couple of feet from them. They braced themselves for it hitting the port quarter, but it didn't touch the boat, and they just stared into its huge eye. It then slowly dipped below the surface and left them in complete awe.

"*Wow.*"

"My God, how did he get so close and not touch us?" Teruyo exclaimed.

"If I wouldn't have been holding on to this bowl of rice, I bet I could have touched him. I've always heard they were curious, but that was amazing how close he came."

That was the most excitement they had encountered since leaving on their cruise to the South Pacific. Now they were settled into the routine of keeping watch on a four-hour rotation and since leaving sight of land, hadn't seen another boat, plane, or anything other than a few flying fish and the Ahi Teruyo caught that morning. The cruising mode was very relaxing, and so far, there were no challenges with the weather or any boat problems. Just smooth sailing off the wind with a following sea.

The last month in Oahu had been quite busy, first with the special equipment additions to *Tranquilo* and their training with Shindo on self-defense. They also more closely charted and coded the many options for destinations they wished to pursue so they could maintain good communications with Shindo while they were gone. The dock master at the Kaneohe Yacht Club generously allowed them to stay to outfit *Tranquilo* for their voyage, so they used their time wisely to supply for many months of cruising. Luke had virtually no major projects to work on with his boat, however, he went through everything carefully to ensure he had necessary spare parts and backups for everything that was important. With no major projects, they had the time to visit with some Luke's friends back at the Hawaii Yacht Club to get advice on cruising the South Pacific from more experienced cruisers and what to supply for their trip.

They were invited by Vern at the Hawaii Yacht Club to spend their last few days in a slip there, and this gave them the chance to finalize the visas they needed for Tahiti and the

Society Islands. They spent some quality time with Gus and Ben as well, and established contacts with local ham radio operators and the maritime network of cruisers so they could keep in touch with Luke's good friends.

The morning they departed was just about as exciting as when they had set sail for Maui on their first crossing together. They'd discussed continuing on with cruising to the big island of Hawaii and spending more time in the Hawaiian Islands, but it was the perfect time to head south and avoid the normal hurricane and unstable weather periods, so full of confidence in each other and enthusiasm for adventure, they decided to go for it.

Of course Mr. Tanaka and Teruyo's mother had to approve. They were hesitant, but with assurances from Shindo and with the trust they had built, they were granted permission to cruise. Even now four days out to sea, Luke still couldn't believe how fortunate he was and how well everything had come together. He was cautious to not get too confident, but it was so relaxing to be at sea and get into the routine of cruising for extended periods.

He was beginning to develop his celestial navigation skills, using a sextant to sight the sun at precisely noon each day. The different math formulas for computing his sights caused some confusion in the beginning, and if it weren't for his ability to compare his figured latitude and longitude with the satellite navigation receiver, he would have been over a hundred miles off from their actual position on the first day. By day four, he was able to estimate their position within one mile of the SatNav fixes. Next he wanted to work on taking star sights at night, but so far, he was having trouble with getting a good sight on the stars while dealing with the motion of the boat. Vern said it would take time and lots of practice to get really accurate.

Each evening at 5 p.m. they would make contact on the ham radio network, and listen in to other cruisers as well as relay information on their progress and location. On day five they made contact with Gus, and it was a big thrill for him to hear how they were doing. Gus had always wanted to go on a long crossing, but he was a very dedicated teacher so he never felt he had the time to get it together. However, talking with Luke and Teruyo was getting him more motivated than ever. Maybe he would sail South during next summer's break from classes.

The winds maintained a steady ten to fifteen-knots off the port quarter with easy four to six-foot seas. The equatorial counter current was setting them to the east, so they were making a good course right for Palmyra Atoll, part of the Line Islands. Luke had heard many stories and seen photographs from a few cruisers who had enjoyed their stopovers on Palmyra, and since they would be coming within a few miles of it, they were anxious to see it themselves.

On the evening of their sixth day, after very careful plotting of their course and location, Teruyo spotted Palmyra off the starboard bow just before sunset. It could easily have been missed, as the highest point was a group of palm trees which reached maybe sixty feet out of the coral outcropping, known as an atoll. How exhilarating it was to reach their first landfall after being at sea for six days.

Luke tried to hail anyone from his VHF radio and almost immediately, was rewarded with a man's voice in broken English, "Yes, sailing vessel *Tranquilo*, this is Palmyra. We read you loud and clear. We are on the catamaran, *Seascape*, from Hamburg, Germany. My name is Uva, and we have been anchored here in the lagoon for about a month."

Luke replied, "What does it look like for us trying to make it into the lagoon by this evening?"

Uva said, "No, do not try to enter tonight. There are no lights or range markers. You will either need to anchor off in the lee of the atoll or hove-to and make your approach in the late morning with the sun at your back."

Teruyo called for Luke to come back to the cockpit, "Hon, we have a squall forming quickly. We better reef the main and the genoa." The clouds were very dark and they could see that rain and waves were building just ahead.

Luke called back to Uva, "We are going to bear off for now as we have some weather forming right in front of us. I'll call you back after we get reefed."

"Yes, we are getting the first of some wind and rain right now. We will standby to hear from you. *Seascape* out."

Teruyo jibed *Tranquilo* to put some distance between them and the atoll. Luke tended to the sails, reducing them in preparation for the fast approaching wind and rain. They discussed whether or not to proceed on to Tahiti, but both were anxious to see Palmyra for themselves, as everyone they had spoken with who'd been there raved so much of its beauty and uniqueness. They decided to sail for six hours on starboard tack, heading east, then hove-to for the rest of the evening and allow the current, which was now coming from the east, to set them back west. The storm continued to pound them on into the night; this was more than just a passing squall.

Chapter 26

As the sun rose the next morning, Palmyra was barely visible in the distance off the starboard bow. Luke had calculated about when they needed to hove-to, so at 1:00 a.m. he had tacked *Tranquilo* and back-winded the reefed headsail. He then locked the helm over which kept them just bobbing on the waves, not making any progress except for what direction and speed the current set them. He was so excited to see Palmyra and proud of his navigation skills, though they were a bit closer than he'd preferred. One of a sailor's greatest fears is running aground in the middle of the night. There were no lights or navigational beacons to alert any passing sailor of the dangerous shallows around Palmyra.

Luke had experienced a terrifying incident during the night. As he tried to haul in more of the headsail when the wind increased, the line in the furler became fouled. Teruyo was down below asleep so he didn't give much thought to going forward to untangle the furler. He had done it before, though in much calmer conditions and in the daylight. A wave came over the bow when he was trying to untangle the fouled line, and almost knocked him off the deck. Only by sheer luck was he able to grab a stanchion and keep himself from falling overboard. With Teruyo asleep and the noise of the wind still whining through the rigging, she would never have heard his cries for help. It was a very near miss at certain death, and Luke was grateful to God he made it back to the safety of the cockpit. After catching his breath and settling down, he put on his safety harness, attached a lifeline, and summoned Teruyo to man the helm before returning to the foredeck and fixing the fouled line. Never again, would he attempt to go to the foredeck alone at night without his harness and lifeline attached.

Now that they were headed back to the atoll, the excitement of making their landfall was bringing back the joy of the cruise. Teruyo fixed fresh coffee and blended a frozen fruit smoothie for breakfast while Luke set out all of his best lures to catch some fish. The morning was beautifully sunny and the trade winds were back to normal for their final approach to Palmyra. Luke again reached Uva on the VHF radio and briefly told of their night sailing away from the atoll to distance them during the storm. Uva gave them additional information on how to identify the channel coming into the lagoon but cautioned them to attempt to approach so the sun would not be in their eyes but over their shoulders. Because the channel was not marked with any navigational buoys and was very narrow, it was critical to be able to distinguish the deep water of the channel, because running into the coral reefs could be disastrous.

The closer they got to the atoll, the more the excitement grew. The jungle was so lush and green, and there were birds everywhere. Because the atoll is uninhabited by humans, hundreds of thousands of sea birds of several species nest there. An escort of Frigates, Brown Boobie and Blue-Footed Boobie birds, which dive for small fish from high aloft, began to dive on Luke's fishing lures. Not wanting any of them to get caught, he immediately reeled in his lures. That would have been an awful mess, and he was not about to sacrifice one of his trusted lures. As they rounded the lee of the atoll, Luke took in the sails and they motored in closer to have a better look at the approach to the channel. They were carefully watching the depth sounder and the chart of Palmyra was with them in the cockpit.

An atoll evolves from coral building up over thousands of years until it reaches the surface then begins attracting dirt and anything else that floats buy on the surface of the water. Eventually, with enough buildup of soil, the seeds of trees and plants, which have also been carried over thousands of miles, sprout and begin a new cycle of life for the area. At low tide, Palmyra measures only six and a half square miles, with a deep lagoon in the middle. The channel was blasted out of the coral by the U.S. military at the beginning of World War II for the purpose of building a refueling depot for Navy submarines and scout planes. Luke and Teruyo could see remains of concrete machine gun bunkers and rusty radio towers. These landmarks were noted on their chart, and they felt comfortable knowing exactly where they were.

It was too early in the morning to attempt their approach to the channel as per Uva's advice to keep the sun over their shoulders. Teruyo held *Tranquilo* steady as Luke busied himself with getting the dinghy out and inflated as well as preparing to anchor. As anxious as they were, they felt it best to heed Uva's advice for navigating the narrow channel. Prior to departing from Honolulu, Luke had stowed the anchor in the engine room so he could seal off the bow to prevent taking on water in the event they hit some extremely rough seas. By the time he had the anchor reattached to the chain and the dinghy inflated, they felt the sun was about right for their approach to the channel.

As they slowly rounded the south islet they could see the channel. It was very narrow, but easily distinguishable from the narrow shallows on each side. They saw sea turtles crossing their path and curious-looking Blue-Footed Boobies watching from the trees along the entrance to the lagoon. As they entered the lagoon, the depth sounder progressively read forty, to sixty, then to seventy feet deep. They were transformed from sailing in rough open seas to the quiet and calm of a mirror-smooth lagoon, surrounded by lush jungle. Ahead at the far end of the lagoon, Teruyo could see another boat at anchor, and they noticed more evidence of the former Navy base. There was a rusty steel pier, and a couple of buildings that appeared to be in relatively good condition.

Uva finally caught sight of them and called over the VHF radio with greetings and advice for a good anchorage. He emphasized that they should consider a spot not too close to the boat already there, which wasn't his, and in a location where they would have plenty of room to swing if another storm came up like the one the night before. He stated he was further up the lagoon and would be finished with his work and would motor over and re-anchor later that evening.

Luke was again grateful for the advice and they eased up to a spot where he released the anchor in eighty feet of water. Teruyo, reversed the engine, allowing the anchor to set, and after checking it carefully with all of the chain he had played out, she cut the engine. They held each other and marveled at their surroundings—what a beautiful place. *"Wow!"*

Before launching the dinghy and exploring, lunch was the first order of business. Luke had been living on coffee and that smoothie for the last twelve hours, and he was hungry. Teruyo warmed up some canned hash and fried eggs. Just as they sat down to eat, they heard strange sounds coming from outside on the water. It was like someone was breathing heavily through their nose and making splashing noises. It seemed to draw closer, so they quickly headed to the cockpit to investigate. Swimming up to the stern of *Tranquilo* were two dogs with just their heads and noses poking out of the water.

One of the stories that had captivated Luke and Teruyo about Palmyra were of the dogs that resided here. Reportedly, a family tried to settle on Palmyra a few years before to start a copra plantation. With Palmyra's abundance of coconut trees, they wanted to harvest the coconuts and process the white meat into coconut oil. They had a couple of dogs that had a small litter of puppies, however when they departed after an unsuccessful attempt with this venture, the dogs had to be left behind due to space restraints on the boat upon which they departed. There now two of the puppies remaining, and they survived by eating baby birds that were hatched on the ground and scraps of food from passing cruisers.

Luke lowered the swim ladder off the stern of Tranquilo to give the dogs something to hang on to, and to his amazement, the dogs climbed right up the stainless steel ladder. They had obviously done this before. With tails wagging and after shaking off on the foredeck, the two new visitors greeted Luke and Teruyo like they were old friends. They were mangled and mangy-looking, had scars and missing hunks of fur and skin, but were so loveable and quite adept at getting treats. Immediately, they were rewarded with a can of dog food that Teruyo had thought to bring along in the event they were able to divert to Palmyra. Actually they brought four cans of dog food, but figured one would be a good start for introductions. The food didn't last long on the two paper plates Teruyo provided to divvy up equal parts for each.

Luke and Teruyo returned to their lunch, and the dogs looked down the companionway opening, but didn't attempt to come below. They seemed to have good boat manners, however they were watching the couple eat with their tails wagging. "What a couple of characters!" Teruyo exclaimed.

Luke replied, "I bet they have some stories to tell."

"Let's go ashore. I'm really anxious to go exploring."

Teruyo helped with lowering the dinghy and the outboard motor, and when all was ready, the dogs jumped on board, preferring to ride rather than swim back. Luke was not at all put off with them jumping into the dinghy, even with their dog smell as they were so lovable and anxious for the attention they were getting.

Teruyo said, "I bet they have been through this with every cruiser that has stopped by."

As soon as they came ashore in front of an old building, which had *Palmyra Yacht Club* painted on a sign, the dogs jumped out and acted like they wanted to show their new guests around their home. The *Palmyra Yacht Club* was all decorated with paints of every color known to man with the boat names of scores of cruising yachts and their crews. There were old chairs and a couch, some tables, paperback books and magazines, and a "welcome notice" posted on one of the walls. The notice stated, "If you are reading this then you are trespassing on private property. However, since you are already here, please be kind to the environment and to leave the atoll as good as or better than when you arrived." A few words about not being responsible for injury or damages and taking your trash with you rather than supporting the rat population were also included.

"Looks like they realize they can't stop cruisers from coming here, but want to cover themselves in case someone gets hurt." Luke said.

Teruyo wanted to relax and enjoy the messages on the walls and ceiling, but said, "The dogs are really anxious for us to follow them. Let's see what's up."

"Yeah, I get the feeling they want to show us something."

They walked out of the building and the dogs immediately led the way down a well-worn path. Another building appeared, this one resembling an old Army barracks for housing the military personnel. *The Palmyra Hilton* was painted on the side in large, bold letters, so Luke and Teruyo couldn't resist taking a look inside. There was no furniture left in any of the rooms, and it reminded Luke of some of the Army barracks he'd been in when he was first drafted in 1971.

Teruyo said, "It's surprising that these two buildings we've been in are in such good shape considering they have had no fresh paint or maintenance, and especially being so close to the equator in such a humid climate."

"Yeah, you'd have thought some storms would have taken them down by now."

They continued following the dogs and wound around a path to a marker where the dogs stopped. It was where Navy, one of their siblings, had been buried. Teruyo read the inscription about how he'd died from shark wounds, and when she was finished, they both looked at the dogs, which seemed to have sober expressions on their faces like they were saying, *"We know who is buried here."*

They continued on down the path and came to a very large concrete tank, next to which were a bathtub and a shower. Luke turned the large faucet and out came clean fresh water. He exclaimed happily, "This must be the fresh water collection tank built back in the 40's to support the troops. We could even fill up our jerry jugs to replenish our water tanks on *Tranquilo* if we need to. This is great!"

Teruyo said, "Look, there is a rope back here to string over the path if we want to take a bath in private. I want to give this a try later."

That was it for the tour. The path ended. The dogs seemed to know all cruisers would want to know where the fresh water tank and bathtub was located.

When they arrived back at the Yacht Club building, Luke and Teruyo met a couple that were from the other sailboat anchored in the lagoon. The men and women paired up by gender after the introductions were made and began talking about their crossings, their boats, where they were from, etc. Steve and Lisa were from Vancouver, Canada and had sailed to Palmyra after spending the last month in Hawaii. After spending so much time with just each other, it was exciting to be talking to another couple, and it dawned on each of them at about the same time that there were four people all talking at once. The couples had spent so much time alone with their partners that everyone was anxious to carry on a conversation with someone else. They all burst out in laughter at the realization and decided to settle down and relax in the chairs of the yacht club and take turns telling their stories.

Later in the afternoon, Uva and Brigitte motored their catamaran into the lagoon and anchored a couple of hundred feet from *Tranquilo*. A week earlier, they had driven their catamaran up on a sandy beach to the northeast of the main lagoon, to paint the bottom with the same anti-fouling paint that Luke had used when he first purchased his boat. The "bottom paint" has a high percentage of copper oxide in it to keep barnacles and other marine creatures from growing on the bottom of boats, which can really slow a boat's ability to track through the water. In order to maintain a smooth surface, sailors need to paint the anti-fouling paint on the bottoms of the boats every year or two. Uva and Brigitte had been cruising for a couple of years and their type of boat, a catamaran, draws very little water so they found a sandy beach and ran it up at high tide so they could paint the bottom at low tide.

They were a very interesting couple, to say the least. Having built their catamaran themselves in the seaport of Hamburg, Germany, they launched and sailed to the Mediterranean Sea during their first summer of cruising. They cruised there for a year and last spring crossed the Atlantic Ocean, the Panama Canal, the Pacific to the Marquesas Islands, up to Hawaii, and now Palmyra. Of all the cruisers Luke and Teruyo had met, they had logged the most miles and were sure to provide many evenings with interesting tales.

Chapter 27

Their second day in the atoll was spent resting with a bit of cleaning occupying them later in the afternoon. Since the previous day had been so intense and he had gotten very little sleep, Luke needed some extra time in the sack. Teruyo was able to make contact with the security team, speaking directly with Shindo. He reported everything was getting back to normal and told them to have a good time. Luke and Teruyo were so infatuated with this new adventure and how their love was growing, there was no way it could have been ruined with more security concerns.

Uva and Brigitte rowed to *Tranquilo* on their way in for baths and invited Luke and Teruyo for a potluck supper. Uva had some fresh-cut heart of palm to make a salad, and they were happy there were other cruisers to share some of their specialty dishes with. Teruyo said that she would bake some bread and bring a couple of side dishes.

Later, as the three couples gathered in the Palmyra Yacht Club, plenty of food of various origins graced the table. There was a broccoli and radish sprout salad, a German cheese casserole, and Steve provided crab claws from the local land crabs, explaining,

"You find a stick and take your machete to trim it so it's two feet long with a 'V-notch' on the end. Then when you find a good-sized crab, you pin 'em down with the 'V' on their largest pincher leg and take your other hand to twist and pull the leg off. If you only take one pincher leg, then they can still survive and will regenerate the other leg in a few months." He sautéed the claws in a skillet over an open fire along with some garlic butter and coconut milk; they were divine.

Uva and Brigitte announced at dinner that they would be leaving for Tahiti in a couple of days and they coordinated ham radio frequencies and times to keep in contact with Luke and Teruyo. They also told some additional stories of their past two years of cruising from Europe to here. The most eye-opening story was of a very large ship coming into a port where they were anchored. The rigging and sail from a sailboat it had hit at some point in its passage had fouled its anchor chain attached at its bow. Uva said the investigation that ensued revealed the ship's crew never realized that they had collided with a sailboat during their passage, and it was assumed the sailboat and crew were lost. Uva stated after witnessing that sight, he and Brigitte never went to sleep while on watch again. "It only takes fifteen minutes for two vessels to reach a collision course coming from different directions over the horizon." That left a very deep impression in the other couples' minds as well.

After arriving back at *Tranquilo*, Luke and Teruyo discussed how once they had gotten settled in on their crossing to Palmyra, it had been so easy to get caught up in a good book during their midnight watches and never get up to look around for other ship traffic. That wouldn't happen again.

Two days later, Uva and Brigitte said their farewells and headed out of the channel, bound for Tahiti. They had reaffirmed their plans to keep in touch with Luke and Teruyo on the ham radio net they established, and hoped to meet up with everyone again "somewhere in the South Pacific."

A few hours after they had left, another sailboat arrived in the lagoon. This was a small sloop from Japan with a Japanese family, Sakai and Tetsuko and their two little boys. As soon as they were anchored, Luke and Teruyo motored over in their dinghy to welcome them, and Teruyo was able to talk with them in Japanese, which made them feel instantly welcome. The boys, Yo and Ko, were so cute and climbed about the rigging of their boat with the agility of little monkeys. They were so excited to see the dogs swimming out to greet them too. After being at sea for a week, it is always good to be greeted by friendly people, and for the boys, two dogs as well.

Teruyo was careful not to go into her family lineage, just that she had family in Japan and had visited there numerous times. She was able to help explain the areas to visit and invited them for the potluck suppers, which were becoming a nightly ritual. It was off to the bath for the new arrivals as their first order of business; their boat obviously didn't have the water capacity that Luke and Teruyo were blessed with on *Tranquilo*.

The next day Luke and Teruyo were anxious to do some exploring on their own and try their luck at harvesting some crab claws for supper. Luke found a stick and broke it to make a notch like Steve instructed, and with the dogs riding along in the dinghy, they headed out to see the rest of the atoll.

After going through a small break from one lagoon to another, they found themselves in a completely different type of lagoon. This lagoon was much shallower, but the bird population and the jungle atmosphere were denser. The dogs immediately began barking and chasing fish, herding them into the shallows and lifting them into their mouths and burying them in the sand. They were baby sharks. Luke was amazed and exclaimed, "No wonder they have so many scars and chunks of fur missing!"

The sharks' skin was so abrasive and

tough, even the dogs' bites could not penetrate them, so they just left them to die in the sand. It was a big game to the dogs. Teruyo said, "Maybe they are taking this game a little too seriously. They probably have been chased out of the water by bigger sharks. Isn't that probably what happened to *Navy*?" The dogs captured and buried seven baby sharks on the beach before Luke and Teruyo got them to venture on into the jungle with them.

The further into the foliage they went, the cooler and darker it became because the taller palm trees shielded out the sunlight. "The trees are so thick through here," Luke commented, "No wonder that family felt it might be a good place for a copra plantation."

Teruyo gasped, "Oh Hon, look at this bird; it's a Fairy Tern." Hovering curiously just in front of them was a pure white bird with black, beady eyes. The little angelic beauty illuminated a glow about it that transformed Luke and Teruyo into a trance-like state. Teruyo knelt down, picked up a stick, and held it out, hoping the tern would land on it. Luke slowly reached into his backpack to get his camera. Just as the bird inched closer to the stick, along came Army and Palmyra wagging their tails and panting. This, of course, scared the tern away just before Luke got the picture, and the dogs received a good scolding from Teruyo. They had no clue why anyone could be upset; *we're just out having fun!*

A little later they found a group of crabs nestled amongst the roots of the mangrove trees, and Luke tried his hand at snatching a few claws for supper. "Damn, these little buggers are tougher than you think!" he exclaimed after wrestling with a few to yank off his prize. He was able to collect eight, which they felt would be enough to add to the pot for supper.

Just before turning back toward the dinghy, they came upon a concrete Quonset hut-style building. "This must be the old hospital Uva spoke about," said Teruyo.

"I wonder if that giant coconut crab he talked about is in there," Luke replied, referring to a chilling discussion over the campfire a few nights ago.

They headed inside. Luckily they had the flashlight in Luke's backpack to help them see. It was very dark and damp inside with such a thick mass of spider webs, so they decided not to venture in too far. The legend of a very large coconut crab that Uva had told may have had something to do with not wanting to deal with the elements that badly.

The next week consisted of exploring, meeting new cruisers coming from or going to the South Pacific, and doing the tasks necessary for surviving on a sailboat in paradise. Uva and Brigitte made contact on the ham net informing Luke and Teruyo they had a great passage to Tahiti and how it is even more beautiful than they'd imagined. They were still in the process of checking in at the capitol city of Papeete and would contact them again on the net in a few days. That motivated Luke and Teruyo to begin thinking about a date to depart Palmyra. They were having so much fun, though, that being on a schedule was just not part of their cruising life.

One of the daily routines of staying in the lagoon was dealing with the afternoon rain showers. One could almost set their watch, as it seemed to begin raining at 2:30 every afternoon. If they were going to do laundry and have it out to dry, they had to be sure to be back to gather it in or it would get an additional rinse. The rain catcher Luke had devised while they were staying in Hanalei Bay was proving very useful as their water tanks were topped off daily. They started the Mercedes diesel once a week and the generator every day to keep the reefers and the batteries charged. Reading books, which took up a big part of the hours during the crossing from Hawaii, was continuing to occupy a large part of their days. They exchanged some of those they'd read with Steve and Lisa as well as leaving some in the "library" in the Palmyra Yacht Club.

The day after first hearing from Uva and

Brigitte, they received another call from them over the ham radio, this time a direct attempt to reach them, not on the net shared with other cruisers. Uva had an urgent tone in his voice.

"This is WH6-BXC, go ahead Uva," Luke responded.

Uva said, "Luke, I'm glad we reached you. When going through our check-in with Tahiti Customs officials, they showed us a photo of your boat at anchor in Hanalei Bay. They asked if we have seen this boat or knew of you. They had an Asian man who really seemed out of place with them, but I told them we hadn't seen you. Something seems wrong here, because they continued going around, asking about you to other cruisers. I hope I did the right thing, but I wanted to alert you first in case you wanted to change your plans about coming here. Over."

"Roger that. I'm grateful for the information. We will look into it. Should be nothing, but I'll let you know what we find out from our end, over."

"We'll go back to our scheduled times on the net. Kilo-Eco-Niner-One, out." Uva signed off.

"Whisky-Hotel-Six-Bravo-Xray-Charlie, out" Luke replied.

Teruyo asked, "What in the world is that all about?"

"I don't know. We've had great communication with your Honolulu base station, and just last week you spoke with Shindo and everything was fine. Let's call and find out if something's up."

Luke changed frequencies to contact the Honolulu base station and called, "Whisky-Hotel-Six-Bravo-Xray-Charlie, calling Whisky-Tango-Charley, over."

After a short pause, "Whisky-Hotel-Six-Bravo-Xray-Charlie, this is Whisky-Tango-Charley, over." They could tell this was not Shindo's voice.

Teruyo replied, "Yes, could you give the following message to Shindo that a photograph of our home and questions about our whereabouts is being circulated at 'B-9'? Do you know of any reason for this? Over."

"Negative, but will relay the message. Suggest you stand by and we will reach you on 'F-6', over."

"Roger, Whisky-Hotel-Six-Bravo-Xray-Charlie, out."

"Whisky-Tango-Charley, out."

Teruyo looked in their radio log for the frequency they had coded for "F-6" and dialed the radio to it. Before leaving Hawaii, Shindo and the couple arranged specific code words and frequencies they could use to help ensure if anyone were listening over the radio waves, they would have a tough time trying to intercept their next transmission.

"Well, I guess all there is to do now is wait," Luke commented. He knew something must be wrong. "You would think the radio operator at the base station would have known something was up if it came from their end."

Teruyo looked worried and said, "Oh Hon, who would be circulating a picture of *Tranquilo* in Hanalei Bay?"

"I don't know, but I'm glad Uva didn't let on that he knew where we are. If someone is looking for us that Shindo doesn't know about, we are going to have to see what he can uncover."

They waited for a couple of hours, not hearing any word. Steve and Lisa came by in their dinghy to see what was up for supper. Teruyo said she wasn't feeling well and that they were sorry, but were going to stay in for the evening. "Please give our regrets to Sakai and his family too," she asked of Lisa.

Just as the darkness of night was turning the stars out in all of their brilliance, a crackle came over the radio, "Whisky-Hotel-Six-Bravo-Xray-Charlie, this is Whisky-Tango-Charley, over." It was Shindo.

Luke replied, "Whisky-Hotel-Six-Bravo-Xray-Charlie, we read you loud and clear, over."

"Yes, be advised we have no knowledge of the inquiry you made. Are you still at Alpha-7, over?

Luke again keyed the mike, "Roger that. The messenger did not disclose our location or any knowledge of us to the officials at B-9. We had been planning to depart but will await further instructions from you, over."

Shindo answered, "10-4, and stay where you are until given instructions. We will get back to you as soon as we can take a flight to B-9 to investigate, over."

Luke responded, "Roger that, and we will stand by on F-6."

"10-4, will contact you as soon as we have any news. Whisky-Tango-Charley, out," and Shindo signed off.

"Luke, you know what I'm thinking?" Teruyo asked rhetorically. "I can only imagine that photo of *Tranquilo* in Hanalei Bay could have come from the North Koreans before they jumped us."

"Yeah, that's what keeps spinning around in my mind, too. I'd give anything to see that photograph right now. We were anchored in two different locations when we were there, and if it was taken after we returned from Tunnels, then I'd say there is someone from your grandfather's organization looking for us, or has sold us out." Luke was thinking out loud, trying to bounce different scenarios off Teruyo.

"Either one doesn't make any sense. My grandfather's organization is impregnable;

there couldn't be someone from inside who would sell this information. And if the North Koreans have the picture of our first anchorage there, then that means there must have been a third agent in Hanalei who got away and got information back to whoever is still pursuing us."

"Whichever it is, I don't like the idea of heading on to Tahiti," Luke said. "Tomorrow night we can try to reach Uva over the net. He may know more."

"Hopefully, we will hear from Shindo before then. This has me really worried." Teruyo was beginning to look distraught.

"Well, let's be strong and not get too worked up. Who knows, this may turn out to be nothing at all." But Luke knew better.

The next morning, after a very restless night with little sleep, Luke and Teruyo made themselves busy doing projects around *Tranquilo*, not wanting to miss a call on the radio. Luke went about checking all of the mechanical and electrical systems, and Teruyo ensured items were repacked and stowed away in the event they needed to depart Palmyra on short notice.

Sakai and the boys rowed over in their dinghy and brought some soup that Tetsuko had sent with the hope of helping Teruyo feel better. The boys were climbing all over *Tranquilo* like they were exploring a new tree.

Just having them aboard broke the tension and helped Teruyo's anxiety subside for a while. The dogs swam out and climbed up the swim ladder to inquire why they hadn't been invited to the party. Soon Steve and Lisa stopped by, so *Tranquilo's* awning provided shade for everyone to be comfortable as they were all concerned about Teruyo. Finding her not to be herself but claiming to be OK, didn't satisfy their concern. They could tell something was wrong, and sensing Luke and Teruyo might want to be alone, everyone decided to just head on their separate ways.

Just as they were rowing away, a noise came out of the sky which none of the cruisers expected. An airplane was descending from the north and began circling Palmyra in a counter-clockwise pattern. As it descended, it became obvious it was a seaplane, and with all of the birds becoming aroused and taking flight, the plane banked to the south away from the atoll. It came in for a landing in the lee of Palmyra and though they couldn't see it land because of the trees, they could hear it bounce off the water and its engines reverse to slow it down as it taxied close to the entrance to the channel leading into the lagoon.

Boobies, Sooty Terns, and Frigate birds were flying out from the trees and going crazy with the approaching *monster*. They were total strangers to the noise and the sight of the seaplane easing up the channel. During the construction of the Navy Base during World War II, an airstrip was built, but was now the nesting grounds for the terns as well as being overgrown with brush. To attempt a landing would have resulted in disaster for the pilot and crew, as the birds would have surely fouled the engines. However, this pilot obviously knew what he was doing, as he stayed high enough above the atoll and chose his landing in the calm waters of the lee, and then bringing the plane through the channel. He shut the engines down about a hundred feet shy of *Tranquilo*.

The cruisers, two sets of them in their dinghies, and Luke and Teruyo still onboard *Tranquilo* were suspended right where they were, watching this unfold. The dogs were going crazy, barking and running back and forth across *Tranquilo's* decks. Luke opened the secret compartment of the binnacle and armed himself with the spear gun "rifle" Shindo trained him with. Likewise, Teruyo grabbed the "flare pistol" and loaded it with the rounds meant for intruders. Luke yelled to Sakai and Steve to head to their own boats, and they promptly rowed on after seeing Luke and Teruyo arming themselves.

The pilot allowed the seaplane to drift to a stop and then he opened a hatch and threw out an anchor, playing enough rope to make-fast the plane. Opening the other hatch on the opposite side from the pilot and waving with a big smile was Shindo.

"Hello, Teruyo-san. Can you please pick me up, or am I to swim to your boat?" Shindo yelled.

Teruyo replied, trying to make herself heard over the barking of the dogs, "I'll be right over."

Luke assisted Teruyo with the dinghy and she motored over to greet her friend. "Shindo, what a surprise, is everything OK?" Teruyo asked.

Stepping very carefully into the dinghy, trying not to tip it over, he replied, "We need to talk, can you allow me to come aboard your boat please?"

Luke waved to Steve to return to get Army and Palmyra, and after the decks were cleared of their canine "watchmen," Teruyo brought the dinghy alongside the ladder and Shindo climbed effortlessly up on deck.

They relaxed under the shade of the awning, and Teruyo pressed Shindo for news of his investigation and why he had to fly to Palmyra. "Shindo, couldn't you have called over the radio? Is something wrong? Why did you come?"

"Teruyo, Kajiki made contact with some friends he has in the government on Papeete, and as far as he can determine, they've been told you have been kidnapped and are being held on this stolen boat by an escaped convict. He is on his way to Papeete right now, but we feel for your safety, you will have to come with me. We are sure the people looking for you in Papeete are North Koreans. We don't know how, but somehow they know you are traveling with Luke. I am sorry, but you must come with me immediately."

Deep down inside them both, over the course of the last 20 hours, they knew this was a possibility. But hearing it from Shindo himself, especially being here right this instant, hit them with a blow that neither were prepared for.

Luke responded, "Shindo, I know you have come at great risk to yourself just to fly into here, but isn't there a way we can sail on back to Hawaii or somewhere else and still be safe? After all, no one knows we are here."

"I'm truly sorry. Teruyo must come with me. Theses are my orders and it is best for her right now until we can put an end to this," he replied.

"No, Luke's right. No one knows we are here! We can sail east to the Marquesas Islands or back to Hawaii. We can't leave Luke here alone!" Teruyo cried.

"Believe me, if we felt there was any other way, we would allow it. However, until we get you to safety, we cannot attempt to solve the problem. Those are my orders, and you must trust me... please I'm very sorry, but you've known all along we have to do what is best," Shindo replied, showing no emotion, just firm with the commitment to Teruyo's safety.

Suddenly turning off her emotions, Teruyo stood up and started down the companionway, "Luke, will you help me gather my things?" She knew not to resist Shindo; she'd tried it before.

"Wait just a damn minute!" Luke exclaimed. "Where do we go from here? Do you know where you're taking her? How am I supposed to find her?"

"Luke, I am so sorry to have to take her. I promise I will allow you to keep in contact; we can keep our codes and radio schedules for now. I'm going to fly her back to Honolulu and we will decide then where we will house Teruyo, probably back in Japan for now." Shindo was sincere but still unwavering with his mission. "We feel that if it really is the North Koreans, they will not hesitate to retaliate for your involvement in the capture of their three agents last month. Safety, for both of you, is paramount. Mr. Tanaka is fully aware of the status at this moment and will divert all of his assets towards putting an end to these people."

Luke replied, "Is there anything I could do to assist you? Maybe sail on into Tahiti?

When they see Teruyo and I are no longer together, it might cause them to come out from behind the Tahitian government and face us directly."

"I will have to wait to hear from Kajiki before agreeing to that. It may be best to handle this in our own covert way, but thank you for your offer," Shindo said.

Teruyo was down below in the cabin, gathering her belongings and any trace of her being on *Tranquilo*. She was also listening to this and quickly came up to the cockpit to emphatically say, "No Shindo, I don't want Luke involved! Luke, I'd really like you to head back to Hawaii and let Shindo and his team deal with this. I don't want you in any danger. We already know these people are deadly serious, and it's not worth it to get you involved!"

Luke went to her and held her in an embrace, "Baby, I want to put an end to this once and for all so we can get on with our lives."

Teruyo rested her head on Luke's chest and began sobbing, "Luke, no... let Shindo take care of it. I can't allow you to get involved with this. Shindo and the team will handle it. Please promise me you will head back to Hawaii... please."

Shindo added, "Luke, that would be best. She is right, we can handle them and the sooner we do, hopefully you can reunite. Now please, we must be off. My pilot made me promise not to be too long as the afternoon winds and rain showers may begin to build."

Luke went below and helped gather everything that looked like it would belong to Teruyo. "Here, take all of this film and have the pictures developed. Maybe someday when we are old and gray we can sit on the front porch in our rocking chairs and reminisce." With that comment, Teruyo and Luke embraced and both broke down and wept.

Chapter 28

All Luke could do as the plane disappeared to the north of Palmyra was dry his eyes and try to deal the terrible ache in his stomach. He felt worse than if he'd been kicked in the sternum and the suddenness of all that had just happened left him totally heartbroken and feeling helpless. Sure it was probably the best thing regarding Teruyo's safety, as well as his. He just wished there were something he could have done to keep them together.

The familiar sound of the heavy breathing approaching his boat broke his thoughts, and he turned to see the dogs swimming out to see him. He went to the stern and invited them up, as if they needed an invitation. After shaking off and searching the decks, they joined Luke in the cockpit and lay at his feet. They were not in a playful mood, but very sober, with *"just want to be here for you, Luke"* expressions on their faces.

He petted them and said, "Thanks guys, I really appreciate you coming out here right now." He got teary-eyed again. Oh how he ached for Teruyo, and now she was gone.

Sakai came over alone, and a few moments later, Steve rowed over as well.

They'd watched Teruyo leave in the seaplane, and wanted to see if they could be of any help as well as find out what was going on.

Luke felt he couldn't tell them the whole story, and although he tried to put on a strong appearance, he even got tearful as he was trying to make up a story to satisfy their curiosity, but at the same time not further endanger the security of Teruyo. He certainly did not want to let on of their involvement with the North Koreans, which could implicate him with the events at Hanalei Bay. He basically spun the yarn of Teruyo having to leave for a family emergency and left it at that.

Sakai, in his broken English, said, "Luke, maybe best to just stay here for few days before deciding where to go. Maybe they bring Teruyo back when family is better."

Luke brought up a bottle of rum and three glasses, and they each had a drink. "To Teruyo's quick and safe return," Steve toasted somberly. After a few more assurances that everything would work out, Sakai and Steve returned to their boats, and Luke was left alone with the dogs and the bottle of rum.

"Whisky-Hotel-Six-Bravo-Xray-Charlie, this is Whisky-Tango-Charley, over." Luke was startled awake with the sound of

Teruyo's voice over the radio.

Jumping up from his nap in the cockpit, he stubbed his toe as he headed down to the chart table where the radio was, hopping on his good foot and trying to squeeze the pain out of the toe as he reached for the mike. "Thissss is Whisky-Hotel-Six-Bravo-Xray-Charlie, is that you, Baby?"

"Hon, are you OK? Is something wrong down there?" Teruyo asked, concerned.

"I... I just stubbed my toe hurrying down into the cabin, that's all. Are you safely back to the base? Over."

"Yes, I couldn't wait to call you. I really miss you, Luke."

"Oh Baby, I miss you so much. Have you made any plans yet?

"Yes, it looks like I'm flying home tonight. They want me at Q-4," she said, referring to the family home in Kobe, "and I have asked to have them set me up a base station there, so we can stay in contact. Have you decided on returning to Hawaii?"

"No, not yet. Sakai and Steve came over right after you left, and the dogs are here now keeping me company. I think I will wait here for a few days to hear from Shindo. I'm hopeful they will bring you back."

"This could take a bit of time. They want to ensure all is taken care of."

"Is he heading to 'B-9' soon?"

"No, he will be accompanying me home. We will stay in contact and I will keep you informed with the first news."

"As soon as you get your base station set up, reach me on F-6 or through *Honolulu Net*."

"OK. Luke, I have to go now. I love you."

"I love you too. Thanks for the call. Take care. See you soon."

"Whisky-Tango-Charley, out."

"Whisky-Hotel-Six-Bravo-Xray-Charlie, out." It was almost time for the daily check-in on the Honolulu ham radio network. Luke switched to the frequency for the net, hoping to hear some news from fellow cruisers, especially Uva.

After fifteen minutes, the radio came alive with cruisers checking in over the net. They would announce their call signs and stand by waiting for other ham operators to check in and try to find information about the weather in the areas where they were sailing or for certain people they wished to speak with to arrange to move to another frequency. When Luke heard Uva check in, he followed and asked him to change to an open frequency, and Uva acknowledged.

When they reestablished contact, Luke asked, "Have you heard why they are looking for us or any further news there?"

Uva replied, "Negative, only the one

incident. They cleared us to continue sailing through the islands. However, a new boat came in this morning, and after they were cleared, we introduced ourselves to them and inquired if they had been asked about you. They also had been asked, but they arrived from the Marquesas Islands, so they didn't know of you either."

"Ok, please keep me informed through the net. Give our best to Brigitte and stay well. Whisky-Hotel-Six-Bravo-Xray-Charlie, out." Luke signed off. He decided he'd better take the dogs back to shore, as they were probably getting anxious *to visit a few trees.*

Upon dropping them off on shore, Luke again felt a deep loneliness he hadn't felt in several years and decided to walk around with the dogs and stretch his legs. They ended up at the old barracks building, the *Palmyra Hilton*, and he wandered inside. Looking down the hallway and into the main sleeping area, he sat down, leaned up against a wall with his knees tucked up to his chest, and his thoughts took him back to a pivotal day in his life in 1970.

He'd just finished his seventh week of Basic Training and was called by his Drill Sergeant to report to Company Headquarters. Luke was left alone to sit outside the company commander's office while his Drill Sergeant was meeting with the Captain.

Captain Ellis was generally feared, as

were the Drill Sergeants, for frequently picking out an individual soldier and having him "drop for fifty pushup's" or take off running around the company holding his M-16 over his head, singing one of the degrading songs about how that soldier's wife was being unfaithful back home while he was fighting for his country.

Luke's platoon Drill Sergeant was a real piece of work. Drill Sergeant Bennett was the meanest of all the Drill Sergeants in the company. He stood only five-foot-six-inches in his combat boots but continually reminded all of the recruits in "Charlie Company" that he was just plain "Arkansas Razorback Mean." Luke actually found humor in watching Drill Sergeant Bennett go about his profession of intimidation and discipline. Humor and looking at the positives in this whole experience was helping him cope with the physical and emotional demands of adjusting to Army life.

Luke had been forced during his sophomore year of high school, as were all of the other male sophomores in his school who were not in the honors program, to take and successfully pass the yearlong Army ROTC course. The year was 1966 and the buildup for the Vietnam War was hitting the nightly news, which continued to become more and more unpopular. The body counts were slowly affecting all sectors of Americans, and Luke's family was no exception. His dad and all of his uncles had served proudly in World War II, however, after one of his cousins returned from Vietnam a very changed man in a way no one could understand, even his conservative family became outright vocal against further involvement in the Southeast Asian "conflict."

Luke actually hoped not to have to serve, but he drew lottery number 36 out of 365. Because he had dropped out of college when he got married, they knew in the back of their minds that it was a good chance he'd be called up. Even though he had detested every minute of ROTC, it turned out to be a tremendous benefit to him after he was drafted. He was the only guy in his platoon that had any clue as to what was going on that first week. He knew his left foot from his right; in other words, he knew how to march. He could polish his boots to a "spit shine" and keep his uniform perfect from the beginning. This proved very beneficial as Drill Sergeant Bennett chose him to become a squad leader, and then after the first platoon leader faltered, Luke was made the platoon leader.

Not that Luke had any military career desires—quite the contrary—but it did give him some privileges over the other recruits, which made life a bit better. Drill Sergeant Bennett expected Luke to help get the platoon from place to place efficiently, and since this also made the Sergeant look good as well, he left Luke alone more than the other men as long as they looked good. Hence, Luke was freer to observe the workings of the "Arkansas Razorback" and it was humorous as long as he wasn't paying the price with extra duties.

As he waited outside the company commander's office, it looked like Luke was getting the double team. Nothing but anxiety kept running through his mind. *What did I do? Why are they singling me out? Is something wrong at home?* He'd heard too many of the ballads of the "Jody back home" who was infamous for stealing one's girl. *Kasey—is she all right? Oh, God no!*

"Private Davis, enter!" yelled Sergeant Bennett. Luke was shaken from his thoughts of doom to come in and stand at attention in front of Captain Ellis's desk with Drill Sergeant Bennett at his side.

Captain Ellis spoke in a cordial manner, "Private Davis, we have called you here to present to you an opportunity, one that frankly is rarely ever offered to a Draftee. You scored in the top 1% of the entire group who entered the reception station on your entrance exams with an aptitude, which the *specialists* say qualify you as a helicopter pilot." The Captain emphasized *specialists* in an uncomplimentary fashion.

He continued, "In addition we've also

had to report to Battalion Headquarters on your progress and leadership so far in Basic Training, and frankly we're pleased to report to them you have shown outstanding leadership and progress." He picked up a brown personnel folder and scanned through it, then continued, "I see here you have led your platoon in many of the physical training standards and have qualified as an expert marksman.

"I know this may come as a sudden shock, since you are a *draftee*," again, in a mocking tone. "You didn't volunteer to serve your country like all of the other Warrant Officers who carried us in and out of the jungle in 'Nam, but all that aside, the *specialists* say you would make a good pilot, and Battalion wants me to offer you a choice to change your volunteer status so you can get into flight school."

Drill Sergeant Bennett shouted, not missing a beat, "Davis, I don't know how in the fuck a Flat Dick like you ever impressed them up at Battalion, but if I were you, I'd seriously consider what Captain Ellis has to say. You'll be cleaning shit out of latrines in Da Nang in about 100 days, boy, as the whole lot of you will be going right on to infantry school as soon as I'm through with your tired asses!"

Captain Ellis resumed in his cordial tone, "Davis, here's the deal. If you take the standard three-year enlistment, which as a *drafteeee* you may end up serving three years anyway, you get to go to flight school. If you graduate there, you will become a Warrant Officer and rather than crawling on your belly in the rice paddies of 'Nam for a private's pay at hundred eighty bucks a month, you'll be living in pilots quarters gettin' sixteen hundred green backs a month and probably flyin' some General around at some stateside post. Hell, they won't send no fucken *drafteeee* pilot to see *real* action." His voice rose with further contempt at Luke's draft status.

Even though Luke was stunned at the suddenness of this opportunity, he couldn't help but laugh inside at the special emphasis these two used to imply their disdain for him being a draftee. *What a piece of work they are,* he thought.

Actually, ever since Luke was eleven and was able to first fly in an airplane, he had wanted to be a pilot. There had been a special promotion at the airstrip at his home to take a flight around the county for "a penny-a-pound," and since Luke probably only weighed ninety-five pounds dripping wet, he was first in line with his own money. When he got on the scales, they said he weighed one hundred-three pounds, which he didn't question but felt he'd been finagled out of eight cents.

That flight was the most thrilling and

unbelievable thirty-nine minutes of his life, and though he'd never flown since, it was so exciting to be offered a chance to go to flight school. And the money—what did he say? Sixteen hundred dollars a month!

Luke cleared his throat and replied, "Sir, I'm flattered and overwhelmed. You say all I'd have to do is enlist for three years?"

"That and pass flight school and get your wings," Captain Ellis answered.

"What if I don't pass flight school?"

Sergeant Bennett jumped in, "You Flat-Dick! If you don't pass flight school, you'd be an embarrassment to me and the Cap'n here, and I'll see you spend the next three years right here peelin' taters and scrubbin' shower stalls! Do you roger that, Flat-Dick?"

"Yes, Drill Sergeant Bennett!" Luke answered emphatically with just a slight grin, which Sergeant Bennett returned. He always laughed to himself whenever the Sergeant called his soldiers "Flat-Dick," though the real humor was the way some of the new recruits would sweat or even break down and cry like babies when Bennett yelled at them, nose-to-nose.

Captain Ellis added in a fatherly way, "Luke, give it some thought. I know this is a sudden development, but it is a great opportunity. I know most of you guys want only to serve the two-year hitch and get back to the world, but as they'd explained to you, you still are eligible for reserve duty call-up into your third year. What Sergeant Bennett said about your company being sent to A.I.T. in Fort Benning, Georgia for infantry training is likely going to happen. Luke, you've done a good job here these past seven weeks and you've earned the chance. If you want, I can have you meet Chief Warrant Officer Rullo tomorrow, and he can give you a better picture. He served two tours in 'Nam, and now has easy duty here flying the General all over the Post."

Thinking this was just too good to be true, but wanting the chance to really evaluate it, Luke replied sincerely, "Thank you, Sir. I would really appreciate the chance to meet him, and if I do choose to accept this opportunity, I *will* get my wings, Sir."

The next day, Luke not only got to meet Chief Warrant Officer Rullo, a crusty old Italian who'd been flying Hueys since they came out seven years earlier, but they took a flight around the Post in the General's "chopper." This made Luke's first flight in that Cessna when he was eleven seem like a merry-go-round ride. It was amazing what this unit could do. Rullo was very candid about flight school and the different challenges of flying helicopters. He said if the assessment of Luke's abilities from the Army's entrance exams were correct, then he must have the aptitude to be a pilot. He knew several men who wanted to become pilots, but just didn't have the coordination and the aptitude to make it. He also confirmed the pay scale, perks, and living conditions for a pilot. Luke decided to call his wife.

Kasey came into Luke's life just after he'd graduated from high school and was entering his first semester of college. She was three years older, recently divorced, and the sexiest girl he'd ever met. She was so unlike any girl he'd ever dated. First of all, she was not only beautiful, but they got right down to having sex on their first date. Now that was a whole new concept. Luke had only made love to two girls by this time in his young life, and found it a real struggle to have to date a girl for a couple of years before she'd consent.

However, Kasey knew what she wanted right from the start, and she took Luke to places he'd never dreamed. Several nights during those first few months, they made love all night long. They were both having the times of their lives and were falling in love from the passion and the virility that Luke possessed, and the needs Kasey had. Luke's parents were not at all happy when they found out about the engagement, as they knew he was rushing into this, but he wasn't listening to any words of advice or caution.

After a simple wedding, Luke found a job working for an engineering company as a surveyor while Kasey continued to stay in school. They lived in a tiny apartment close to the campus, and though barely getting by, they were very happy. Then came the news: Luke's draft notice. The saddest day in his life came at four-thirty in the morning one Friday when Kasey and Luke's Dad took him to the bus station for the ride to Kansas City for his induction into the Army.

At first, they figured he'd just wiggle out of his service obligation by faking medical problems at the physical, but as it turned out, the doctors there had seen every trick in the book. Before Luke knew it, he was on another bus heading to Fort Leonard Wood, Missouri to Basic Training. He called and assured Kasey everything would be all right, and for her to stay in school. He would send his money back home to support her, so she wouldn't have to get a job. Luke's Dad also promised to help out.

Luke was unable to reach Kasey on the phone from the hangar after his flight with Chief Warrant Officer Rullo, and it was only very late that night into the early morning hours that he finally reached her. She'd been to a concert and he could tell she was either sleepy or had been drinking, but that didn't keep him from expressing his excitement and telling her all about it.

All she kept saying was, "That's cool man, flyin' helicopters around... Hell yeah."

Luke took this as a sign of approval. He was still so "high" from his flight and this whole opportunity that she could have protested and he still would have taken it as an endorsement. The next morning he returned to Captain Ellis's office and signed the enlistment papers.

Chapter 29

Roger Bryan, the narrator in the book *Mutiny on the Bounty*, stated upon his first sight of Tahiti, "*There, many leagues away, I saw the outlines of a mighty mountain rising from the sea—sweeping ridges falling away symmetrically from a tall central peak, all pale blue and ghostly in the morning light.*"

Luke had that same feeling of awe as he approached Tahiti early in the morning of his sixth day sailing from Palmyra. He had a fast and uneventful passage, though much more sleep-deprived without Teruyo splitting the watch duties. He tried his best to keep a constant watch, but hour-long naps were required about every six hours.

He did see one freighter coming on an opposite course, but she was about a quarter-mile off to port. When he tried to hail her crew with his VHF radio on the hailing channel #16, he received no response. This made for an eerie reminder of the story Uva and Brigitte told of the freighter with the sailboat rigging fouled in its bow. Uva had said, "They set the auto pilot on their desired heading and sometimes leave the pilot house without a watchman for hours on end."

Luke did the best he could to maintain a

constant watch, thinking of the wonderful times he and Teruyo had shared. She was such a special lady and her absence was giving him time to reflect on how truly magical their short time together was. He was bound and determined to get her back.

They had been able to make contact about every other evening. Some nights the conditions were not right for them to receive each other's signals. But for the most part, they were able to keep in touch and keep the fire burning, even at this great distance. She was with her mother in the family estate in Kobe, Japan. Michi had been flown there too, much to her great dismay as well, but they were making the best of it until solid information on the situation could be confirmed and a plan to deal with it implemented.

Kajiki was in Papeete investigating the situation, and he'd sent for two members from the Hawaii security team, Kimo and Benny, who were of Polynesian ancestry, so they could help him with the investigation without looking too out of place. They had grown up together on the island of Maui and upon graduation from High School, went on to become Navy Seals. Neither man was someone you wanted to mess with. Kimo was six-foot-two and a solid 240 pounds and Benny, though smaller at five-foot-ten and 190, more than made up for Kimo's huge presence with lightning speed as well as great knowledge of the newest electronics of the day.

They set up a ham radio base station and were able to communicate directly with Luke. Kajiki liked Luke's plan to come on into Papeete and try to draw out whoever was circulating the picture and the rumors of Luke kidnapping Teruyo. So far, Kajiki was unable to penetrate the Tahitian authorities to discover who was behind the scam. Not wanting to jeopardize his cover, he did not try to convince the Tahitians that this information was false. Their real mission was to covertly uncover who was behind this and deal with them in their own way.

When Teruyo was told Luke had made up his mind to help, she became furious. However, by the time she found out, Luke was already on his way south, and he insisted to her that his only role was to convince the Tahitian authorities there was no kidnapping and hopefully draw out who was behind this. Unannounced to Luke, she tried to collaborate with Shindo to fly to Tahiti, but Kajiki would not allow it.

Luke surveyed the harbor in Papeete as he motored in from the channel entrance and was able to hail the Harbor Master on the VHF radio. The customs officials gave him directions to park "stern-to" at a courtesy dock and to prepare for boarding. After locating the spot he was directed to, he grabbed the mooring and tied off his bow, then backed *Tranquilo's* stern into the dock. As he was preparing to set ashore to cleat his stern line, a young man of Tahitian origin with a big smile offered to assist, so Luke tossed him the stern line. The young man introduced himself as Taeio and after securing a line to another cleat, was welcomed aboard by Luke. They shook hands with their introductions, and in a low voice, Taeio stated, "I am here on behalf of Kajiki to assist you. There may be some delay with clearance."

Luke replied, "I'm grateful, as I am expecting some problems and I really appreciate you just hanging out in the event there are any. Is Kajiki close by?"

"Yes, he can see us, but I don't see him." Taeio laughed in his peculiar way.

Luke spotted some official-looking men hurrying his way. Obviously his announcement over the VHF radio to the Harbor Master got plenty of attention. There were a couple of local *Gendarmes*—police-like men dressed just like *"Louie"* in the movie *Casablanca*, only they wore shorts rather than long pants. Their typical French-style, flat, cream-colored hats and starch-pressed uniforms with polished leather pistol holsters and "bowie belts" gave them the look that they meant *serious business*.

"Tell me, Taeio, do all cruisers get this

much of a welcome?" Luke asked as he watched the approaching procession.

"No, no, no, Mr. Davis. You are getting special welcome." Again Taeio answered laughing. Taeio was putting on an act to appear to be a dumb harbor kid looking to scam a few dollars off an unsuspecting American.

The first "official" leading the parade of men spoke as they reached *Tranquilo*, "Mr. Davis, welcome to Papeete. I'm Monsieur Bogenville, Director of Customs. May I introduce Captain Follet and Lieutenant Pallen. We are here to inspect your vessel and process your visa. May we come aboard? "

Luke replied with a smile, "Yes, please step aboard. This young man, what did you say your name is?" Luke turned to Taeio.

"Taeio, Sir." Turning to the customs official, Taeio continued, "I was offering to help the American tie up since he appeared to be alone."

Luke stated, "Yes, Taeio… uh, thank you. Can I offer you something for your help?"

Monsieur Bogenville interrupted, "Excuse me, Mr. Davis, may we proceed? You will need your passport, visa, proof of financial means, and vessel documentation. How many passengers are with you?"

Taeio interrupted, "Good luck, Sir. I be on my way." He left laughing, as if he hadn't a care in the world.

"I'll catch you later if you are around, Taeio. Thanks a lot," Luke said as he turned to go down into the cabin. "This way gentleman, or would you prefer to stay in the cockpit?"

"We will need to inspect your vessel, so we might as well have a look. How many passengers are with you?" the customs official asked again.

"Just me, Sir." Luke answered. "I single-handed here from Hawaii. The last leg from Palmyra took me six and a half days, and I couldn't have asked for a better trip."

"Didn't you leave Hawaii with a Miss Teruyo Boudreaux?" This time it was Captain Follet getting involved.

"Yeah, we started out together, but she got terribly seasick and begged me to return her to Hawaii. I took her back to the first island we came to, Lanai, and she took a flight back to Honolulu and that is the last I've heard from her. Frankly damn glad to be rid of her. All she did was complain the whole time," Luke replied.

Without asking, the two Gendarmes split up, one going to the aft cabin and the other forward to search Luke's boat. Luke calmly gathered his documents out of the chart table and presented them to Bogenville.

The Director of Customs inspected the documents very thoroughly, asking, "What proof do you have that what you say about

Miss Boudreaux is true?"

"Well, she isn't here is she? Why don't you call her up and find out?" Luke answered.

The Gendarmes returned to the main cabin. Captain Follet stated, "No sign of her or any trace of a woman traveling with him."

Turning to Luke, Follet continued, "Mr. Davis, I'm afraid you will have to come with us for further questioning. You may secure your vessel, and if you like, we can make arrangements to have it watched. I am placing you under arrest for the kidnapping of Miss Teruyo Boudreaux, and until we confirm her safety, you'll be detained pending the outcome of the investigation."

"Whoa there, guys. I don't know anything about any kidnapping. Teruyo wanted to sail with me, and there was never any force on my part at all," Luke emphasized in a louder tone.

Just then, the Gendarmes grabbed Luke by both arms and handcuffed his hands behind his back. He didn't resist, as Kajiki had briefed him that this would most likely happen. Instead, he asked, "Hey, do I get a chance to lock up my boat?"

Follet replied, "We still have to inspect your vessel, and we will take responsibility for it."

"Wait a minute, fellows, why can't we be civil about this. I've done nothing wrong, and you can't just arrest me without any proof, can you? Can't we take care of this right here? How do I know my boat is going to be OK?"

Bogenville answered, "Where is the lock to your hatch? Lieutenant Pallen will secure your vessel."

"Top drawer of the chart table and the washboard is in the portside lazarete." Luke answered.

Captain Follet tugged at Luke's arm and motioned for him to ascend the stairs out to the cockpit. He said something in French to his Lieutenant and they stepped off the stern of *Tranquilo*. Luke was walked to a police car waiting at the end of the dock, like they'd had it all arranged. Just as Luke was ducking to get into the car, he noticed Kajiki across the street, dressed like a tourist complete with flowered shirt, shorts, black shoes and socks, shopping bag, and camera around his neck. Kajiki gave Luke a slight nod of assurance as the car drove away.

As they drove to the police station, Luke thought, *I wonder what their story would have been if Teruyo were with me?*

After waiting for over two hours in a room with only a wooden chair, still handcuffed, Luke was wondering if he were really in for major problems. He wished he didn't have those weapons Kajiki gave him. What if they discovered them in the binnacle? Sure, it seemed to be the perfect hiding place— the workmanship was so well-machined that no one would suspect it, but what if they did find them? He could lose his boat and be put in jail just for a weapons violation.

Finally *"Louie"*—Captain Follet—and Bogenville entered the room. Follet began, "Mr. Davis, is this your boat?" and he held up an eight by ten color glossy photograph of *Tranquilo* in Hanalei Bay.

Luke looked the photo over carefully, noting the location of *Tranquilo* at anchor, and stated, "Yes Sir, looks like when Teruyo and I were anchored there about two months ago. Where did you get this?"

"Never mind, that is not important for now. We have a statement that you were last seen having bound Miss Boudreaux's hands behind her back and carrying her in your launch out to your sailboat. Is that true Mr. Davis?" Follet asked.

"Hell no, that's not true! And who in God's name told you that?"

"That's not important right now," said Bogenville. "Tell me, Mr. Davis, where is Miss Boudreaux?"

"Like I told you, I took her back to Lanai and she took a plane on to Honolulu. I haven't heard of or seen her since. Do I get a phone call? Is there an American Consul here?" Luke asked.

Just then, the door opened and an Asian man entered the room. He was Korean, Luke could tell, having about the same features as their attackers in Hanalei Bay, just before he'd changed their complexions with his hands and feet.

"Mr. Davis, this is Masashi Tanaka, grandfather of Teruyo Boudreaux. He is the one who is accusing you of kidnapping."

"Masashi Tanaka" walked up to Luke, who was still sitting, and hit him squarely in his jaw, knocking him completely out of his chair. The blow was totally unexpected and came with such lightning speed, Luke didn't see it coming. He began seeing light flashes, on the verge of unconsciousness.

Almost dislocating Luke's shoulders, Follet and Bogenville roughly lifted Luke up and forced him back in the chair. The Asian man asked, "Where is my granddaughter?" and struck Luke again, this time from the other side and higher up next to his eye, again knocking Luke to the floor. This blow didn't hurt as badly, but swelling began immediately under Luke's left eye.

Luke gasped, trying to find in his memory the names of the men who were first interrogating him, "Hey guys, what's this? You gonna allow this? What kind of bullshit investigation are you trying to run here?"

Again, Follet and Bogenville lifted Luke off the floor and roughly threw him into the chair, almost flipping him backwards.

The Korean got right in Luke's face. "What did you do with her?"

Luke yelled, "Captain, get this imposter out of here. He knows I have met Teruyo's real grandfather! This is **not** Masashi Tanaka!" The customs officer's name finally came back to Luke. "Bogenville, this is not Tanaka! Give me a chance to prove myself and I'll save you a lot of wasted time and a chance to arrest this son-of-a-bitch!"

Again the Korean knocked Luke out of his chair, this time hitting Luke again on his right side. The Captain and Custom's Officer grabbed "Tanaka" and ushered him out of the room. Luke, while lying on the floor, half unconscious, heard them yell to a Gendarme by the door to take Mr. Tanaka to his hotel. "We will contact you when we have further information," Follet said loudly as the Gendarme ushered "Tanaka" out the door of the Police Station.

They returned and lifted Luke back into the chair and Bogenville yelled for another Gendarme to bring in a wet towel. *"Oh great,"* Luke thought. *"Now they're going to beat me with a wet towel."* Then Luke passed out and again fell to the floor.

Chapter 30

Kajiki had pretended to want to make a police report for a theft from his rental car and was in the Police Station trying to observe where they had taken Luke. He was able to use just enough broken English, with mostly Japanese mixed between words, to thoroughly confuse the Gendarme at the desk. When the Korean was being escorted out, Kajiki acted frustrated and left a short distance behind. The Gendarme who was escorting the Korean had ahold of his arm and directed him into taxi and off they sped. Benny, in an awaiting car pulled up, Kajiki jumped in, and they followed the taxi.

Keeping a safe distance, and contacting Kimo over a handheld radio, they set up a "tail" to track the taxi without being spotted. Once Kimo was behind them, Kajiki and Benny turned right and then Kimo took over the tail. After a few blocks, Benny returned and got behind Kimo and they were able to tail the taxi inconspicuously until the Korean was delivered to a house near a condominium complex on the outskirts of Papeete.

Kajiki and his men set up positions in the condominium parking lot across the street to discretely observe the house. He contacted his base station with the address for them to run a check on the owner of the property.

A faint glow of light crept in at about the same time the pounding throb of pain startled Luke awake. Someone was patting his forehead with a damp cloth, and he was feeling cold and clammy. Luke wasn't sure where he was, or why his head hurt so much. Trying to get up, his mind began to race. *Don't just lie there; get up. You've got to get back on deck and keep watch... can't let too much time go by or a collision could happen, even way out here in the Pacific.*

"Monsieur, can you hear me?" asked a young lady's voice that Luke didn't recognize.

Trying to rise, but feeling her gently restrain him on his shoulders, he heard her continue, "Monsieur, you have suffered a concussion, can you open your eyes and look at me?"

Luke struggled and with great effort, was able to focus one eye on a slender woman in a white clinical-type jacket with a stethoscope around her neck sitting to his left. She asked, "How do you feel?"

Luke replied, "Ma'am, I promise I'll behave. Please don't hit me anymore. Whatever I said, I didn't mean it. The rum... it was just the rum talking."

Smiling at his humor, she answered, "Monsieur, I'm Doctor Parant. It appears you have suffered a head injury. I am going to admit you to the hospital for evaluation and some tests, so I want you to know that you are being cared for and you will be moved to a room shortly."

"Tell me, did they get the license number of that truck?"

"Monsieur? What truck is it that you speak of?"

"Just an American joke. Are we alone or am I being escorted?"

"Captain Follet and two Gendarmes are waiting outside. He is anxious to talk with you as soon as you are awake. However, I feel you need rest and regardless how he protests, I am not going to allow him access to you for the rest of today."

"Tell me, does he send a lot of business your way?"

"Monsieur? What is it you mean... business?"

"Did he tell you what happened to me?"

"Only that you have been the victim of a beating."

"Doctor... what did you say your name is?"

"Parant, but you mustn't try talking too much. You need to rest and stay calm."

"Doctor, please do me a big favor. In the elastic band of my shorts is a piece of paper. Could you find it for me please?" Luke struggled to think.

Luke had written the telephone number of Kajiki's base station on a strip of paper and inserted it into the elastic band of his nylon shorts. He could feel her fold the elastic band down to expose the opening where the drawstrings exited. "Just pull the left side string and the paper is rolled around the string."

After she found the paper, he said, "Yes, that's it. The phone number is to a man I know here in Papeete who needs to find me. It is very important he gets word I am here. Please, without Follet knowing, will you call him? His name is Kajiki, and he will be grateful to know I'm OK. You see, Follet allowed this to happen, and if I don't make contact with Kajiki and Follet gets me back, I'm sure they will have me killed," Luke pleaded.

"Yes, I can imagine Follet is behind this. He thinks of himself so powerful. What is your name, Monsieur?" the doctor asked.

"Luke Davis. I just sailed here from Hawaii, and Follet and a man who said he was from the Customs Office, Bogenville, I believe he said his name was, arrested me and as you see, *interrogated* me."

"Ssshh... not so loud. They may hear

you. Stay calm and rest. I will call this Mr. Kajiki, but you must stay quiet. You don't want to complicate your head injuries," she replied.

Luke had momentarily forgotten the pain, but as he struggled to look at the doctor, he was quickly reminded he was not having a good day. He added, "Please don't let Follet know you called Kajiki."

"Very well, Mr. Davis, stay calm and I will see you get moved to a private room. Of course, they will probably stand guard, but I am in control here, not Follet."

She applied a fresh damp cloth to Luke's forehead, and gave him a sip of water through one of those bendy hospital straws. "Thank you so much. Do you have anything for a headache?"

Kajiki was called away to contact the base station by phone. He called from a payphone and was informed the owner of the house was a wealthy businessman from Indonesia who seldom used the property. According to what his agent at the base station could determine, the owner was not on the island. Kajiki told him that they would maintain surveillance until dark and decide when to move in.

Not long after resuming his position in front of the house, and just before dark, Kajiki received another call over the radio to again contact the base. He returned to the payphone to discover that a Dr. Parant had called from the hospital and Luke had requested Kajiki be notified that he had been beaten and was being held under house arrest in room 341. Kajiki decided to place a call to Japan.

Captain Follet was furious. This was the third time that Dr. Parant had not allowed him to question a prisoner. *Who does she think she is? Just because she doesn't like me, she tries to keep me from doing my duties!* he cursed to himself as he left the hospital. He'd left strict instructions to the Gendarme posted outside Luke's room that no one other than hospital personnel were to see Luke Davis.

Luke, although he didn't understand French, heard the shouting outside of his room just after being moved there and gained some solace at the thought that the doctor was coming to his aid. Now he needed to get in touch with Kajiki. That photograph he saw of *Tranquilo* in Hanalei Bay was taken when he and Teruyo had come back from Tunnels. It was taken from the Sheraton, the same spot where they overlooked the entrance to the bay when they had brunch. Someone from the inside of the Tanaka organization was involved. Luke was sure of it.

Dr. Parant returned with a nurse. "Oh, Mr. Davis, did I not ask you to get some sleep?"

"I want to thank you for making sure Follet was not able to get to me. I feel that's the best medicine I could have for now," Luke replied.

"Let's see how you are doing." She took his pulse then looked into his eyes. "So you sailed here from Hawaii? Were you all by yourself?"

"Yes, Ma'am, I've got a beautiful boat and have always wanted to sail the Pacific," he cautiously replied. *Is she working with Follet?*

She kept looking into his eyes with a light and continued, "You must be an excellent sailor to navigate and withstand the hardships all by yourself."

Luke decided to play along, "Have you ever been sailing?"

"Yes, a few days I spent on a charter to Moorea. I must say it was wonderful, and we caught the most beautiful fish on the way back. I believe they called it a Mahi-Mahi?"

"I caught one of those up by Maui a few months ago. I didn't know who would win that fight. Did you bring it in?"

"Oh no, one of the deckhands on the

charter boat did the honors. It was amazing how the fish turned colors just as it was dying," she reflected.

Luke relaxed his suspicions of her just a bit after hearing that. Maybe she was OK. "Were you able to contact my friend?" he whispered.

"I was able to leave a message. He wasn't in. I did give him my direct line to call, but I haven't heard anything as yet. Since our rooms do not have individual phones, I'll let you know when he calls. Can I get you anything to make you more comfortable?" the pretty doctor asked.

"Rum... do you have any rum?" Luke teased in his best pirate voice.

"No, Captain Bligh, not just yet." She smiled in a flirtatious way and walked out of the room.

It was beginning to get dark outside. *Maybe I can catch a few winks.* After all he'd been through—the lack of sleep on the voyage and then the welcome to Tahiti—he was asleep in just a few seconds.

Kajiki was able to finally get through to Dr. Parant and she filled him in on the extent of Luke's injuries and the situation with the Gendarme. She explained to him that Captain

307

Follet had most likely been involved in other "assaults," but she had no proof until now, since hearing it directly from Luke. He was most grateful to her for informing him of the situation and asked, "Could I beg of you just one more favor?"

"Certainly, if I can," she answered.

"Is there any way you can get me into see Luke for just a few minutes?" Kajiki asked.

"Well, I'd have to make you look like a member of the staff, and it would be easier if we could do it late at night when there is only minimal staff here. I wouldn't want to trust anyone here to see you, fearing they may report it to Follet."

"I wouldn't ask if I did not think it was urgent. Since the Customs Official and the Captain seem to be involved, Luke is in serious danger," Kajiki emphasized.

"Yes, Mr. Davis feels the same way. Be here at the emergency entrance at 1:30 in the morning. I will meet you and see if I can get you into his room."

Kajiki felt his men could continue handling the surveillance. He instructed them to watch for anyone else entering the property and for now, just follow him should he leave.

Luke heard the same voice from before

as he felt someone gently shaking his shoulder. "Mr. Davis, it's time for your medication. Sorry to disturb you, but you need to wake up and take your pill," the Doctor stated, just loud enough for the Gendarme standing guard to hear as the door closed.

Luke was sleeping comfortably, maybe too soundly, as Dr. Parant gently shook him awake. As he climbed out of the depths of a dream and slowly focused his eyes in the dimly lit room, he said, "You don't realize how many times the Army Medics used to wake me and Willy up to take our medication. We probably would have healed faster if we could have just slept through the rest of the war."

"Easy Luke, don't question this Doc; she is on our side," Kajiki replied, dressed in a starched white coat, complete with a stethoscope around his neck.

Luke was surprised to see Kajiki and said, "So far this isn't quite going like I'd hoped."

Dr. Parant interjected, "Sshh, Mr. Davis. We don't want to alert the Gendarme. Has the pain subsided?"

"It's still there but not as bad. I think."

Kajiki leaned towards Luke, "Easy, we don't have much time. Is there anything you can tell me about the Korean who was escorted out of the police station?"

"Yeah, he claimed to be Teruyo's

grandfather. He packs a pretty good wallop too! Oh, they showed me the photo of my boat in Hanalei Bay, and it was taken from the Sheraton after we came to meet Mr. Tanaka and you all. They are claiming I took Teruyo by force in my dinghy from there and he's acting like I've kidnapped her."

"Is there anything else?" Kajiki inquired.

"I don't remember much after he started wailing on me. However, Follet and Bogenville didn't do much to stop him. They may be involved."

"Yes, Dr. Parant is helping us because she suspects they've been responsible for other beatings as well," Kajiki added.

"Are you going to get me out of here?"

Dr. Parant answered, "No, you must stay here for now. You have a concussion, and it could be very dangerous for you to get up too soon. I'll see that you are not moved."

"Thanks, Doc. Kajiki, don't let Teruyo find out about this. She doesn't need to worry about me."

"If you don't mind, Doctor, I'd like to keep in touch with you and would appreciate it very much if you will call me at the first sign of any problems or changes," Kajiki said.

Kimo and Benny were still watching the

house for any movement. Kajiki wanted to alert Mr. Tanaka personally of Luke's condition and of the news about the photo. Kajiki also felt there must be someone from Tanaka's own team collaborating with the North Koreans and this "mole" needed to be discovered quickly. The whole family could be at risk.

Two more staff from the security team were ordered to fly into Papeete immediately, and Shindo would be coordinating the security of the family in Japan. Kajiki wished he could be in both places at once to initiate the investigation in Japan, but he was gambling he could get the information he needed here.

There had been no movement of people in or out of the Indonesian's property, and they had not determined how many people were there. Just before sunrise, a car entered the drive, driven by Bogenville. An hour later, two more cars entered, one with Captain Follet in the backseat, and both cars were full of uniformed Gendarmes.

Kajiki and his team waited for over an hour to see if an arrest was being made, but it was taking a long time if, in fact, that was that they were doing. He sent Benny to the airport to meet the additional security team members who were about to arrive on one of Mr. Tanaka's private jets. They were bringing some equipment he requested, and he wanted to be sure everyone was promptly brought up to speed on the situation.

Another hour passed, and Kajiki relieved Benny and Kimo, who'd been up all night, with two fresh team members, although they were not quite well rested either having had to depart Honolulu early in the morning. One thing nice about working for Mr. Tanaka was there were plenty of private jets around and it made for "importing" surveillance equipment easier. Kajiki ensured everyone's radios were still ready to go and then headed back to his base headquarters, a rented warehouse close to the harbor.

Just as he arrived, he received a call from Dr. Parant. She reported that Captain Follet had just called to see what time she was releasing Luke. She had told Follet that Luke had a setback during the night and would need further x-rays and certainly more rest. She told Kajiki that Follet slammed the receiver down on the phone.

Kajiki thanked her and asked how Luke was doing and she assured him he was still sleeping. She said, "Considering the lack of sleep and the rough beating he took, plus the fact we need to keep waking him up to observe him to ensure no blood clots go to the brain, rest and quiet is what he needs most."

Shortly after her call, Kajiki was notified by radio that the two police cars had left the house, and the Korean was with Follet. Kajiki had one agent follow and one remain to ensure there was no one else there. He gathered the equipment and headed back to the house.

"Mr. Davis, it's time for some lunch. How about some soup this afternoon?" the nurse suggested.

"Oh please, what does it take to get more than an hour's sleep around here without being woken up for another 'eye check' or pill?"

"Now, Mr. Davis, Dr. Parant told you with head injuries like you have, we need to watch you carefully," she replied in her heavy French accent.

"Well, do you at least have something with some flavor in it this time? That last batch you brought for 'breakfast' did nothing for me."

Dr. Parant interrupted as she entered the room, "Frances, is Mr. Davis being difficult this afternoon?"

"No, Doctor, nothing we can't handle. Maybe if he gets a good shave and a haircut, he will be much more cooperative," she laughed.

"OK, OK, I'll behave. Please, Doc, just don't let Frances here near me with a pair of scissors." Luke motioned for Dr. Parant to come closer and whispered, "I'm actually traveling incognito. I'm a famous American Rock Star and I don't want anyone to know who I am."

"Oh really?" the Doctor whispered back, "And just who are you actually?"

"You promise you won't tell anyone?" He received a nod. "I'm really Jim Morrison; everyone thinks I'm dead."

"Ohooooo, Mr. Morrison." With a snicker, she continued, "We'll keep that between you and me, and if you eat all of your soup like a good 'rock star,' we will let you keep your beard."

She motioned for Nurse Frances to go on about her duties, and when the door closed, Dr. Parant said, "Would you rather me call you Luke or Jim?"

"Luke would be better; we wouldn't want to blow my cover," he replied with a grin, knowing she wasn't falling for this a bit.

"Luke it is then." Dr. Parant began looking into Luke's eyes with a penlight and continued, "I received a call from Captain Follet, and he is furious that I won't release you to him yet. I am still truly concerned with your injury, although I see some improvement. However, Kajiki needs time to sort things out, so in order for me to maintain my authority over you, you will need to play along with being sick. So when the nurses come in, don't be too spirited with them or they may leak it to the wrong people that you are getting better." She tilted her head to the door where the Gendarme was still posted.

"Doctor, I'm grateful for your help and working with Kajiki. He is very talented in his profession, and I am sure glad he's on my side in this mess. If he's on to something, you can be sure he'll see the right thing is done."

"Last night you spoke of a lady. I take it you have a companion?"

"Yeah, we've had to part for a while, and Kajiki works for her family. With his help, maybe we can get back together soon," Luke replied, but as soon as he had spoken he thought, *I hope I haven't said anything that will fall into the wrong hands.* Oh, how he missed Teruyo. Just someone asking about her, and he let his guard down.

With a softening tone of disappointment in her voice she added, "I'm sorry for inquiring, but I just wanted to know if you wanted me to contact someone else for you."

"No, please don't contact Teruyo. If she were to find out I'm in the hospital, she'd come here, and it's her they're really after! This is a very dangerous situation I've gotten myself into. I'm sorry to involve you, but those are dangerous people out there, and now to find out that Follet and Bogenville are involved with them... you better be very careful as well."

"It's suspected all over Papeete that they are corrupt, but there has never been anyone able to stand up to them. Don't worry; I have connections with government officials from the political side whom I can go to at the first sign of trouble from them. However, if Kajiki can uncover a plot or evidence of corruption, then I'm most interested in seeing them implicated."

"Thank you, Doc, I'm really at your mercy. There's one other thing you could do for me if you could. My boat really means a lot to me. Her name is *Tranquilo,* and she is tied up in the harbor. Do you suppose if Kajiki calls back you could ask him if she is being looked after?"

"Oui, I'll ask him as soon as he calls. I frequently stroll down there for lunch. I will see if I can find it and let you know," she replied, and left Luke with his broth.

Kajiki received word from Kimo, who was following Follet and his two cars, that they all went to the airport and were waiting at the arriving passengers gate. Upon the reassurance that there was no further visible movement in the Indonesian's house, he decided to go in and plant bugs and tap the phone. He and Benny dressed in uniforms from the local phone company, which they'd "acquired" from a phone repair van. They approached the house and knocked on the door... no answer, so they picked the lock and were in the house in less than a minute.

Kajiki immediately went to work installing remote battery-powered transmitters in each room, while Benny placed a tap on the phone line. They were very careful to conceal their work; after all, this was one of their specialties. In less than ten minutes, they were out of the house and back across the street. Fortunately, they had several parked cars in the parking lot that they could blend in with, so it was now just a matter of listening in when the suspects returned.

A few minutes later, Kajiki received a call over their radio that three more Asians were met at the airport, and the Korean joined them in a rental car. Kimo was just falling in behind the three cars, and it appeared they were heading back to the house.

The base station operator called as soon as that radio traffic cleared, "Dr. Parant called to inquire who was watching Luke's boat."

"What?" Kajiki replied. *Great timing: who cares about the damn boat at a time like this? We're about to get to the bottom of this, and the Doctor is worried about Luke's boat?* "Call her back and tell her its being watched by a boy named Taeio."

Kajiki was feeling edgy; he hadn't slept in about thirty-five hours. *I've got to stay focused.* He crawled in the back seat of the car to take a nap. Benny, in the front seat, was told to monitor the receivers and recorder and to wake him if something developed. *Who's watching the damn boat? Are you kidding me?!*

Dr. Parant strolled along the harbor until she spotted *Tranquilo.* Sitting in the shade of the bimini top, reading a magazine was a local man.

"Excuse me," she asked. "Are you Taeio?"

In his friendly style, he laughed, "That I am. How do you know me?"

"Luke was wondering about his boat. Can I come aboard?"

"Sure, let me pull her a little closer." Taeio winched the stern line closer to the dock so she could step up the swim ladder.

"I'm Dr. Parant, Luke's attending physician. He is in the hospital."

Taeio replied, "Yeah, I heard." And in a whisper, he asked, "Did Kajiki send you?"

"Well sort of. Kajiki sent word back to Luke and me that you were watching his boat for him, and as soon as Luke heard that, he was relieved. I was just strolling by and thought I would look in on you. Is there anything I can get for you?" she asked.

"No, no, plenty to eat and drink here." Taeio laughed. "I watch from the dock as the Customs Inspectors and the Gendarmes went through the boat. Really tore it up! Don't know what they looking for, but left frustrated that they didn't find nothin'. Tell Luke I straightened up as best as I could, but I'm sure he will have plenty to do when he get back."

"I'll tell him. He will be so grateful to know you are here."

"How is he doing?" Taeio asked.

Not totally sure about this boy's loyalty, she answered, "He's hurt pretty badly but hopefully will be able to get back in a week or two."

Chapter 31

The boredom of being in a hospital was bad enough, but having to pretend he was not recuperating in order to stay under Dr. Parant's authority was making it even harder. The doctor or a nurse continued to come in every hour to check Luke's eyes and condition. She had thoroughly convinced the nurses that Luke's injuries were serious and he was not doing well. He also played along, sometimes acting a bit too sick in her opinion. She had him taken to the radiology department for further x-rays, and that gave Luke his first look outside his room. However, the Gendarme followed and Luke had to continue to pretend he was not well.

The Gendarmes rotated their guard duty over Luke's door every four hours. They were using a lot of manpower to ensure he didn't go anywhere. Sometimes, they would get bored with waiting, occasionally pacing back and forth down the hall, but always keeping an eye on Luke's door. Fortunately for the guards, the men's restroom was only twenty paces down the hall, so there were short times when the door was left unattended. However, they were left with strict orders to not allow any unauthorized person in the room and to keep close attention to all conversations and changes in Luke's condition.

Luke was unable to have books or magazines, and of course no television or phone. He worried and longed for Teruyo. Other than the times he spent trying to figure out this whole bizarre involvement, his thoughts returned to how much he still yearned to have Teruyo back at his side in the cockpit of his boat. They should be anchored in the Lagoon of Bora Bora under the shadow of Mounts Pahia and Otemanu right now, not separated and fearful for their lives with her living under the strict security of her grandfather's realm.

The Tanaka family estate with its beautiful gardens and orchards, streams and waterfalls, was located in Kobe, Japan, nestled at the base of Mount Rokko. "The compound," as Michi called it because she and Teruyo felt so confined, had plenty of guest houses and room to roam in quiet solitude, wearing the traditional dress, kimonos, or their more casual western-style clothing, whichever they preferred.

"This is so boring. How long is this going to go on?" Michi protested. She was really upset that she had been pulled out of school in the middle of the semester. Now she would have to start those classes all over again.

Teruyo replied, "I don't know, but I'm so worried about Luke. I can't stand not hearing from him. Something's gone wrong. He should be able to receive my radio transmissions." She had asked Shindo to find Kajiki and look for Luke, but so far there had been no word. Shindo was obligated with strict orders from Mr. Tanaka not to tell Teruyo anything about the operation in Papeete or of Luke's injuries. Mr. Tanaka had his hands full enough with all of these new security concerns as well as handling the protests of his two granddaughters. He didn't need any further arguing about whether or not she needed to be with Luke.

Shindo was not only heading the security detail for the family in Kobe, but also investigating who could have taken the photograph from the Sheraton, Kauai. Only he and Mr. Tanaka knew of the photograph, and they had no developments with finding a disloyal employee. They needed more information from Papeete.

The "bugs" Kajiki planted in the house were all transmitting well, and the battery-operated recorders were getting all of the telephone conversations on tape, however, nothing relevant had surfaced yet. The only information of any use was that Captain Follet and Monsieur Bogenville were being paid "handsomely" for helping the Korean, whom they believed was Mr. Tanaka of Tanaka Industries. The Korean repeatedly pressed the two men to get Luke out of the hospital for further interrogation.

One of the Korean men who were picked up at the airport had found no trace of Teruyo flying from Lanai. There was no record of her on any of the flights from Lanai or out of Honolulu. "She would have most likely paid in cash and used another name anyway," he suggested to his boss.

Kajiki was perplexed by how Follet and Bogenville could actually believe this guy was Mr. Tanaka and why they believed his story, since there was nothing on any of the wire services or through the embassies regarding Teruyo being kidnapped. He was having his Honolulu office look into how the story could possibly be verified by the government in Papeete. Surely Follet would have verified the story. Kajiki drove back to the warehouse to call Japan.

"But Grandfather, I need to talk with

Luke!" Teruyo cried to Mr. Tanaka. "You have denied knowing how he is, but I think you're keeping information from me. I know you have the ability to contact him. Please!" she begged.

"My beautiful Teruyo-san." Mr. Tanaka embraced his granddaughter. "You are correct, I do have the ability to contact Luke, and I have been avoiding telling you with the hope you would be patient until we discovered all we could about the people who are after us." He then filled Teruyo in on Luke's situation and the investigation to this point.

"Grandfather, I need to be with him! What if his injuries are more serious? We must fly to Papeete immediately, and I want you to send a doctor with me to assist!"

"No, Teruyo. I forbid it! I will not jeopardize your safety, and Kajiki assures me that Luke will be all right. We must be patient!" he stated firmly.

Shindo interrupted, "Sir, maybe it would be good if Teruyo and I did go to Papeete as a way to draw out someone here in our organization who is involved with this security breach. If a call comes in to the Korean imposter stating Teruyo is coming to Papeete, then we will have the break in the case we need. If no call comes, then we could concentrate on eliminating the Korean and seeing the Police Captain and the Customs Official are exposed for their corruption in this scandal."

Teruyo agreed, "Grandfather, that's a great idea. That would be the only way we could expose the informant. I'm sure Luke is right about the photograph, and we need to catch this bastard immediately before there are any further security threats on you or other members of our family."

Mr. Tanaka was taken aback with Teruyo's language, but added, "But if something happens to you, I'd never forgive myself."

Shindo replied, "Mr. Tanaka, I assure you nothing will happen to Teruyo. I give you my word."

Mr. Tanaka hesitated, and then hit the call button to his secretary, "Get me Kajiki, and then arrange a conference call to all the heads of the security teams to begin in one hour."

"Hello Mr. Morrison, I mean Mr. Davis. How are you feeling?" Dr. Parant asked with a grin.

"Oh. Hello, Mom. Is it time to get up and milk the cows?" Luke replied loud enough for the Gendarme to hear just as the door was closing.

"Milk the cows? Mom?" the doctor

asked. "Luke, maybe you really *are* seriously injured. I'll have to keep you here longer even if we get these corrupt officials arrested."

"Is that the plan?" Luke whispered. "Is Kajiki going after them too?"

"I'm not sure, but if he doesn't, then I will," she replied. "I met Taeio yesterday. He assured me that everything is all right with your boat, aside from the mess. He said the customs people really went through your boat, but didn't find anything. It is a very beautiful boat."

"So did you go aboard?" Luke asked anxiously. "Did anything look torn up or broken?"

"I didn't go below; I only sat in the cockpit with Taeio, but nothing looked broken," she replied.

Whew, they didn't find the weapons in the binnacle. Luke thought to himself. Even though Kajiki assured him that no one would suspect it or find the way to open it up, it had still worried him.

"Well, you've given me the best medicine you could have. Thanks for taking the trouble to look in on her for me," Luke said. "Now if we could only find a way to get this whole mess solved and get me back to exploring these beautiful islands of yours."

"I think for now you really need a lot of rest. I'm going to have the nurses refrain from the hourly visits, so you can get some sleep. Please remember, though, you must not be too lively so word gets back to Follet that you're well enough for him to take you back. Kajiki said he still needs more time to piece everything together."

"Doc, I wish there was something I could do to pay you back," Luke said sincerely. "I'm really not anxious to have any more time with him or the Korean. Except for the protection you've given me, I really feel vulnerable."

"Don't worry about that. If we can expose Follet and Bogenville for how corrupt they are, that will be worth all of this risk and effort," she answered firmly.

"You know, I made a career out of being able to read people's faces, and if you don't mind me saying, I see some genuine hatred in you for those two. What's that all about?"

She sat down on the side of Luke's bed and answered, "When I returned to Papeete from France after completing medical school and my internship, I had all of the enthusiasm of a first-year doctor and I was ready to solve all of the ongoing medical problems these islands fight year after year. My first day back, Bogenville, who thinks he is God's gift to my gender, tried to force himself on me and because I refused, he used his position to delay my processing back into my own country!" she exclaimed with a rising voice, but caught herself before alerting the Gendarme standing outside the door. She continued in almost a whisper, "Then, after my aunt came to my rescue and was able to keep me from being detained any longer, Bogenville and Follet continued to team up to delay shipments of medicines and antibiotics we needed here and for some of the clinics on the outer islands.

"A typhoon that hit the Marquesas last year and caused very heavy damage, leading to an outbreak of cholera. Bogenville and Follet confiscated the antibiotics and medicines we prepared to fly over there for the disaster. Scores of natives would have died had they not received that shipment! Bogenville came to me and said he would be able to see the shipments arrived immediately, if only I would be more 'cooperative.' I had to give myself to him in order for that medicine to be released," she cried in disgust.

Tears forming in her eyes, she continued, "He is the most despicable man ever to live, and I swore that one day he and Follet would pay. If it were not for the Ministry of Health, who was instrumental in sending me to France for my education, I would most assuredly have given up my desire to practice here and I would have moved back to Europe. I am able to have some control here at the hospital, and they have backed off from further harassment of me lately, but I swear on the graves of my parents, I will see them brought to justice!"

Kajiki agreed for Mr. Tanaka to announce that he was allowing Teruyo, "after all of her constant whining and pleading," to go to Papeete and bring Luke back to Japan for his recuperation. Mr. Tanaka would announce in the conference call that Luke had gotten word to Teruyo that interrogators had beaten him upon his arrival in Papeete, and that she feared for his life. Mr. Tanaka of course never informed his other department heads of Kajiki being in Papeete and, in fact, upon Kajiki's suggestion, he pretended Kajiki was in Honolulu for the conference call, and that he would immediately depart Honolulu for Papeete to assist with Teruyo's security.

Now all they could do was to wait and see if the word leaked out to someone in the organization.

After a few well-deserved hours of sleep, Benny and Kimo returned to take over the surveillance of the Indonesian's house. So far, nothing was reported worthy of contacting

Kajiki; he needed some rest as well. Kajiki was able to rent an empty condominium just across the street to make the job of monitoring the house and the listening devices they'd placed there more comfortable and efficient.

Benny and Kimo were fully trusted and briefed on what to look for. They were very dedicated to Mr. Tanaka and their team members, as well as very anxious to uncover the "mole" if one existed. They had some close associates murdered along with Mr. Tanaka's friend in Honolulu two months ago and they couldn't wait for revenge.

About the time the sun was rising on this, the second full day of surveillance of the Korean, a phone call came in.

"Let me speak with Suh Byung-su. Tell him this is Aurio."

Both Benny and Kimo looked shocked. "Aurio!" Benny exclaimed, "Mr. Tanaka's driver? How could he... why?"

Kimo replied, "Quiet. Let's listen."

"Aurio, what do you have?" Suh Byung-su asked.

"I just drove Tanaka's granddaughter, Teruyo Boudreaux, and her security director, Shindo, to the airport. They are taking an international flight, Japan Air Lines #61 to Tahiti and should be arriving in the morning."

Suh Byung-su replied, "Are you sure? Why would they come here?"

"They are pretending to be newlyweds and celebrating their honeymoon. That's all I know, and felt you needed to hear this."

"How about Tanaka? Any further movement or trips scheduled for him? He is the one I want!" Suh Byung-su shouted back into the phone.

"No. Nothing yet. I will let you know as soon as I hear of anything."

Suh Byung-su hung up the phone without saying thank you or goodbye.

Kimo said, "Let's get this to Kajiki right away," and he dialed the base station on the newly installed phone.

Kimo played the tape to Kajiki while Benny stood watch over the other receivers. Kajiki hung up and immediately called Mr. Tanaka in Japan to see if it was too late to prevent Teruyo and Shindo from flying on and to let him know they'd found the "mole."

Chapter 32

Kimo and Benny were unable to understand all of the conversation Suh Byung-su and his new guests were having as they all spoke Korean. However, they were getting it all on tape and would phone it on to Tanaka's headquarters for translation as soon as there was a break. It was obvious with the urgency they spoke, that they were planning something.

Kajiki arrived shortly and informed them that Teruyo and Shindo's flight had just departed, so they were in route with a stopover in Auckland, New Zealand. Mr. Tanaka was going to have a jet flown directly there and stop them from continuing on to Papeete. Aurio was being detained for questioning, and they would be informed immediately concerning any further information he would "provide" to the Korean and his team here.

Kimo said, "I wouldn't want to be in Aurio's shoes right now! I wonder why he did this."

Benny replied, "I'd sure like to get my hands on him for his part in the murders in Honolulu!"

"Hey brah, let's stay focused on these men across the street for now," Kimo encouraged. "That will be our revenge."

The "bug" placed on the telephone came alive with another call. This time, it was Suh Byung-su calling Bogenville. "Hello, Bogenville? I need a meeting with you and Follet as soon as possible."

"Monsieur Tanaka, I assure you, as soon as the doctor releases Davis, we will find out what he did with your granddaughter. Until then, there is nothing we can do," the Customs Officer stated.

"Yes, I realize you are doing your best," Suh Byung-su responded. "I now have another request which may help speed up this process. Could you and Follet meet me here alone like we did for our first meeting?"

Excited at the assumption this meant another cash transaction, Bogenville replied, "Oui, I will get in touch with him. Good day, Monsieur Tanaka."

Kajiki called the base station. "Assemble everyone immediately. I'll be there in ten minutes."

He turned to Kimo and Benny, "I need one of you to stay and man the recorders and the other to come with me. If what I think is going to happen, Bogenville and Follet should be meeting with Suh Byung-su and his people alone. As long as none of Follet's men come along, I want to be able to storm the house and take them all by surprise. Which one of you wants some action?"

They were both anxious, but Kimo being the larger and stronger of the two, got the nod. Plus, he'd been a good friend to the radio operator who was killed in Honolulu.

Kajiki had sketched the floor plan of the house when he and Benny installed the bugs. He explained the mission to Kimo and the other two agents who had brought the surveillance equipment to Papeete. Kajiki had smuggled a nice assortment of automatic pistols with silencers in a false panel of the private jet he'd brought into Tahiti, and of course, each of his men were experts with them.

Follet and Bogenville arrived at the house just after dark. Bogenville had called Suh Byung-su back and apologized for being late, but Suh Byung-su encouraged them to come over right away.

This worked out in Kajiki's favor, for now they could approach the house under cover of darkness. They were even prepared with dark clothing and everyone, as former Special Forces soldiers, were expert in the craft of surprise and engagement.

Suh Byung-su greeted his visitors at the door and brought them into the dining room.

Benny, across the street in the condo,

had good reception from the bugs and communicated to Kajiki and his men via their hand-held radios, "They're in the dining room, seated at the table."

Kajiki and his men moved into place: two at the front door, two at the back door, and one standing by crouched down between the cars.

Suh Byung-su began, "Gentlemen, my name is not Tanaka. I paid you the $20,000 and made the story up about the kidnapping, all as a way to see if you were the type of men we could work with for a much bigger operation." Suh Byung-su opened a suitcase full of U.S. $100.00 bills and continued, "Gentlemen, you see in front of you $150,000 in unmarked American dollars. Early tomorrow morning, Japan Airlines flight #61 will be arriving at the Papeete airport with the real granddaughter of Tanaka, and you are to bring her to me."

The looks on the faces of Bogenville and Follet were like those of children on Christmas morning. Trying to gather some semblance of composure, Bogenville spoke first, "Who are you really and what is it you want with this girl?"

Suh Byung-su replied, "That's not for you to know… if you want this money."

At that, Benny called to Kajiki over the radio, "Move in now!"

Kajiki called to Kimo over the radio,

"Kimo, are you ready on the front?"

Kimo answered, "10-4, on your call."

Kajiki stated, "On one—three, two, one!"

Both the front and back doors burst open in unison with shattered wood and glass. An instant later, the four team members converged on the dining room, firing from crouched positions. Kimo instantly killed the two new Koreans with single shots to their foreheads, and then Bogenville and Follet met with the same fate, except that they took three shots each to their chests. Only Suh Byung-su was to be spared, and he was shot in the shoulder before being subdued by Kimo.

Kajiki called to his watch outside, "Three, all clear?"

The base station operator who was watching from the driveway responded, "Three back to one, all clear out here... didn't even hear you after you entered."

Kajiki to Benny, "One to base, we're coming out."

Benny replied, "Copy, I'm on my way," and he started the car and drove across the street to pick up the "passenger."

Kimo applied tape to Suh Byung-su's mouth to ensure his cries of pain were not heard. Kimo then taped both of Suh Byung-su's hands behind his back and lifted him up off the floor. Suh Byung-su was not only feeling the effects of Kimo's rough handling, but when he saw his men along with Bogenville and Follet lying dead around the table, the expression on his face changed from pain to fear.

Benny came into the house and began helping Kajiki remove all of the bugs, and they discussed what to do next. He suggested to Kajiki that they leave the tape recorder with Suh Byung-su's proposal to Bogenville and Follet, and Kajiki agreed. "Be sure not to leave any fingerprints on the tape or recorder," Kajiki ordered, as Benny and Kimo muscled Suh Byung-su out to their awaiting car. They took him into the rented condo and Kimo stood guard over their wounded captive while Benny went to work on his recording.

Kajiki and his men were careful to search each of Koreans, hoping to find weapons and identification. They recorded all of their names and passport numbers and took the semiautomatic pistols two of the men held. Kajiki and his agent carefully placed their pistols in the hands of the slain Koreans. The pistol, minus its silencer, that Kimo used to kill the Koreans was placed in Bogenville's hand.

Benny returned a few minutes later with the portable recorder and a cassette tape that began with Suh Byung-su stating he was not Tanaka and stopped just prior to Kajiki and his men breaking down the doors. Kajiki placed it under the table and carefully checked all angles of the bodies to ensure the room looked like a gunfight had occurred over the money, which they'd left lying on the table. When everything looked perfect, they dispersed in different directions to meet back at the warehouse.

Kajiki joined Kimo in the condo and they were able to get Suh Byung-su back in the car without being seen. They drove back to the warehouse. It was time for a little talk.

Chapter 33

The next morning, Luke was groggy from almost nine hours of sleep, the most rest he'd had since departing Palmyra. The nurses had left him alone all night, and as he tried to clear the cobwebs, he could hardly believe that he'd been allowed to sleep all night without interruption. He sat up in the bed and, as nature called, he shuffled to the door to have the Gendarme get a nurse to escort him down the hall to the restroom. He was startled to see that there was no guard.

Shall I make a run for it? Probably won't get too far before being noticed dressed like this. First things first, I've got to pee! And Luke headed for the restroom.

After taking care of business, Luke poked his head out of the restroom and looked up and down the hallway. Still no guard and the guard chair was gone. A nurse walked by, and Luke asked, "Is Dr. Parant around?"

"No Monsieur, she is out. We expect her back this afternoon," the nurse replied.

"Do you know where the Gendarme has gone?"

"I'm sorry, Monsieur, I don't know. There was not a Gendarme when I came on duty at 8:00 this morning. We were instructed to look in on you and to let you sleep as long as you were resting comfortably. You must be hungry, no?"

"Yeah, mighty hungry. Do you have anything besides soup?" Luke asked.

"If you feel strong enough, why don't you take a shower while I see what the kitchen can fix for you?"

She got Luke some towels and a fresh gown and directed him to a private room that had its own bathroom and shower. Luke reveled in the steam and unlimited hot water for almost a half-hour—a forgotten luxury since moving aboard his boat.

Physically weakened from the lack of food and the intense heat of the shower, he was barely able to dry himself and make it back to his room. He thought he was feeling almost back to normal, until he lay down, so he decided he might still have some recuperating to do yet. He fell asleep.

"Monsieur Davis, your breakfast is ready. Monsieur Davis, are you not hungry?" asked a familiar voice.

Luke slowly opened his eyes and tried to focus. *Who is that? Am I dreaming?* he asked himself as he focused on the lady standing over him... Teruyo! He shot up off the pillow, "Baby, it's you!"

With tears in her eyes and a big smile, she embraced Luke and cried, "Oh Hon, are you alright? I missed you so much. I can't believe what you have gone through," and her grip on Luke tightened as she started crying.

Luke was completely stunned. After spending what seemed like an eternity in this hospital bed with the tenuous hope of ever seeing Teruyo again, he was now holding her in his arms. As he opened his eyes again, while still being squeezed by Teruyo's emotional grasp, he noticed Shindo and Dr. Parant standing by the door.

Tears were welling up in his eyes too, and after a few moments, he was able to get Teruyo to ease her embrace so he could get his hands to each side of her face and kiss her cheeks. "Easy, Baby, we're together. Oh, I can't believe you're here."

She continued crying, "Oh Luke, I never should have left you. Look at you... you could have been killed. I'm so sorry, Honey... I, I..."

"Hey, it's alright. Don't blame yourself; I got myself into this mess. You're here now... we're together again. That's all that matters," he said, gently easing her slightly back so he could look into her eyes. Wiping away her tears with his thumbs, he said, "Oh Baby, I love you."

Breaking back into the uncontrolled sobbing, she tried replying, "I... I love... love you... you too, Luke."

Repressing his happiness and joy, he

almost laughed as he said in a slight giggle, "Hey, where is my breakfast?"

That got Teruyo to ease into a laugh, though her clasp on Luke remained as firm as a baby monkey on its mother's back.

Dr. Parant interrupted, "Miss Boudreaux, could I have a look at Mr. Davis's bandage? We need to see if he is fit enough to have some solid food."

Teruyo pulled back and said, "Oh, I'm sorry. Luke, how are you feeling?" she asked. "I lost it seeing you. I didn't even consider you are still sick."

"Hey, I'm OK. Other than being hungry, I'm feeling a lot better," he replied. "Hey, Shindo. Good to see you. What's happening?"

"Easy there, Jim, I mean Luke," the doctor inserted with a grin. "Lay back down and let me have a look for a moment first." She looked into Luke's eyes with the little flashlight again.

Teruyo said, "Shindo and I arrived early this morning. We heard from Kajiki that they were able to secure things and you were no longer going to be detained."

Dr. Parant said gleefully, "Yes Luke, our friends have met with a very, sudden... end. I was called this morning to assist in the investigation of their murders, and it appears they were involved in a gun battle over bribes and a plot that implicated you. You have been cleared from all charges, and the local authorities are now fully involved in the investigation of Bogenville and Follet."

Teruyo exclaimed, "As soon as you are all better, the doctor says you are free to leave!"

After a thorough examination of Luke's eyes and response to movements of her penlight, the doctor asked, "Other than the emotional euphoria you have, how are you really feeling?"

"Actually, I'm really hungry!" Luke emphasized.

"Good! That is just what we needed to hear," Dr. Parant said. "We can ease you into some solid foods and watch your progress for the rest of today.

Shindo asked, "Doctor, you called him Jim?"

"Oh I'm sorry if I almost blew Mr. Morrison's cover," she replied with a smile.

The investigators were almost running into each other, pouring over the Indonesian's house, searching for evidence and more clues into Papeete's highest government corruption scandal in history. Now that Follet was dead, the struggle for power within the police department was hindering the effectiveness of the investigation, not that they were equipped or experienced in this type of high-profile investigation anyway.

Benny, using his electronics skills, was able to tune into the radio frequencies used by the Gendarmes and hear the disorganized chaos of the investigation. Kajiki was amused by the way they were bickering over who was in charge and how they violated good investigative practices to determine what had actually happened there the previous night.

Kajiki was more concerned with Suh Byung-su and how far up the intelligence ladder of the North Korean government he went. The danger now was where they would strike next. So far, Suh Byung-su would not talk, but eventually he would. Kajiki was sure of his abilities to "interview" subjects.

So far, the translation of the tapes they'd sent to Tanaka Industries indicated no contacts with North Korea. The two Korean associates killed in the dining room, whom Suh Byung-su had just picked up from the airport, were not on any international "watch list" as being spies or counter-intelligence agents. Both had South Korean passports, and their addresses were from the same town as the agents whom Luke and Teruyo had repelled back in Hanalei Bay, Kauai, making it seem more of a "family type" operation than an intelligence operation from North Korea. Kajiki had a lot of experience with spying on the North Koreans and investigating Japan's security vulnerabilities, and this was not adding up yet. He decided to get Suh Bung-su on one of Mr. Tanaka's private jets bound for Kobe, Japan immediately, before the local authorities realized who they were looking for.

Epilogue

Kajiki, the experienced interrogator he was, determined the operation against Mr. Tanaka and his associates and family was a personal vendetta, which was began by Suh Byung-su and his brother Suh Byung-min. Their father, who had been a leader in the Korean resistance, was killed during the Japanese occupation of Korea in World War II. After his sons became adults, they had traced the blame back to Masashi Tanaka, the young Japanese officer they believed had led the eradication of their father's village.

The two brothers had dedicated their lives to finding ways at getting back at Mr. Tanaka, but upon finding this news, Mr. Tanaka dispelled the story as he was never in the Army. During World War II, as a young engineer, his skills were more needed in the manufacturing sector. Tanaka Industries was established and grew after the end of the war. The two brothers had made a crucial mistake and all of these years were after the wrong man.

After Kajiki felt confident this was not a North Korean government operation, he of course felt he had to eliminate his captive. Aurio, Mr. Tanaka's driver, was also thoroughly "interviewed." The Korean brothers had approached him about eight months ago and enticed him with several thousand dollars in cash to keep them informed of Mr. Tanaka's, his family's, and close associates' movements. Aurio met the same fate as Suh Byung-su when it was determined he had no other contacts.

After meeting with Mr. Tanaka, Michi and Teruyo were allowed to resume their lives. Shindo stayed in Tahiti to continue to monitor Teruyo and Luke's travels while they were in the Society Islands.

Each day brought more press releases about the continuing investigation into Bogenville and Follet. The investigators were having a field day uncovering corrupt dealings between the police and customs departments.

Luke was discharged from the hospital the same evening that he and Teruyo had been reunited, and after expressing their sincere gratitude to Dr. Parant, they headed straight for *Tranquilo*. Dr. Parant insisted the police and customs departments would take care of Luke's financial responsibilities to the hospital.

As faithful as a good friend could ever be, Taeio was still on the boat and welcomed them in his usual happy, carefree manner. After refusing at first, Luke convinced Taeio to accept an envelope with a nice sum of cash for looking out for *Tranquilo* and keeping her from being pilfered.

As soon as they coordinated communication with Shindo and had his blessing, Teruyo and Luke provisioned *Tranquilo* with as much as she would hold and set sail.

Coming up for air after free diving to photograph some tropical fish, Teruyo and Luke were back where they wanted to be. The waters were pristine, having at least one hundred-foot visibility. Now that they were closer to the Equator and in warmer waters than those in Hawaii, the colors and varieties of species of coral were even more vibrant and diverse.

"You know, I could really get used to this," Luke said after removing his snorkel.

"I'm all out of film and starting to shrivel up like a prune. How about going topside for a beer?" Teruyo suggested.

"Now you're beginning to sound like an ole salt!"

After rinsing off with some freshwater that had been warming up in Luke's solar-heated water container on the deck while they swam, they lay down to soak up the sun themselves. Holding hands as they allowed the sun to dry them out, Teruyo exclaimed, "I can't believe I actually photographed a rock fish! My first one!"

"You know, the next port we make for, I hope they have a good supply of photo albums and film for the camera. We're almost out, Mademoiselle Boudreaux," Luke said.

Teruyo rolled over to let her head rest on her lover's chest. "I've been meaning to ask you, what was all that back at the hospital about Jim Morrison?"

Luke stuttered, "I... um, was just trying to convince the good doctor I was traveling incognito as Jim Morrison, but she didn't take the bait at all. One of her nurses threatened to shave my beard and I was so bored just having to lie there pretending to be in worse condition than I really was, I tried havin' a little fun to break the monotony."

"You weren't being a little too playful with the pretty young doctor now were you?" Teruyo asked with a jealous tone and an inquiring eye.

Luke rose up to look Teruyo in the eyes, "Baby, don't ever think my love for you will stray."

Teruyo's heart melted. Luke was so sincere. She laid her head back on his warm chest.

"I'll never have desires for another woman... now Wanda, where's that beer you promised me?" he continued, jokingly.

"Wanda!" Teruyo yelled, hopping up

and giving him a scornful look. "Wanda is it? Well I've got your *Wanda*, you ole flirt!" and she pulled her towel up off the deck and started snapping him with it.

"Hey easy, Baby. Remember my head injury!" he cried as he tried crawling backwards, laughing.

"You'll have more than a head injury to worry about if you pull an act like that again!" She yelled, trying to act angry, but not able to totally suppress her smile.

His only refuge was the water, so under the lifeline he slithered. Looking back up from the water at his beautiful lady standing on the deck with her hands resting on her hips like the *Queen of the Hill*, he laughed with her like silly children.

That evening after grilling and eating three of the lobster tails they'd caught the night before while night diving, they snuggled in the cockpit of *Tranquilo* as happy and content as any two people have ever been. The sun was just setting over the clear horizon, and the last puff of light it shed was a brilliant flash of green.

"Wow."

A Message From the Author:

Thank you for taking the time to read my book.
I would be honored if you would consider
leaving a review for it on *Amazon*.

About the Author:

This story was based on the true adventures of the author when he left-it-all-behind, went to Hawaii and began cruising on his first sailboat. This photo was taken with the author's wife and the real "Dogs of Palmyra," Army & Palmyra, in front of the Palmyra Yacht Club. Palmyra Atoll has since been purchased by the Nature Conservancy and is protected from development, remaining a largely undisturbed island paradise for its wildlife inhabitants. Cruisers may request permission to take brief rest stops, and while Army and Palmyra have long since passed, the memory of their joyful spirits live on in those who met them.

The author as Capt'n

The author with two Papio

The author with the "Dogs of Palmyra"

The author's wife on the inflatable dinghy

Yo and Ko

The author with an Ono

Acknowledgements

My late father, Vern Walton Daise, would occasionally reminisce about his adventures in the South Pacific during his time in the US Navy during WWII. He'd tell of swimming in the crystal-clear waters and white sandy beaches (usually after we'd put up hay for our cattle on hot, humid August days). Those seeds he sowed, as well as the encouragement to fulfill my dreams, led me to leave my very successful career and sail into experiences and adventures way beyond my wildest imagination.

Having lived a very similar adventure to that of "Luke Davis," though without the drama of having been accompanied by the granddaughter of one of the wealthiest men in Asia, I would like to express my sincerest Mahalo Nui Loa to the following friends and mentors who helped shape my sailing and cruising experiences:

Gary Larsen, my first friend in Hawaii and sailing mentor. We sailed his Columbia sloop to Maui together and that "hooked me" for life. I'll forever be grateful for his teachings and for befriending me.

Captain Albertson, founder of The Pacific Maritime Academy, for his great sea stories, celestial navigation and US Coast Guard navigation rules and aids to navigation training... I never intended to become a professional mariner, but he inspires me to this day.

Jimmy English, who taught me the art of bartending and fishing so I could supplement my lifestyle and pursue my dreams of cruising.

Fred Branum, the best friend and dive-buddy one could ever hope to have. Rest in peace dear Bubba, we shared the best diving and sailing adventures ever!

Tanna Swanson for not allowing this Captain to ever get too full of himself.

And finally my best friend and wife Vashti, who was my love-at-first-sight just like with Teruyo and Luke. Thank you for believing in me and trusting your life in my hands as we cruise together.

Check out these titles from
Amazing Things Press

Keeper of the Mountain by Nshan Erganian

Rare Blood Sect by Robert L. Justus

Evoloving by James Fly

Survival In the Kitchen by Sharon Boyle

Stop Beating the Dead Horse by Julie L. Casey

In Daddy's Hands by Julie L. Casey

Time Lost: Teenage Survivalist II by Julie L. Casey

Starlings by Jeff Foster

MariKay's Rainbow by Marilyn Weimer

Convolutions by Vashti Daise

Seeking the Green Flash by Lanny Daise

Nikki's Heart by Nona j. Moss

Nightmares or Memories by Nona j. Moss

Amazing Things Press

www.amazingthingspress.com

Check out these children's titles from
Amazing Things Press

The Boy Who Loved the Sky by Donna E. Hart

Terreben by Donna E. Hart

Sherry Strawberry's Clubhouse by Donna E. Hart

Finally Fall by Donna E. Hart

Thankful for Thanksgiving by Donna E. Hart

Make Room for Maggie by Donna E. Hart

Toddler Tales by Kathy Blair

Amazing Things Press

www.amazingthingspress.com

Made in the USA
Charleston, SC
07 November 2014